MESSENGER

OF

DEATH

MESSENGER

OF DEATH

BY

ALEX MARKMAN

ASTEROID
PUBLISHING

MESSENGER OF DEATH

Asteroid Publishing, Inc.

ISBN 978-0-9811637-9-6

MESSENGER OF DEATH is a work of fiction. Names, characters and events are the products of author's imagination. Any resemblance to real persons, organizations or events is coincidental and not intended by the author.

Book cover by Julia Chabad and Anna Philippova

Table of Contents

Chapter 1

I

August 1995. It was a sunny afternoon, the time when the streets of St. Michel are flooded with people. Hordes of office workers invade restaurants, bars, and cafes; competing for tables on sidewalks; and chatting and laughing under the accompanying ring of forks, knifes, plates, and glasses. In a short Quebec summer, clients prefer to sit under the sky, enjoying the fresh air and nice views of the city, while watching crowds of passersby.

A man in his middle thirties entered a small, but rather charming restaurant at the corner of two streets and took his place at the most distant table outside, by the railing separating pedestrians from the clients. He was neatly groomed with a touch of gray hair and a casual, but expensive, dress; he had the respectable look of a white-collar worker. The only dissonance to his otherwise peaceful impression was his wrestler-sized neck, not that conspicuous at the moment when hidden by an oversized turtleneck.

"Just coffee," he requested, and the waiter rushed off. *This client always gave good tips, no matter how big or small his order,* was the waiter's thought. The waiter had another incentive, too. He was dead scared of this visitor.

No sooner was the coffee served when a different kind of man sat at the table. He had a short and tidy beard and brownish, with a shade of red, hair, which was combed back into a thick ponytail. His drawn, wrinkled, suntanned

1

face made him look like a sailor who had just crossed the ocean on a small yacht.

"Hi," he said in greeting, and, after shaking hands, diverted his attention to a young woman in a tight miniskirt, passing by the separating fence. "Nice ass, ah?" he asked with a smile, as if looking for approval of his taste for female beauty. His dark eyes were alert, as if he was waiting for something. The question hung in the air. He put a cigarette in his mouth and clicked his golden lighter.

"What's the rush, Marcel?" he continued, drawing in the smoke with apparent delight. "You could've told me about the meeting yesterday."

"Too busy with skirts lately, Stash?" Marcel asked. Stash exhaled a huge puff of smoke, diverting his attention to other seductively swaying hips.

"We work to enjoy life, don't we?"

"We do," agreed Marcel with a smile, which had nothing kind in it. "So do many others, who we don't like."

"Here's Machete," Stash remarked. It was an opportunity to change the direction of the not-so-pleasant conversation.

A touch of contempt spread across Marcel's face as a large man approached their table, unceremoniously grabbed a chair from a neighboring table, and dropped onto it. He leaned back, making the wood under him squeak. Marcel pulled up a sleeve on his left arm, flashing a Rolex wristwatch.

"Hard to beat the traffic," said Machete, explaining his being late, his coarse, rough voice supplementing the obvious absence of rudimentary manners. The waiter brought another two cups of coffee, although only one had been requested, and asked, "Anything else, gentlemen?"

"Beat it," Machete grumbled. The waiter bowed politely and quickly stepped back, like people do at the sight of a rattlesnake. Marcel observed Machete disapprovingly. Machete wore a T-shirt, tightly stretched over large, but sagging muscles. His thick arms—those of a former athlete—were densely wrapped in tasteless, colorful tattoos. He had a disheveled beard and long, uncombed hair. He looked like a pirate from a sunken ship. Marcel sighed and shrugged his shoulders. It was too late to teach this hoodlum anything. This was Machete, well known in the criminal world by his physical strength and pathological brutality. About 10 years ago, he had earned a black belt in karate. Now, however, excesses of drugs and alcohol had taken their toll on his body.

Marcel did not like Machete. Like a mad dog, this biker resorted to violence, whether it was necessary or not—even when it was detrimental to the interests of the gang. However, all members stayed behind him in times of trouble—as this was the code of the club—especially when tough guys, so plentiful in the underworld, sought revenge. However, Marcel needed Machete. The man was a leader in his own right. He controlled several violent gangs, which served him well when beatings, murder, or destruction was being contemplated.

"I was about to say to Stash," Marcel began speaking, "that we are at the point when some decisions must be made. We can't sell our stuff in some areas, like before, because the Ghosts have a cleaner product."

"Don't look at me, man," cut in Machete, returning the grim stare. "I told you to get rid of them, but you didn't listen. Who in his right mind would set up an outlaw biker club without our permission? And you—you put up with it."

3

"I told you before that you're dumb. Did it help?" asked Marcel in false kindness. Machete's eyes narrowed, but Stash intervened, depriving him a chance to demonstrate the biker's dirty vocabulary.

"What do you suggest we do with the Ghosts, Marcel?"

"I will take care of them," Machete stated, and lit a cigarette.

"You know that they don't wear colors," Marcel said. "You can't make them out on the street."

"Gimme one of them, and I can find out where everyone else is. It won't take long until all of them are out of the game."

"I know only one." Marcel said mockingly. "Jason. He's the president."

"Let's start with him," suggested Machete.

"You've smoked too much pot lately," Stash chuckled. "Jason is well connected with the Italians and Columbians. They do a lot of business together. You know that."

Machete's answer was populated with dirty words. The meaning of his response was *Let's take care of business, no matter what*.

"That's not the way to deal with them," Marcel said. "Too much trouble."

Machete uttered a strange sound.

"Never heard you bothering about troubles. What then?"

"We'll tell them to close the club. Jason will know what that means. For sure, he has tough guys around him, and that's okay, but he's the clever one among them. He knows that they are too small. He would understand that eventually none of them would survive. Let's give them a choice. I'm pretty sure that they are not mad dogs, crazy for a fight. On the contrary, most, if not all, of them are businesspeople. There is a good chance that they will come to their senses."

"When and how are you going to do this?" Stash asked, as Machete spit on the floor.

"Today. I've already talked to Jason over the phone," Marcel said. "The meeting is in an hour, at 2 o'clock. I have already told everyone in our other chapters that we have a meeting with the Iron Ghosts."

Machete and Stash exchanged glances. Marcel enjoyed the effect of his words. He liked surprises.

The last time they had seen Jason had been at least 15 years ago. Since then, Jason had led a very secretive life and, as the entire underworld knew, was flying high. Marcel remembered Jason as a cunning and diplomatic business guy, who enjoyed swimming with sharks in the dark waters of the drug trade. He always tried first to find a peaceful solution with his foes, and was surprisingly good at that, if one takes into consideration that very few in this business accept a compromise. Jason never used drugs, very seldom used alcohol, and knew well what is right or wrong in the underworld. With all that, he was capable of making terrifying decisions in a split second and executing them with speed and ferocity, which impressed even the most daring gangsters. Marcel was sure that fighting with him would be costly and deadly.

"How'd yah find him?" Machete asked.

"An Italian helped me. Do you have your colors with you?"

"In the car," Stash said. Machete nodded silently.

"Let's go now. Follow me."

Marcel rose to his feet and threw a fistful of dollars on the table, not waiting for the waiter to bring the bill. He led the way; the other two followed him to their cars. Marcel's new jeep started with a hardly audible crank. The jeep and the other two cars cruised along the crowded streets. At the outskirts of the city, the traffic subsided and at last disappeared as they entered a rural area. Marcel pulled up in front of a lonely, strange-looking building, hidden almost to the roof behind a high, brick fence. The other two cars parked behind him.

Marcel put on his colors—his biker's jacket with insignia, emblems, and other imprints of their club. The very sign of all these attributes meant to intimidate anyone who would dare to mess with one of the most powerful outlaw motorcycle gangs in the world.

"Almost 2 o'clock," he commented. "We got here in time."

They passed through the gate in the brick fence and approached the entrance to a large one-story building, on the wall of which the emblem "Iron Ghosts" had been painted like a large seal. The guard at the door, a menacing-looking and sturdy fellow, looked them up and down with a suspicious, hostile stare.

"Carrying toys with you?" the guard asked. Marcel spread his hands like the wings of a bird, exposing his whole body for observation.

"Wanna search?"

"Go ahead." The guard nodded and stepped aside, allowing the three bikers to enter.

Marcel threw a quick glance around as the door behind them closed with a metal click. The windows facing the yard were large, admitting plenty of light, some of it drawing attention to a bar overflowing with bottles in the left distant corner. Sofas, chairs, and coffee tables had been set up around the floor with a purposeful disorder that was, apparently, meant to encourage casual, informal sitting. Everything was new, of good quality, and sparkling clean.

A skinny man in tight jeans and a T-shirt—he looked less than thirty—was sitting in an easy chair. As the three bikers entered, he got up and gave a brief nod, inviting them to follow him down a narrow corridor. He swung open one of the doors before them and led them through it, his face emotionless, like a stone. Marcel and Stash found themselves in a room brightly lit by fluorescent lamps. Unlike the previous room, this one had no windows, no other light. A long, polished table stretched before them, 10 people sitting around it. None of the men looked older than forty; they watched their guests with serious, calm faces that showed more than a bit of contempt. The skinny guide closed the door and pointed to the end of the table, where a few chairs were vacant.

"You can sit there," he stated curtly before moving to the other end to take a place beside a man who had the sharp, abrupt facial features of a boxer and dark hair with contrasting white skin. Marcel took the offered chair. As he moved, he observed each set of eyes at the table, testing its owner's guts with a momentary, penetrating stare. No one blinked.

"Jason." Marcel greeted the man at the opposite end of the table. Jason gave a nod in return.

"Wanna talk business, I s'pose."

Jason was a leader—an obvious conclusion even by casual observation. But it was the man beside him, the self-confident fellow who had led them in, who truly interested Marcel. The bastard had been examining Marcel with keen interest. Marcel reciprocated, calmly studying the longish, pale face, the blond, shortly cut hair, the icy cold blue eyes, and the small scar that accented his left jaw. Leaning back

7

in a relaxed pose, smoking leisurely, he exuded calmness and confidence. Undoubtedly, this guy was one any leader would chose to be close by his side.

"So, you guys call yourselves an outlaw motorcycle club." Marcel started with the heart of the matter. He paused, testing the reaction to his statement. Jason's expression did not change. He did not say a word. No, a man with a lazy eye, halfway down one side of the table, was first to react.

"What business is it of yours?"

"You haven't asked our permission," explained Marcel. Someone at the table hissed, as if suppressing a laugh.

"And, we won't," the guide responded matter-of-factly.

"What is your name?" asked Marcel.

"None of your business."

"Okay, look, None-of-Your-Business," Marcel raised his voice slightly, hardly able to contain his boiling rage. "*You* don't even wear colors. Who could tell who you are?"

"Nobody," Jason interrupted. "Neither you, nor the cops. Is that what you want?"

Marcel let this question hang in the air. He directed his attention to the fellow with the small scar.

"I'd like to talk to *you*," he said. "What should I call you?"

"Stanley."

"Stanley, then. You should know, Stanley, that you can't set up an outlaw motorcycle club without our permission. You should also know what happens to those who think differently."

Messenger of Death

"Who the fuck are you to tell us what we should or shouldn't do?" Stanley asked, shooting Marcel a look of cold steel.

Marcel turned directly to him with a sudden jerk, his chin up, his right hand stretched aside and slightly back, as if ready to throw a grenade or a knife. Everyone in the room knew he was the president of the most powerful Devil's Knights biker chapter. Anyone speaking to him with such disrespect should be dead on the spot.

"Who the fuck are we?" Marcel repeated the phrase, now in a lower tone. His anger had suddenly subsided, and he composed himself, putting on the air of a businessman. After this pause, he added, "You should know by now. Wanna know us better?"

"Better," Stanley echoed, not so irritating but with mocking contempt.

"Better," nodded Marcel.

Stanley laughed. A splash of laughter from others around the table joined him. Bikers appreciated the opportunity to show their contempt and defiance to the "almighty" Devil's Knights.

Marcel fixed his frozen stare upon Stanley; his eyelids opened wide, showing white space all around his irises. It was the look of an insane, outraged animal whose only instinct was to bite off live flesh. And yet, his body and gestures were calm and reflective. This combination was so ominous and impressive that the gangsters of the Iron Ghosts club gave him a moment of respectful silence.

"Fuck you," said someone at the back. All three Devil's Knights looked at the one who said it.

"I'll remember you," promised Machete, stretching his lips in a hateful grin. He stood up and walked toward the door; the other two followed him. Everyone around the

9

table understood that these guys would take care of business. Everyone smiled.

The guard at the door blocked their way.

"Hold on," he said. He looked the Devil's Knights up and down.

Marcel couldn't believe what was happening. Would they dare to kill him right here, in the club? Were they *that* stupid, to start a war this way?

The sound of steps made him turn back. He saw Jason approaching in a steady, unhurried pace.

"Let's talk outside," he said to Marcel, giving a nod to the guard.

The door opened wide, letting them out into the parking lot. Agitated guard dogs, restricted by long leashes, jumped back and forth for a few moments and then sat, watching the group with tongues hanging out. The sun, lingering above the horizon, showed its red edge in the crack of thick, black clouds. Dusk was quickly turning into darkness.

"Is this your fucking way to negotiate?" Jason asked, fixing Marcel with a glare of malice. "Give me an ultimatum? You think we are a bunch of scared broads here?"

"You know as well as I do that the guys in America press upon me. I have no choice."

"Look, Marcel," Jason began, talking in a calmer manner. "There is always a way to cut a deal. After all, we can at least agree not to cross each other's domains."

"There is another way of doing things," Marcel responded, "and that is for you to work for us. We will give a name to your club, a prospect status, you know, all that. . . ."

"Move your ass out of here," Jason demanded. He gave Marcel a burning glare, turned around and disappeared behind doors. Marcel had no illusion; Jason's outrage meant something.

Before opening the door of his car, Marcel turned toward his followers.

"The only thing we can do is wait and see what the Ghosts do now. Anyway, none of their club members should be killed without my permission. We'll set up a special commission, which will make decisions as to who to take care of. Understand, Machete?"

II

Claude was slowly coming to the end of his prison term. Placed in the wing where the Devil's Knights held an upper hand, he had kept a low profile, trying not to jeopardize his timely release.

For the last few days, Claude had stared through the grid of metal bars that covered his window. He looked at the sky, fancying the biker's life, with its unrestricted freedoms and cruel, dangerous adventures on the edge of survival. He would use his favored weapon, a piece of metal rod, to beat the shit out of those who stood in his way. He would obtain "hangaround" status in the Devil's Knights club and steal cars with his childhood friend, Hans. Hans was a good thief, but did not have as much guts as Claude. When someone refused to pay a debt for a stolen car or parts, Hans used to ask Claude to "educate" the debtor in the morality of financial obligations. In the criminal world, when almost everyone was able to kill, it was not an easy task. Claude, however, always got the money he earned.

Finally, the day came when he could take his first steps on free ground again, unsupervised by jail wardens. Outside the gate, in the dreamland of freedom, the sun shone differently: It generously shed warmth and welcome smiles on him. A black muscle car, an impeccably clean Mustang, blocked his way. Its shiny surface, throwing back the sun's rays like a huge mirror, was adorned with polished, black-painted, and chrome-plated parts, the metal emblem of a leaping horse at the front edge of its frame. Leaning against the left door stood a short, lean fellow, his head shaven and shiny like the surface of his car. This was Hans, the only one close to him whom he had never beaten. He wore a T-shirt and worn-out jeans and smiled in unison with the sun. An expert in car theft, Hans knew just as well how to buy cars, fix them up, and sell them. For his own use, he was accustomed to keeping sports cars and taking very good care of them.

They hugged each other, and rushed to take seats and head down the road. Hans stomped on the gas pedal, the motor rumbled agreeably in response with all its 250-horsepower, and the tires screamed, pushing the pavement under them at breathtaking speed. They laughed and shouted.

"Where're we goin'?" Claude asked.

"To your apartment," Hans answered with a sly grin.

"Yer kiddin'," Claude said, and gave Hans a light slap on the neck. "I don't have one."

"You do, too. I rented one for yah. Gave the super some dough. Paid for the first and last month."

Claude uttered his rowdy, barking laugh.

"Son of a gun. Do you have any broads for tonight?"

"Of course. That's the first thing."

"Is there a telephone?"

"'Course. But why do you need it so soon?"

"'Cause I have to call my buddy from the slumber. Trasher his name is. A Devil's Knights guy, you know." Claude spoke casually, as if he were a big shot in the biker's world.

"Bullshit," Hans said. He gave Claude a serious, questioning look, as if to say, you're pulling my leg, buddy.

"No kiddin'. He wants to meet me. We'll do big business, Hans."

"I'm not from the biker's stock," Hans said. "I'm in the car business."

"You don't make much in it," Claude noticed.

"'Cause I'm lazy. But I do a good job, you know. And I'm not greedy. That's why I've stayed away from the joint for so long."

"Let's talk later," suggested Claude, looking out his window at fast-running pictures of the road: green, tidy, mowed lawns; tall lampposts; small houses under the sleepy afternoon sun; and bridges with a rare pedestrian moving along their walkways.

Hans turned the Mustang into a rundown quarter of the city and soon stopped at the back of a dilapidated apartment building, where a few rusty, battered cars were parked.

"Here we are," Hans said with pride, taking care not to step in the greenish puddle of liquid that smelled like a clogged toilet. "There is an entrance from here. I find it kinda handy sometimes to sneak in from the back. Don't yah think so?"

"Handy it is," Claude agreed. Hans unlocked the door, and led Claude to the second floor, where he opened the first apartment on the right. Claude was impressed: Although the furniture was old and half-broken, it was furniture, nonetheless. The kitchen was equipped with refrigerator, toaster, and gas stove. What else could one dream of?

"This is to start with," said Hans, alluding to the not-so-presentable ambience. "When you start making money, you can buy something better."

"I don't give a damn," Claude said with a rowdy laugh. He sounded like a mad, happy horse. "This is good for me."

Hans grabbed the phone and dialed.

"I'll have a couple of broads here ASAP," he explained, while waiting for the response.

Indeed, two plump, short-legged birds arrived soon, not bad for the first day after three years in a high-security jail, although any would have done for such an occasion, even one from an old-folks home. And a real, beautiful life began: plenty of booze, pot smoking, fucking, pizzas, and Chinese food, delivered from the local restaurant. Two days later, after the crazy smokes and fires had settled a bit, just when he needed a break, Trasher, his former cellmate, dropped by. Claude didn't even remember calling him, but it didn't matter; they had business to discuss, anyway.

Trasher, tall and lean, dressed in a black jacket and leather trousers, came in without a knock on the door, which was not locked. Claude reasoned that no thief in his right mind would break into an apartment that had no valuables inside and was guarded by a former con from a high-security prison. Claude jumped up from the sofa and exchanged strong, friendly hugs with the guest.

"Hay, old buddy," Trasher said, placing a big bottle of whisky on the table with a knocking sound. At thirty-three, he was seven years older, and yet he called Claude "old," alluding to years in jail. "Life's good?"

He fell into a dilapidated easy chair that complained against such abuse with a squeaking sound of its wooden joints.

"Getting better," nodded Claude, settling on the sofa. "And you?"

He observed Trasher with friendly interest, but with a touch of envy. Trasher dressed well, which meant that he had money. His thin, but long bony nose and dark questioning eyes gave him a hawkish look. His suntanned skin, untidy beard and thinning, receding long hair made him look like an Indian chief.

"Not bad either," assured Trasher, with a nod. "Not bad at all. Let's crack the bottle."

"Naw," refused Claude. "Can't take it anymore."

"No rush," agreed Trasher. He stood up, took off his jacket, and hung it on the easy char. On the back of his T-shirt was a huge sign, looking like a corporate seal, with his club insignia along its edges: "Devil's Knights."

"So, what are you gonna do now?" Trasher asked, returning to the squeaking chair and leaning back. "Any plans?"

"Naw. Any suggestions?"

"'Course." Trasher stretched his legs, as if preparing for a long conversation. "I'm selling stuff, you know. Lots of money. That's what I wanna talk about."

"Naw, Trasher. I'm not cut for selling. Can't do it, man."

"What do you wanna do?"

"Action. Rob banks, beat the hell outta somebody. You know me, Trasher."

Claude stood up, went to the refrigerator, and took out a jar of tomato juice.

"Wan' some?" he asked Trasher. Not getting a response, he began drinking from the container.

"I need exactly your type of man," Trasher shouted cheerfully, and hit the table with his bony fist. Empty bottles and dirty dishes jumped noisily, as if sharing their excitement with Trasher. "That's what I'm gonna suggest to you."

"Shoot."

Claude returned to the sofa and stretched his legs, as well.

"Some jerk from the Iron Ghosts visits my territory. This chickenshit sells stuff better than mine. I told him to fuck off, but he doesn't. He has his backup, too, you know. I gotta beat the shit outta this fuckhead to make others think twice before coming to my place." He clenched his fists. "Wanna help me?"

Claude uttered a sadistic guffaw.

"'Course! What and when?"

"In two days. I'll pick you up. In the meantime. . . ." He pulled his jacket from the chair, removed a roll of money from the inner pocket, and threw it carelessly on the sofa.

"Two grand," he said. "To start with."

"Shit," Claude exclaimed in pleasant excitement. "Let's go to a good bar tonight. Ah? May be we could hook up with a good-looking broad."

"Sure, Claude. I have to rush now, though. I'll be back at eight." He stood up. "See you soon."

And he did. The destination that night was one of the strip bars close to downtown, about half an hour from where Claude lived. As Trasher explained, the place had a reputation for having the best girls in town, young and pretty, and a fairly peaceful crowd of professional men. With this well-to-do clientele, security was tight. Claude, however, had his own notions of security. He knew too well that fights sought out those who had no intention of avoiding them. His favorite weapon, a short and heavy metal rod, was stashed behind his belt and hidden under his jacket.

Half an hour later, Trasher parked his Harley Davidson close to the bar entrance and the two buddies went inside. Two grim fellows examined them at the door with menacingly narrowed eyes. Claude chuckled. They had chosen the wrong targets for their intimidation tactics. A few moments later, they were seated at the far end of the first row of chairs.

In the middle of the stage, a narrow pillar had been erected, and around it, a very pretty young woman was dancing with almost professional grace, completely naked. In the next round of the show, she lay down on the floor and, moving her knees and thighs in impossible twists, exposed herself to the fullest. Then, she stood up and began weaving her legs and arms around the pillar, like a liana around a tree, holding it from time to time close to her loins and gliding up and down it in a very suggestive manner. In one of her turns, she noticed Claude's inflamed eyes and paused for a moment to give him the sweetest smile he had ever seen. An invisible needle pierced him from his groin to his throat, causing a strange feeling of acute itching and sweet pain. He took two big gulps of beer to wet his dry mouth. Never before would he have dreamed of approaching such a beauty. But now, with plenty of money filling his pocket, she might be affordable. He smiled back. She winked. His heart began pounding against his ribs.

"Hot little pussy," commented Trasher with an approving smile.

The girl finished her show and nodded to the enthusiastic applause of her spectators. She smiled into space, to no one in particular, and threw her arms up and backward, behind her neck, her elbows pointing to the ceiling, to make her breasts push forward in a seductive way. She then began walking out while another girl stepped in for the next performance.

Claude stood up and quickly reached the stairs leading to the stage. The beauty descended confidently, like a woman dressed in the most decent outfit.

"Hi," Claude said.

"Let me pass, please." She gave him a friendly smile.

"I'm Claude," he introduced himself, stepping aside. "I wanna meet you tonight."

"I'm Leila, and I can't." She rejected his advances with a promising smile. "Someone already takes care of me," she explained in an apologetic tone. "You'd better run from here. It could be too dangerous for you."

She passed by and climbed the short flight of stairs leading to the dressing room. Claude stared greedily at her pretty bum, which swayed femininely at each step. After the girl disappeared behind the door, somebody tapped him on the shoulder. Claude looked cautiously around. Who the hell dared to touch him?

"Don't hit on that girl again." A rather tall and strong-looking black guy stood there, his brutal face matching his powerful physique. His advice came with a frown.

"Why not?" Claude asked mockingly; then, he laughed. The fellow was visibly perturbed by the fact that someone was not afraid of him. Apparently he had not expected any resistance.

"Don't ask questions, you son of a bitch," he said, slightly raising his voice. "Beat it. Or I'll hang you by your balls."

His stare was heavy. He was a real brute, Claude recognized at once. His attention was diverted momentarily to the changing room door, where the beauty was coming out again, this time with a light, transparent piece of cloth over her shoulders. She flashed Claude a short and scared smile. That was Cupid's last arrow, and it hit his heart with deadly accuracy.

"Why don't we go outside and discuss that idea?" Claude suggested. In reality, he was trying to feign naivete and friendship to disorient his antagonist. He could hardly contain a boiling fury that had risen inside. How good it would be to tear this bastard to pieces here, on the spot, and run away . . .

If not for the girl.

The guy looked at him, puzzled.

"Are you stupid, or what?" he asked, and then exchanged quick glances with two other men who had rushed to his side. He shrugged his shoulders and led the way to the back door.

"I'm with you," said Trasher from behind his right ear.

"Go to your bike. I don't need you."

"There are three of them."

"Do it. It's more important to get outta here fast. Turn your bike on and wait."

Claude didn't look back and didn't know whether Trasher had gone or not. He followed the one who led the way, feeling with his sixth sense the two others behind him.

It was already dark outside, but the streetlights made sufficient illumination for a fight. Claude pulled the metal rod from under his belt, and with a quick twist of his body, he hit the black man in an attempt to crush his skull. The man dodged; the rod missed the right spot but landed on a shoulder. The blow was still devastating, and the man collapsed, uttering a desperate, roaring sound like a mortally wounded large animal. Though the other two guys had already jumped out of the rear door toward him, Claude indulged himself in a second blow, which landed with a cracking sound on the head of his opponent. The man fell silent onto his back and stretched his arms wide, as if dead.

Claude hit the second man, but received a hard blow from the third, who then grasped Claude by the arm that was holding the rod. Claude hit the man's face with his forehead and felt the bones of the guy's nose crush; he collapsed, screaming. The second man had recovered and jumped to his feet, but did not dare attack alone. He limped away in awkward, jerky movements.

Not in the mood to chase him, Claude went back into the bar, where he found the beauty standing in a transparent bikini by the door of the dressing room, anxiously looking around. At the first sight of him, she approached the decorative fence that separated the showgirls from the public.

"You have blood on your mouth," she said, her eyes opening wide from fear. "Where are they? Where is Jessie?"

"Who is Jessie?" asked Claude, wiping his lips where he figured the blood was.

"The black one."

"Jessie, son of a bitch, won't come back today," Claude said. "He will be busy with health problems." He laughed rowdily. "I have to go, though. When do you finish?"

"Soon. I want to leave at midnight."

"Very good. I'll catch you. Just walk slowly along the street." Claude paced briskly out of the bar and disappeared into the darkness, like a raccoon in the forest.

When he went out, Trasher gunned the engine, filling the quiet street with rough, growling sounds. Claude hopped onto the back, and the mighty bike jumped forward like a mad horse. Nobody chased them though. As they mingled with the other cars, two police cars approached on the opposite side of the road, their deafening sirens and flashing lights stopping oncoming traffic. Soon Trasher pulled up at the apartment building.

"Good job," commented Trasher. "See you the day after tomorrow."

When in the apartment, Claude dialed Hans.

"Wanna help me tonight?" he asked.

"I'm dead tired," Hans moaned, half asleep, far from being pleased with a late call.

"I need your help, buddy."

"What's up?"

"I have to pick up a broad. Do you have any hot wheels?"

"I do. A jeep. Only 'til tomorrow, though."

"That's okay. For an hour, at midnight. Okay?"

Hans expressed his lack of enthusiasm with a short but impressive shower of dirty words.

"Okay," he agreed at last. "I'll pick you up."

Claude needed a stolen car. In case of a police chase, they could abandon it and run away. Hans, sleepy and angry, met him in the jeep, which he had brought from its hiding place. Close to midnight, they parked about 50 meters from the entrance of the bar, where it could be conveniently observed.

At exactly 12 o'clock, Leila came out and began walking along the poorly lit street. She had taken hardly a dozen steps when the Jeep Cherokee pulled up near her. Its back door opened.

"Get in," Claude said from the front passenger seat. His tone suggested no disobedience. Leila hesitated, but after he repeated his command in a more menacing tone, she climbed onto the back seat.

"How are you?" asked Claude, turning back. "Everything was well in the bar?"

"Where are we going?" asked Leila, her voice trembling in fear.

"To my place. Don't you worry, everything will be okay. How was at your place?"

"Jessie was taken to the hospital. He's in a coma, and they say his life is in danger. The other two are also in the hospital, one of them with a serious injury."

Claude roared in sadistic laughter.

"Jessie will survive," he assured her. "These guys have two skulls. I broke only one of his." He laughed again. Hans echoed his laugh, but with less enthusiasm.

"Are you going to kill me?" Leila asked as she began to cry.

"Stop it," demanded Claude. "Nobody would dare to touch you. You are under my protection."

Leila used her sleeve to wipe away some tears.

"Please, let me go," she kept crying. "Please."

"Stupid broad." Claude was now talking to Hans. "I'd kill anyone who'd even look at her."

"Please." Leila was shaking, as if in a fever. In a few minutes, she was able to calm herself and the car grew silent, with only sporadic weeping sounds that expressed her fear. Soon, the Jeep came to a stop. Claude jumped out and opened the rear door.

"Come out, bunny," he said, offering his hand. His gesture had a sudden and unexpected effect on Leila. She stopped crying, took his hand, and stepped down to the ground. Claude closed the rear door of the car; its tires screamed from the strong push to get away. A moment later, its rear lights disappeared around a corner.

"Where are you taking me?" asked Leila with renewed fear.

"To my apartment. I live on the second floor. Usually I use stairs from the rear entrance. Don't like to see people that late."

"I'm scared," complained Leila.

"Stop it. Trust me. Okay?"

"Okay," agreed Leila, somewhat reassured. She followed Claude up the staircase and watched as he opened the door of his apartment.

He led her inside. The light switch clicked, and the bright glare of a bare bulb hanging from the ceiling on a white cable brought to view the ugly, screaming poverty of the room before her. A shabby sofa bed stood in one corner, dark, dirty stains covering its bumpy surface; a worn-out table was littered with empty bottles, remnants of food, and cigarette butts; the thick odor of never-cleaned ashtrays mingled with the sticky smell of spilled beer; a few stools had been scattered on the floor, some of them upside down, as if they had been shoved about in a battle.

"Sit down." Claude pointed to the sofa with a wide, generous gesture of his hand. Leila sat and leaned back, her legs crossed.

"Wanna whiskey? Some pot?" Claude asked. He threw a hungry glance at her knees. Leila nodded. Claude pulled a small metal box out of his pants.

"Here you are," he said, giving her a handmade joint from the box. "Let me find you some whiskey."

He opened the door of a kitchen cabinet.

"I'll ask the superintendent to clean up the place," he said. "Here it is." He returned with a bottle. "She does this job for me, from time to time," he lied, while pouring some golden liquid into glasses. "I pay her well."

Leila took a sip, and then quickly complemented it with a puff of pot. Still holding her breath, she fixed her green eyes on Claude. He half closed his eyelids, as if dazzled by too bright a light, but she was already turning her head around to examine the room.

Claude saw wrinkles of surprise on her forehead. "I won't live like this forever," he said, finishing his glass. "I just don't have time to buy new furniture."

Leila responded with an indifferent nod.

"You don't believe me," Claude pronounced as a statement of fact. "Wait a sec."

He went to the kitchen cabinet again and came back with a sizable roll of money in his hands.

"You see? Soon there will be more—plenty of dough." He threw the roll at the table. "Will you help me buy new furniture?"

Leila was visibly impressed and looked him up and down with a fresh interest.

"Yes, I will."

"Where are you from?" Claude asked.

"Vancouver. I ran away from home 'cause my parents bugged me all the time. They shouted at me for fooling around with guys. They wanted me to study and get a profession and do housework. They wanted me to do everything I hated to do. I don't want a profession; I don't want to work. I like pot. I like to drink. I can't live without a good fuck. I don't want their boring life."

Leila stopped. She probably thought she had talked too much, since a renewed fear blinked in her eyes. But Claude smiled encouragingly.

"Keep talking," he said, helping himself to another glass of whiskey. "It's rather interesting. Tell me, how did you end up with this shit-box, Jessie? Did he push you to the street?"

"Oh—Jessie." Leila took another confidence-boosting sip from her glass. "He was the first one who picked me up here. But no, he did not push me. He said he would keep me only for himself. Dancing was the only thing he allowed me to do. He said he would crush anyone who approached me. Until today, no one had dared."

"Did you like him?" Claude asked, looking down at the bottom of his glass. He did not want the girl to see his face while she answered the question.

"At first, I did," she admitted. "I thought it sort of interesting. The girls at school always said that the blacks have big cocks and can fuck a lot. He really had a big one, but I didn't like it, after all. I even wanted to run away from him, but I didn't have enough money or a place to run to."

"Was he nice to you?" Claude asked.

"Yes, he was. But I didn't really like him." She paused for another sip. "I liked you at once, when I saw you. I thought I saw something very scary in you, though."

Claude looked up.

"Are you scared of me now?" Claude met the beautiful girl's eyes.

"Not at all." Leila giggled. Some sparkles of joy began to flicker in her eyes. "You turned out to be very nice. Nothing to be scared about. It was silly of me."

"Right you are," Claude laughed.

"What did you do to Jessie, though?" Leila asked. "The police said he was badly hurt. The ambulance picked him up almost dead."

"I guess I hit him a couple of times. He must've fallen and hit his head against something on the ground. But it doesn't matter. I don't give a fuck. I don't want to talk about him anymore."

"What would you like to talk about?" Leila asked. She was getting tipsy.

"About you—I want you to be my girl. You won't be dancing anymore. I'll give you a good life. I will treat you well. Do you wish to be with me?"

"Yes, I do," Leila said solemnly, as women do in front of a priest at their marriage ceremony. "I like you."

This was the first night in Claude's life that he understood how happy a man could be with a woman. The miracle of love stunned him. After the girl had fallen asleep, tired of his insatiable hunger for her body, he placed his rough palm on her tender breasts, kissed her neck, and fell asleep.

In the morning, he woke up still holding her in his arms. Her right hand was on his shoulder, her head on his chest. Claude lay still until her lashes trembled. He felt a strange burning in his heart when she looked up at him with half-closed, sleepy eyes and a lazy, dreamy smile.

III

In the fall of 1995, the new head of the anti-biker squad had arrived. It was Serge Gorte, a detective with a well-established reputation. Nothing in his unremarkable appearance suggested he was suitable for the task. Yes, he was a homicide detective—and a good one, too—but to strangers, his well-used civilian clothes, his average height, round puffy face, and expressionless blue eyes gave the impression of a homely family man. The fact that he was only thirty-five years old and already had a visible tire around his waist probably did not improve this image.

Being expert in complicated detective's work, Serge realized that gathering evidence against top-ranking bikers was not going to be an easy task. These men do not commit crimes themselves: They delegate them to subordinates. But Serge also new that they, as all humans, make mistakes and wrong judgments, haunting their criminal careers to the end.

Already, information about them was flowing into police databases from undercover agents, informants, conversation taps, and other sources, seemingly with no connection to these individuals. The task of the investigator, Serge thought, was to assemble these bits and pieces into a clear picture of criminal activity, to define the most important targets, and to concentrate major efforts on them. That is what Serge, obsessed with his work, knew how to do best. Written notes, photographs, copies of documents, and physical artifacts had their proper places in his archives. He collected data not only on the known suspects, but also on their friends, their relatives, their acquaintances, the places they visited, their habits, anything—even if it seemed to not have a relation to their criminal activity. Although he had an excellent memory, he did not rely on it with confidence. He was constantly preparing and updating a matrix of relationships of people, events, evidences, and logically related facts. The job took enormous amounts of time, of course, to the great dislike of his wife and kids. But that is what the success of any activity is about. One either devotes himself entirely to his vocation, or he lingers around mediocre achievements.

His predecessor, a man who was invariably upset and unhappy, drew his attention to a biker named Stanley Mathews, suspected of being one of the key figures among the Iron Ghosts. The police risked their best undercover agent to set him up. The agent was found dead in the basement of a house under construction. A few other deaths of valuable informants among lower bikers' ranks were grim evidence of corruption in law enforcement agencies.

Serge pulled some photographs and a few documents from the tower of binders and arranged the materials in order of importance. Everything was related to Stanley Mathews. Serge examined his sharp features: the skin, tightly stretched across his bony face, with no flesh in between; hard, examining stare; neat and tidy otherwise, not much different from an ordinary man. A very tough criminal, Serge thought. The first thing to do was to find where he lives and his hiding places, and install listening devices. It would be nice to arrange surveillance around his dwelling, but a staff shortage would likely not afford that.

Serge leaned back and looked at his watch. The funeral of the Iron Ghost drug dealer, killed two days ago and set up for today, must be already over; however, no news about it had arrived yet. The gang, according to scarce police data, was not big yet, although it was quickly gathering strength. Where could Patrick, his help, be? He should have been here at least an hour ago.

Thoughts brought him back to a disgusting crime scene in a shish-kebob restaurant two days ago.

"Two people broke in," said the waitress telling the story, shivering violently as if she had malaria. "They wore masks. One of them covered only the lower part of his face. The one in the half-mask hit the poor guy on the head, it was with something heavy, I guess—I didn't notice exactly what it was. The man started to collapse, but the other one picked him up by his armpits. They twisted his arms behind his back, yanked him to the kitchen, and pushed his head— *his face*—down, onto the grill where shish kebobs were cooking. His cry . . . Oh, God—I have never heard such a scream. He was shaking and twisting, but those guys held him, his face on that red-hot grill—it was terrifying, and that awful smell of burning human flesh . . .

"One of the killers, I think the one with only half a mask, was laughing. His sadistic laugh . . . there was nothing human about it. Then . . . I don't know how he picked it up, or where he got it . . . I just saw that he was suddenly swinging a cleaver. And still holding an arm of the poor man . . .

"He chopped off his head—and left it on the grill . . .

"The body fell to the floor, of course . . .

"Blood shot out of the neck; it suddenly shrunk, got thinner—you know? It was . . . unreal. I don't know why I noticed it. Anyway, I think it was an act of mercy, as I could imagine the suffering of that poor guy.

"Excuse me . . . , " she sobbed.

Serge had seen many gruesome scenes during his intense years in various special police units: disfigured corpses in morgues; exhumed remains from graves; assault victims dying in hospitals or at crime scenes. Nothing was as nauseating as this cooked human head. There was no mustache, no blue eyes, or any other features mentioned by the waitress that could help identify it, if not for the IDs in his wallet.

The door to his small office opened with a metallic screeching of hinges, and Patrick, a young detective who had recently been assigned as help, stepped in. Tall, blond, and always in good humor, he was good looking and nice to work with. Today, though, he had no self-confident countenance or merry smile. He pulled up a chair, dropped onto it, and wiped the sweat from his forehead.

"You'd have to see it to believe it," he said with a frown. "About 200 Iron Ghosts attended the funeral. It was quite a motorcade! They were all on good Harley Davidsons, with their insignia on their backs. Can you believe that they are already such a big gang? It was a show of strength, that's what it was."

"Did you take pictures of them?"

"No. It was impossible, Serge, trust me. They took control of the streets. They blocked some of them with pickup trucks to ensure a smooth procession to the cemetery. They didn't care about traffic lights: They stopped traffic, as cops do, where they wanted. There were only a few of us. We expected 20 to 30 people, not more, you know, but that many . . . Gosh, it's scary what these guys can do. . . ."

"What do you mean?" asked Serge.

"I mean, how they will respond. For sure, they have already figured out that the Devil's Knights are involved. We don't have enough cops to prevent a war between them."

Serge rubbed his chin. Patrick was right. The fight for a $1 billion Quebec drug market could be horrific. If the Iron Ghosts gang was that big, how big were Devil's Knights?

IV

They met in the park, after dark, far away from the eyes and ears of police. Machete was smoking pot; Marcel was pulling a cigarette out of a pack. Tension was high, as it was well known in the club that in the past Marcel had killed those who disobeyed his orders.

"What's the fuss, man?" Machete asked.

"The fuss?" Marcel echoed Machete in a menacing, questioning voice as he settled himself onto one of the fallen trees.

"Do I need to get news of your hits from the TV?"

"I meant to talk to you about that," Machete said. "I was busy, kinda. What's the fucking difference?"

"Shit!" Marcel hissed emphatically, clicking a cigarette lighter. In its feeble flame his narrowed eyes glowed in rage. "Don't you remember our decision not to clash with the Ghosts, yet? We have to wait until Jason is locked. They'll put him in the cooler for good soon—after all, seven tons of coke is not easy to shake off."

"My guys talked to this jerk three times before." Machete lit up again, his handmade cigarette dying and the tart smell of marijuana spreading over the area. "The last time, when he was told to beat it, he told 'em, 'fuck yah.' You think, Marcel, that I'll let any chickenshit talk this way in my backyard?"

"How'd yah set it up?" asked Stash from the darkness. "Who did it?"

"One of the kitchen help in the Greek Delight tipped us off that the shithead was there. At first I wanna dispatch my hit brigade, but then Trasher, the man whose territory it is, you know him, tells me that he has a good guy, just out of the slammer, who wants to join our club. Trasher said to him, 'Do something to prove your worth.'"

"What's the name of the guy?" Marcel asked.

"Claude. Claude Pichette."

"Doesn't ring a bell."

"Trasher called me and asked to let him do the job. I said 'yes.' I said, scare the shit out of those who even think of working in our territory. Trasher said, 'Don't you worry; Claude will do a good job.' He did, actually."

"I wanna talk to him," Marcel said.

"These bloody Ghosts are on my heels," Machete said. "What are we waiting for, Marcel?"

Marcel was quick to respond.

"You are a piece of shit, Machete. Piece of shit. We either have to wait for their blow, or do it first. There is no other option, thanks to you."

Next day, Marcel set up a very important meeting at a restaurant in Submarine Plaza. The busy food court was crowded at lunchtime, and he could easily disappear among the massive influx of noon diners. He arrived early so he could choose a table with a good observation angle, from which he could capture any unusual detail that might provoke his suspicion. He was about to meet an insurance agent—"the Golden Boy," as the head of the Mafia family had dubbed him.

The place he had chosen was the most expensive one among the eating establishments. It had only a single entry point where guests had to wait to be seated. The spacious booths had soft benches and comfortable chairs, and hid everyone inside. No sooner had he taken a seat in the far corner than a tall, lean figure appeared across the table. Having never seen the man before, Marcel easily recognized Raymond Jacques by his description.

This rascal had rather respectable looks. At twenty-eight years of age, he gave the impression of a much older and more mature man, a serious and responsible professional. His balding head helped—his hairline was retreating from his temples like soldiers in a disciplined army, which in turn made his forehead appear much larger than it was. But, it was his manner that made him seem like a trusted lawyer or a family physician with a successful practice. He had been in business 6 years and had learned all the tricks of the trade. Large round glasses enhanced the image of a learned person, though Marcel had been told that they were a sheer decoration—the lenses were made with clear glass, as his vision was quite normal. This was the face of a thinker, observant and attentive to tiny details. What could be better for a financial advisor?

Marcel's connection, who was close to the Italian Mafia, had privately revealed a few details of Raymond's biography and career that would never be recorded in his professional resume. After graduating from a secondary school with good credits, he had been admitted to the most prestigious university in the city. He had wanted to become a criminal lawyer, but found that 6 years of study and hard work would be a fairly boring proposition. The third year finally broke his patience. He left the university and chose, to the great surprise of all who knew him (if only anyone knew him well), the career of an insurance agent.

The decision appeared to be a stupid choice for such a good and promising student. But Raymond new what he wanted. With a clear understanding of his goals and how to achieve them, a good memory, an analytical mind, and an aptitude for all adventures in life—no matter how risky they might be—he rolled up his sleeves and took the matter into his own hands.

As an insurance agent, he gathered information about businesses and individuals, missing no detail pertinent to financial matters. Soon, he became a jack-of-all-trades: insurance agent, financial advisor, income tax specialist, and so on. He knew exactly where a client's money was, which businesses were heavily involved in cash transactions, what transactions were of a questionable nature, and where rich people held their fortunes (as well as how they got them in the first place). With this information at his disposal, he found his way to the Italian Mafia. Although the price for his services was extremely high, so was the return.

Marcel's contact expressed his suspicion that Raymond might have been involved in operations of his own, but it was more speculation than an established fact. Raymond was very secretive—no one knew more about him than he deemed necessary.

"May I sit here?" Raymond asked, bending over the table.

"Sure." Marcel pointed to the chair. "Sit down, Raymond."

"You recognized me at once," Raymond stated with an amiable smile. He sat where Marcel showed him.

"I had a good verbal description of you," Marcel explained.

"Oh—the balding head!" He responded with a note of contentment, as if the lack of hair was something he was proud of. "I recognized you at once, as well. Your photograph appears in newspapers once in awhile."

Marcel shrugged his shoulders as if to say, "That is the price for being famous."

A waitress appeared and stood close to their table, waiting for their orders. She was pretty: blond with very white, smooth skin and nice, full lips. Raymond stared at her with unceremonious interest. The waitress, a bit embarrassed under such unwelcome attention, took the order and left, the corners of her mouth turned down in a disapproving grimace.

"Nice girl," Raymond commented, raising his eyebrows, as if asking, "Isn't she?"

"Don't pick her up here," Marcel warned. A vertical wrinkle between his eyebrows vividly conveyed his disapproval.

"I know, I know," Raymond sighed. "Business first. What can I do for you?"

Marcel delayed his answer until the pretty waitress, who had already come back with a tray, served their drinks and arranged flatware at their places. This time, Raymond ignored her presence, patiently regarding Marcel with a trace of curiosity.

"There is a new biker's club in our backyard," Marcel began, once the waitress left.

"I know," Raymond nodded. "Iron Ghosts."

"There wasn't much hoopla about it," Marcel said, wrinkles of surprise creasing his forehead.

"Until the last funeral. But I knew about them before. I have some connections . . . " Raymond let Marcel guess what the rest of the phrase was supposed to be.

"I see. I hope they are not the same as Jason's."

"No, no," Raymond assured emphatically. "I wouldn't play such a risky game."

"Good. We need information on all of them. The problem is that we know nothing about them, with the exception of Jason, their president. This group is not like other biker clubs. They do not wear colors that would help distinguish them in a crowd. As far as I know right now, Jason has gathered some fairly tough guys around him."

"That is true," agreed Raymond. "They all are businesspeople."

"How'd yah know?"

"A friend of mine is a former cop," Raymond whispered. "He told me that it's impossible to penetrate Jason's circle—as is the case with your club. But there are many sympathizers and associates that could be employed by the police."

"What else did he say?" Marcel straightened up, impatient for an answer.

"The police believe that a biker war is imminent. They are preparing for the worst."

"Do you know any details?"

Raymond gave him a polite, mysterious smile.

"Not yet."

Marcel frowned.

"Any chance of gathering the information I want?" he asked.

"It would take time," Raymond said evasively.

"You've made my day." Marcel's eyes were glowing with appreciation.

"Do you wish to visit our clubhouse this Saturday?" Marcel's tone suggested that Raymond should accept his invitation as a great honor. But Raymond shook his head in rejection.

"You guys are under police scrutiny. Any association with you would draw their attention my way. Besides, you are a very strange lot—very unpredictable."

Marcel raised his eyebrows.

"What do you mean?"

"I mean one never knows what offends you and what might be the reason for one of you to pick a fight. I am no contest for hoodlums. Look at my hands."

Raymond stretched his arms out to show Marcel his long, elegant fingers and smooth skin, and placed them close to Marcel's left hand, its hairy fingers folded into the large, heavy fist of a weightlifter.

"Hoodlums?" repeated Marcel with metal in his voice. He gave a brief glance to Raymond's hands, and then tried to meet his eyes. The bastard across the table did not blink.

"Yes."

Raymond folded his arms against his chest and stared back with the patience of a trainer dealing with an irritated tiger.

"What's wrong? You guys like fighting, don't you? That is what your culture is all about, isn't it?

"If only one could call it 'culture.' But hey, that's how poorly educated journalists hail any weird lifestyle—culture." A sardonic, contemptuous smile appeared on his face. It was not clear whether his regrets were regarding culture, poorly educated journalists, bikers, or any of these. However, this was absolutely clear: Raymond had no fear of Marcel, not even a shade of it.

"In our business one has to have sufficient strength to defend himself," Marcel insisted, suppressing his first impulse to hit Raymond square in the face. "Sometimes we need to silence people. Besides, physical treatment can be very convincing." He released the tight grip of his fist and spread the fingers in a relaxed way.

"I understand," Raymond nodded. "But modern technology is at your disposal. Works nice, if you know how to use it."

Marcel examined Raymond's face with keen interest. Had this bastard ever killed anyone? Marcel had a strange feeling that the snob sitting across the table would not have hesitated one split second if a murder were more expedient.

"You've picked up a lot of garbage from the press and literature on bikers. First of all, we never fight in the clubhouse. It's against the rules even to curse there." Marcel continued to stare into Raymond's face, debating what to say or not to say. He decided to get back to the reason for their meeting. "So, Raymond, I need addresses of the Iron Ghosts, the locations of their businesses, if any, their relatives, friends, license plate numbers, anything."

Raymond's head was turning after a pretty girl, walking toward a distant corner of the restaurant, her shapely behind stretching her skirt into appealing curves.

"Such a broad," he commented in apparent appreciation. "A nice girl is the worst distraction to a conversation. And, I missed something. What was your point?"

Marcel had no doubt that Raymond hadn't missed a tiny bit of what he was saying. This was a maneuver to win time for finding the best answer. Marcel frowned.

"Don't give me any bullshit. How much do you want for your services?"

"It's negotiable. Let's postpone this topic until I find something. In my practice, I've found that I can open the hearts and purses of my clients by telling them what particular information I have."

"We have other sources of information, as well," Marcel remarked. "Hurry up."

Raymond smiled.

"I will. I know how to make my living."

"Okay, then. We also need to know construction sites with explosives—where they stockpile them, possibly who is responsible for their safekeeping, who will take money in exchange for goods. But remember: The Iron Ghosts will be after this stuff about us as well."

"I'll do my best," Raymond said. "Let's keep our business confidential."

"What do you mean?" Marcel raised his voice slightly, enough to intimidate any tough guy.

"None of your colleagues must know that you are dealing with me. You may trust them as much as you wish, but I don't have to."

"You don't understand how the Devil's Knights are organized. No one knows the business of others unless it is absolutely necessary. Everyone has his own people elsewhere. Don't worry, nobody would know about your existence. Let's agree on places to meet and what we shall call them, as well as what kinds of messages you can leave on my pager, if need be."

Raymond was nodding in acceptance of the instructions Marcel was giving him. When the lunch was over, he got up and put his hand in his pocket.

"Don't bother," Marcel dismissed him with a gesture of his hand. "I'll foot the bill."

"Thanks," Raymond said. Within moments, he had disappeared into the crowd.

V

Leila picked up the phone. "Just a moment," she said, and stretched it to Claude. When the voice on the other end of the line said a cool and polite, "Hello, Claude?" he snapped, "Yes."

"Come at 2 o'clock to the Rodeo Bar and wait outside," was the anonymous instruction. The line went dead. Claude knew where the Rodeo Bar was. He knew who wanted him.

"I have to go," he said to Leila, dressing in a hurry. "Will be back at night."

At exactly 2 o'clock, he was there. A car stopped in front of the bar. The driver motioned him to get in.

"Marcel is waiting for you," a middle-aged man at the steering wheel said. "Let's make sure that there's no tail, and then I'll take you to the restaurant where Marcel is waiting for you."

"How'd yah know it was me?" Claude asked.

"I've a good description of yah," explained the driver. He made a few sudden turns and eventually pulled the car to the edge of the road.

"Here," he said. "Get out." The driver led the way inside the restaurant and stopped by the table where a man with a protruding bony nose was sitting. Claude recognized him from photographs he had seen before. This was the legendary Marcel.

"Sit down." Marcel pointed with a nod at the chair across the table. Claude obeyed, making the best effort to conceal his admiration for everything around—tall and nicely draped windows, high ceilings, polished mahogany, and sparkling crystal glass. He was turning his head, trying to understand what this luxury was needed for, but stopped short when he noticed Marcel watching him with an understanding smile. Marcel gave the driver a look, and he disappeared.

"Like the place?" asked Marcel. Claude nodded and pointed his finger to the piece of snow-white cone-shaped cloth on the table to his right.

"What's this bloody rag for?" he asked.

"It's a cloth napkin," explained Marcel. "Now, look at the menu. Choose what you like. In the meantime, I want to talk business to you. Do you mind?"

"What d'yah want me to do?"

"Machete told me 'bout you and Trasher. Good job, but never again do anything without my command. Got it?" Marcel sighed. "I think you'd be able to take care of two Iron Ghosts."

Marcel began, helping himself to a glass of red Italian wine.

"We know the restaurant they have been frequenting lately. We cannot get them anywhere other than this place. That is unfortunate. I don't like a show of force in public places. But what am I supposed to do?" Marcel shrugged his shoulders and showed his palms, as if saying. "I give up. In spite of the best of my intentions, I have to kill them in public places."

"You wanna shoot 'em?" asked Claude. Marcel nodded.

"There is no other way, I gather. Our people will contact you when these guys are there. Usually they spend more than an hour at a table."

"How'd I recognize them?" Claude asked. Marcel took two photographs out of his breast pocket and placed them on the table in front of Claude.

"Do you know them?"

"No."

Their waiter brought the steak Marcel had ordered, expressing with his posture the desire to serve and please. He took the white napkin off the table, unrolled it with a swift flap, and placed it on Marcel's lap.

"Enjoy your meal, sir," said the waiter.

"Fuck off," Claude said to the waiter's retreating back. He turned back to Marcel and swallowed nervously when he noticed Marcel's disapproving and contemptuous grimace. Claude managed to force a feeble smile on his closed lips and looked into Marcel's unblinking, frozen stare. A few butterflies fluttered their wings inside Claude's stomach.

"A recent blast near our clubhouse was the deed of this one," Marcel went on talking, while pointing a finger at one of the photographs. "We need to get him, to strike back as quickly as possible. Everyone should know how we respond. We are Devil's Knights. That means something."

Claude nodded contentedly. The waiter now brought his steak, placed the plate in front of him, spread his napkin on his knees, and retreated with the same "Enjoy your meal, sir," comment. This time, Claude nodded "Thank you" and Marcel granted him a short smile. He liked how quickly Claude learned.

"I will give you $15,000 bucks for the deal," continued Marcel. "Five thousand today and ten after it's done. Seven thousand, five hundred for each head."

The gleam in Claude's eyes gave the proposal a wholehearted welcome. He cut an impressive piece of steak and shoved it into his mouth.

"Is that okay?" asked Marcel.

"Uh-huh," murmured Claude, his jaws working hard on too large a piece of meat. He used his palm to wipe up a thin stream of sauce that rolled from the corner of his mouth. He had never eaten anything that tasty. The promised pay for his service added a sense of good life to the conversation. Marcel picked up the napkin from his lap and dabbed his lips. Claude swallowed, took his napkin in his fist, and did the same.

"Good," said Marcel. He did not specify to what he was referring: Claude's improving manners or his acceptance of the pay.

"Do you have a gun?" Marcel gave him an inquisitive look.

"Not yet. But I have someone who will sell one to me. No sweat."

"Don't worry about that. My people will give you a good one. You need a gun that never fails."

"Cool."

"Now. When you go, dress in a jogging suit. This way, nobody will recognize you by your clothes. Take a ski mask with you. Do not put it on until you decide to shoot. Nobody will remember your looks before the mask is on. Clear?"

"I know that much," grumbled Claude.

"Of course. But I want to make sure we are thinking alike. Drop the gun right after the shoot. Remember to stick to the major rules. The most important one is not to kill bystanders. We've had enough bad publicity lately. Another one with innocent victims and all the newspapers will scream and yell. Some bloody journalists are always on the lookout for something resembling Hollywood-style murder."

"I know," agreed Claude. The thought of being such a hero made him smile.

"Try to make it quick, in a matter of seconds. Remember, if you do get caught, do not even think about selling me out to the police."

"What are you talking about?" Claude interrupted indignantly. He exchanged menacing glances with Marcel. He did not give a shit for any authority when his own reputation was questioned.

"Devil's Knights will haunt you for the rest of your days," Marcel said, dismissing Claude's reaction. "And I don't think I need to mention what would happen when they found you."

He paused. Claude stopped chewing and stared at Marcel as if he wanted to hit him.

"Who are you taking me for?" he asked, about to explode in a filthy outburst of rage, but Marcel raised his hand as a warning sign.

"Okay, okay. I have to tell you that, you know. Don't take it too personally. Let's get back to business. People arranging the deal will be in contact with you over a pager. They will let you know when these two are in the restaurant. All other planning, as well as execution of the hit, will be up to you. I do trust you."

"I don't have a pager."

"I know. We will provide you with one tomorrow."

"I like it." Claude uttered a short laugh, returning to a good mood. "Will do. But would you promote me after that?"

"Oh, yes," agreed Marcel hurriedly, as if he had forgotten an important thing. "Sure. I'll propose to give you 'hangaround' status. You are a good chap. I like you."

Claude leaned back in his chair and relaxed. He was pleased. This was a happy day in his life. The leader of the Devil's Knights had treated him to lunch in the fanciest restaurant, talking to him like an equal. Money, the most desirable thing in his life, would soon be in abundance. And, also soon, maybe very soon, he would become a full member of the Devil's Knights motorcycle club.

VI

"I can't believe it," Claude shouted, shifting his eyes from the sleek Honda Civic to his friend's smiling face. "This is jus' three grand? Are you sure, old buddy, that this is a clean car?"

"I told you, I know how to buy wheels." Hans pointed his finger, like a barrel of a gun, at Claude. He was swelling with pride. "The car is clean, don't you worry."

"Now we'll make tons of money," Claude assured him, his eyes on the car. "Let's drive!"

"When can you give me the money for it?" Hans asked, taking the passenger seat.

"Right now. But you have to help me, Hans." Claude let the car leap forward, as if they were on a racing track.

"Cool down," Hans grumbled.

"Will you help me?"

"How?"

"First, we need another car. Just for a few hours. Okay?"

"Yah. What's next?" Hans turned his face to Claude. He listened with grim attention to the plan of action that Claude had thought over in great detail. The Honda would be parked at the plaza, 5 minutes' driving time from the restaurant. The hit must be conducted quickly, 10 minutes at the most, including driving from the restaurant to the plaza. Hans would get three grand for a few hours of trouble.

"Hey—hey—hey," Hans began protesting after Claude had finished speaking. "You know, Claude, I'm in a different business. I'm not a biker and never wanna be. Besides, hits are not my bread and butter. I'm in the car business, you know."

"That's right," Claude insisted. "I'll do the hitting. Just driving, that's what I need from you. C'mon, Hans. Three grand for a few minutes. Good dough, eh? I'll pay you next day. Okay?"

Hans shrugged his shoulders.

"Fine."

As promised, a man on an errand from Marcel brought a pager. Then, on the day that the hit was to take place, Hans stole a car and parked it in the chosen plaza, not far from Claude's Honda. Claude was waiting for the signal in his Honda, just an extra precaution in case the police were already in search of the stolen car. A few minutes past 1 o'clock in the afternoon, the pager beeped. Claude glanced at the display, got out of his car, and went to Hans.

"Let's go."

Hans was apparently nervous, but drove well. His eyes were pale; his lips, tight.

Claude was edgy, as well. Murder did not worry him— he had killed people before. But in the past, except for the hit at the shish-kebab house, it had happened in fights, sometimes premeditated, sometimes not. This time the game was different. The shooting would be in a public place and follow strict adherence to Marcel's rules.

This son-of-a-bitch Stanley might have a gun, he suddenly thought. His face on the photograph wasn't the one of a college boy: He would react quickly at the first sight of a masked man. He would likely sit in a place from which he could observe the whole restaurant. The bastard might pull out his own gun and shoot, for sure, with deadly precision.

Claude touched the gun under the top of his jogging suite. The exhilarating feeling of its strength and uncontested power over other people overwhelmed him. A tide of energy stiffened the muscles in his hands; he held the card that beats all other odds.

I'll do my best, he said to himself with tight lips. The train of his thought was crushed by another beep of the pager.

"They are there," he told Hans. Hans nodded, drove to the restaurant, and stopped the car at the entrance.

"I'll wait for you over there, by the parking meter." Hans pointed to a short metal post half a block down the road.

"It won't take long."

Claude pushed the door open and went inside. To his left was a sign in a frame, fixed on a thin metal pole: "Please wait to be seated." Nobody was around, as all the waitresses were busy. Almost every table in the spacious dining room was taken. To find Stanley in such a crowded place and not draw his attention would take a stroke of good luck. But Claude had a pretty good idea where to look for him. He and the other man would likely choose a table in one of the corners to secure their rear with two walls. At the same time, the place would have to be in a good observation point from which any suspicious move would be immediately detected.

He was right. Three men were sitting at the far end of the room, to the right, at a large square table. One of them was for sure one of those in the photograph Marcel had shown him. But Claude had never seen the other two. That meant that they should not be shot at. However, the most wanted target—Stanley—was not there. In an instant, Claude changed the plan. With a steady pace and a carefree, absent-minded air, he proceeded to the washroom, where Stanley most likely would be. Kill him there, he thought, then rush back and try to kill the other one. Even if the second man, alarmed by the sound of a shot, managed to escape, the hit would be good enough; without Stanley, though, the task would not be completed.

He entered the washroom. Nobody was there. Claude put on the ski mask—it was a cylindrical cloth covering only the lower part of his face—and went back, holding the handle of the gun under his jogging jacket.

The target was very quick to react. As Claude had suspected, at the first sight of a masked man, he jumped from his seat at the table and rushed to the exit door. Claude fired. The bullet hit the man somewhere and made him stumble. Screaming, twisting, and shivering in agony, he ran again, but Claude let a few more bullets fly toward him. Someone else shrieked in horror and pain. The wounded target fell. Claude darted to him, fired two more shots into his head, and briskly walked off to the exit. He turned around at the door to make sure that nobody was following him. Nobody was. Claude stretched his arm, released his grip, and let the gun drop. It hit the floor with a metal sound, bounced, and landed again, this time immobile and quiet. Claude rushed outside, took off the mask on the way to the car, jumped into the passenger seat, and commanded, "Full speed!"

Hans was waiting with the engine idling. He sped up until the car reached the street speed limit and then drove smoothly, obeying road rules and street signs.

"Right, Hans," Claude said, slapping his shoulder. Hans knew very well that many were caught when tough guys like Claude, trying to leave a crime scene as quickly as possible, provoked a police chase.

Hans was about to stop at a traffic light when both of them noticed a police car in the rearview mirror, flashing its warning lights. It was far away, but approaching fast, in an apparent rush to get somewhere.

"They may be after us," Claude growled. "Someone in the restaurant could've made a call. Push it, Hans."

And Hans did. He made a very dangerous turn. The tires of oncoming cars screamed, but they escaped a seemingly inevitable collision. He maneuvered past a few cars on the way to the next turn, then twisted the steering wheel to the right, and kept moving toward the plaza. The police car had disappeared from the rearview mirrors. Hans turned into the parking lot.

"Good," Claude said. "It'll be much harder for them to find the car in the plaza. They may block roads, thinking that we are on the run, but they shouldn't look in a parking lot."

Hans knew his part of the game well. He stopped at the first available vacant spot, not far from Claude's Honda. Now, the police would have a nearly impossible task. There was little, if any, chance of them seeing the car if it was not moving.

They left the stolen car and walked to the Honda. Nobody paid attention to two guys in jogging suits striding leisurely along the rows of cars. Claude took the driver's seat in the Honda and turned the key. The engine came to life, and he steered the car to the exit, past the incoming police car, whose deafening siren made all traffic stop.

Claude made another turn, then another one, and in a few minutes entered the highway.

"Good job, Hans," he said and roared with laughter. "Good job! You've made three grand in a few minutes, as I promised. Not bad, eh?"

Hans did not share Claude's merry mood. He sat, his face without a trace of a smile, still not recovered from the fear of the police chase.

"It's over, Hans, over," Claude shouted again and gave his friend a pat on his back. "There is nobody on earth who could point a finger at you. Take your gloves off and give them to me. It's over."

Hans forced a feeble smile onto his face.

"Let's go to my place. I'll give you three grand now. Good job, Hans."

Marcel met Claude the next day in a park located on the outskirts of the city. The sun had already sunk below the horizon and darkness was making the woods dangerous to both the police and the public. They walked along a narrow path among the trees and bushes, speaking in low voices and listening to the silence around them.

"All the newspapers are screaming about this hit," Marcel was saying. "The problem is that a woman was hit by one of your bullets. Don't you remember what I said? Under no circumstance were you to harm anyone except those two. Bad publicity—that is what will eventually get us."

"I did my best," Claude said in a slightly apologetic tone. "There was no choice." He gave Marcel a detailed account of what had happened. Marcel listened with intense interest. When Claude finished, Marcel gave him a hug.

"Now I see. It's good that you wanted to find Stanley. But you've gotta get some training in shooting. I'll arrange that."

"I just . . . " Claude stopped, apparently hesitant to continue.

"Go ahead," Marcel demanded. "What's up?"

"You promised seven-and-a-half grand for each."

"Oh, that. I know. I will give you five, two-and-a-half extra. After all, it was not your fault that Stanley was not there. Good enough?"

"Thanks." Claude was very grateful. He felt that he could kill anybody for Marcel.

"There will be plenty for you to do soon," Marcel promised, as if answering his thoughts. "Are you ready?"

"Yes."

"Do you sniff? Smoke pot?"

"Yes. But not much."

"Good. We don't need anyone who uses those things too much. They become useless. Remember: you will never become a Devil's Knight if you take too much stuff up your nose. Better yet, stay away from it altogether. You have to have a firm hand and a clear mind. You need to work with the precision of a surgeon. Understand?"

"Yes."

"Good." Marcel took a pack of money out of his pocket and handed it over to Claude.

"Here it is. Go back alone. I will go a different way. Have fun."

VII

As the feeble light of a November morning crawled through the half-closed shutters, Claude sneaked out of the sofa bed, put a pile of money on the table, and got back to where warm, soft, and tender Leila was sleeping. Feeling his arm around her, she moved closer, still in deep sleep. He was lying motionless, waiting patiently, looking at her parted lips and closed eyes. Soon her lashes trembled and she woke up.

"Morning," she whispered, still in the grips of sweet dreams. Claude smiled and pushed a thick wisp of hair off her forehead. She kissed him, raised to her knees, and stretched. The first glance at the table made her utter a joyful cry.

"Wow! This will make for good shopping!"

"Sure. Why not?"

"How much may I take off the pile?"

"Take it all."

"Kiddn' me?"

"Nope. Take it."

She hopped on him and jumped a few times, as if riding a horse.

"Should we buy new furniture?" she asked.

"Anything."

"Love you. Sweet boy. We need some clothes. I wanna buy something for you, too. Handsome guy, but dresses like a peasant."

"Good idea," he agreed, although a much better plan preoccupied him at that moment. There was a bar, which was so far nobody's territory. It would be nice to meet there with Trasher and show off his riches. Let Trasher guess who did the hit—the hottest media topic of the week. Every gangster wants fame and recognition more than money. He picked up the phone and dialed.

"Hello," rasped Trasher at the other end of the line.

"Can we meet at the Brussel bar today?" asked Claude.

"M–m–m. When?"

"At three."

"Okay. Somtn' important?"

"Not much. Jus . . . I'm gonna be at the plaza there, while Leila shops. We can talk."

"Sure."

At the plaza, Leila changed her plan. It was the furniture store that distracted her attention.

"Let's buy a bed," she suggested. "Ours is completely ruined, partly through your efforts."

Claude smiled and gave her a friendly, gentle, and loving tap with his fist.

"You worked hard as well to deserve it," he said. "Choose whatever you like, and arrange the delivery with the store. After that, go to Holt Renfrew. I'll meet you there."

"You are leaving me alone?" she exclaimed capriciously.

"I have to meet Trasher at the bar. It won't take long."

Claude found him sitting at the table with a glass of beer.

"Your hit?" he asked, when Claude took a chair.

"Wanna drink somtn' better?" asked Claude. "My treat."

"Nah. Maybe later. Doing well?"

"Not bad."

They sat in silence, and when a double shot of Scotch was served for Claude, they drank, exchanging meaningless remarks. Suddenly a tight knot squeezed Claude's stomach.

"What's wrong?" Trasher asked, throwing suspicious glances around.

"Turn back, but very slowly. There is a skinny guy at the bar stand."

"Yes. I see."

"That is Stanley, the big shot at Iron Ghosts. Marcel showed me his photograph."

"Do you have a piece with you?" asked Trasher.

"Nothing."

"Me neither. But don't you worry. One blow of this hand," he showed his large, hairy fist, "will break his neck."

"I'll do it," Claude said. "See, he's skinny like a starving horse. I'll break his jaw with one punch."

"Don't," insisted Trasher. "Stay as a cover, in case he's not alone."

"He noticed us," Claude warned.

"You see, it's even better for you not to move while I approach him."

Trasher stood up and walked, looking in the opposite direction, as if Stanley was of no interest to him. For a split second, Claude froze in horrific amazement. Stanley dove under Trasher's assaulting hand, which was supposed to have dealt a devastating blow, but missed. Trasher took an expert punch in the jaw. While he was off balance, Stanley grabbed his jacket and threw him backward. Trasher's head hit the bar stand with the sound of crushed bones; his lifeless body fell on the floor.

Claude rushed toward Stanley. This time, though, he had bad luck: Stanley's fist stopped him. It was the punch of an expert boxer, too fast to avoid, too hard to withstand. With lightning speed, Stanley's left hook landed under Claude's right rib, near the liver. A wrenching spasm of pain gripped Claude's body from head to toe. He bent over and got another blow, this time in the jaw, very accurate as well, but not as painful, although his brain almost stopped working. With inhuman effort, motivated by intense hatred and an insane rejection of defeat, Claude darted forward and clutched Stanley, like a wrestler. A few moments of wrestling gave him a break. The acute pain subsided; his sadistic rage and energy returned. He did not manage to do much, though. With a powerful twist, Stanley threw him against the bar counter. Claude felt terrible pain again, but this time at the back of his head. Blood was now running down his face and body. Claude groped forward only to encounter another blow, which, it seemed, crushed everything inside his skull. He fell to his knees, hands planted on the tile floor, spitting thick, red saliva and crumbs of broken teeth. With the detached curiosity of an outsider, he saw a tiny dark stream pouring from his face into a growing dark puddle on the floor.

"This is the end," he said to himself. This thought did not frighten him, but the sour feeling of defeat, mixed with the greasy flow of blood, gave him a bad taste in his mouth.

To his surprise, the beating stopped. Somebody lifted him and placed him on a chair. He raised his head. Two cops stood in front of him, observing him with apparent hostility.

"What happened?" asked one of them. Claude shrugged his shoulders. A few steps away another cop was helping Trasher; blood was streaming from a wound at the back of Trasher's head, but he was still alive. Stanley was nowhere to be seen.

"I will get you, Stanley," Claude said to himself.

Chapter 2

I

Camilla thought of herself as an extraordinary, exceptional girl, although nothing in her biography had so far been remarkable enough to defend such an inordinate notion. She was tall, blonde, and pretty, with an artistic look. She had wits and a good sense of humor, but an actress, she was not. Instead, she was on the last leg of her studies to become a registered nurse. At twenty years of age, she had already had a few lovers, all of whom she'd left behind with broken hearts. These affairs would have been of interest to her close friends and admirers, but they were not significant enough for any biographer to record. Her fate, however, was about to take an unpredictable twist.

The day was overcast, as many were in January 1996. Camilla was standing in line to board a chairlift at the Mont Tremblant ski resort. Over her shoulders, she wore a backpack with a colorful patch that read "McMichaels School of Nursing." Next to her was her closest friend and roommate Shelly—a petite, sweet little woman with large, dark eyes like those of a defenseless gazelle. Though Shelly was a student at the art institute, her goal was a successful marriage, not a career in the arts. To that effect, she considered every male who approached her to be a potential groom. The long line of skiers was advancing slowly toward the chairlift. Just outside the boundaries of the stretched ropes stood a man talking on a cell phone. Camilla gave him a quick look.

Not bad, she thought. Like Shelly, and most young women, she loved to flirt. Usually, men accepted her advances gladly, but this one stared right through her, as if she did not exist, and said something into his cell phone. Camilla could not make out the words, in spite of his close proximity. As the line moved forward and she passed by, she noticed a small scar under his left jaw and cold, ruthless rage in his eyes. She dropped her game and resumed talking with Shelly.

The girls were getting very close to a four-seat bench on the chairlift when Camilla heard indignant, irritated voices behind them.

"You have to stay in line like everyone else, sir," a man was saying, reprimanding someone rather angrily.

"Next time—," she heard. Presumably, this was the response of the man to whom the reprimand had been directed. "I promise."

"Outrageous," a woman's voice proclaimed solemnly.

"I will change for the better, ma'am, I swear," promised the voice.

"Stop him!" the woman demanded. Nobody obeyed her command.

"This would be my last run today, ma'am," the man said. That was easy to promise because the chairlift was shutting down in ten minutes.

Shelly stopped talking and glanced over Camilla's shoulder. Camilla turned around, too, to see what was causing the disturbance. She noticed a man struggling awkwardly to get through the line of skiers. Jostling with enviable energy, he advanced at last to the place where Camilla stood and asked her rather politely, "May I join you girls?"

He was the man who had not responded to her glance just a minute before. Camilla shrugged her shoulders and looked the guy up and down. Medium height, slim but apparently strong, a sporty, very fit man. The blue, piercing eyes on his skinny face reminded her of a marathon runner. She noticed again the small scar under his left jaw.

"You may. The lift is for four."

The next moment they were in a rush to be seated on the moving bench.

"My name is Stanley." The man introduced himself as the lift began moving.

"And your name?"

The question was directed to Camilla, as she was next, on his left.

"Leave us alone," responded Camilla. She did not like these kinds of advances.

"That's not polite," commented the man. Camilla turned her head and looked disapprovingly into his unblinking eyes. An expression of unrestrained force in them was frightening. She did not say a word.

"What are you doing tonight?" Stanley asked.

"Indeed, Camilla, what are we gonna do tonight?" asked Shelly. "Let's go to the spa first. I love to sit in the hot tub outside when the snow is all around."

"Good idea," agreed Stanley. Shelly bent forward to look at Stanley with her "would-you-marry-me?" eyes. When their stares met, she flapped her eyelashes but then, disturbed and embarrassed, she leaned back and fell silent.

Stanley tried to strike up a conversation a few more times, but his attempts were not well received. He then sat quietly for a while, bending forward and shifting his eyes from one woman to another. Camilla, however, felt that most of his attention was directed toward her. As the lift approached the top of the hill, she turned to Shelly.

"I'm gonna try the Diamond Run this time. You go on Green, Shelly."

"Please don't, Camilla," Shelly begged. "Look—there are icy moguls all the way down. And it's getting dark."

"I don't care," Camilla said, jumping off the bench and pushing ahead with both poles. "I'll see you down there."

She slid to the start of the run and looked back. Stanley stood right there behind her, smiling.

"I can't let you run alone," he explained. "Nobody goes there. What if you break a leg?"

"I wouldn't advise you to go after me, unless you are a really good skier. The slope is very steep. See those moguls? They are all ice."

With another push of her poles, she began making the slalom descent, elegantly making quick, deft turns on parallel skis. She stopped where the moguls began and looked back. Stanley was catching up, trying to make the same turns and twists that she had. No doubt he was a poor skier. He wasn't even able to keep his skis parallel, let alone demonstrate elementary slalom techniques.

"Please, be careful. Don't try to follow my tracks," Camilla warned him again when he stopped beside her. "This is really dangerous."

"Everything dangerous is worthwhile for me."

"You are crazy." She tried to convince him: "If you do that, the paramedics would bring your body down the slope in parts. Don't exhibit your stupid bravado here."

Having said that, she pushed forward and rushed between the moguls, fully enjoying the strength of her legs, the speed, the twists, turns, and jumps—all attributes of a body's physical superiority over the challenges of the world. A noise behind made her stop. To her horror, she saw Stanley rolling on the snow. His skis—which were off his boots—were scattered far away from where he was tumbling downhill. At last, his body ceased its terrifying roll. He lay on his back, arms spread wide, motionless. Camilla looked around in search of anyone who could help. Only the icy moguls and the still trees, clad in their white winter dresses of snow, were in sight. She took off her skis and walked up as quickly as she could, but the climb was not easy in heavy alpine boots. When she got close, she knelt beside him and touched the artery in his throat. Suddenly, Stanley opened his eyes, grabbed her with both hands, threw her on the snow, and bent over her, smiling.

"A-a-ah!" Camilla screamed, frightened. "Let me go!"

"I will. But tell me first, why did you touch my throat?"

"I was trying to feel your pulse. Let me go. Now!"

He held her tight. It was useless to struggle against such a strong man.

"How'd you know about feeling for a pulse in the throat?" he insisted.

"Because I am a medical student. Next year I will be a registered nurse. Why do you care?"

"I almost lost my life chasing you," he complained.

"I warned you," Camilla objected. She sat up, looking at him as a nurse would a patient. "How do you feel?"

"My hip hurts. But, I'm okay."

"Can you get down alone, or shall I call the paramedics?"

"No, no help at all," commanded Stanley decisively. "I'll manage."

"I'll go get your skis and poles. Sit here for now, okay?"

Stanley nodded. She brought him his equipment and helped him get ready. The guy was apparently in pain, but was trying not to show it.

She walked back down the slope and put her skis on. In the meantime, Stanley slid past her—this time with caution—and then turned left to the easier run, disappearing behind the trees.

It was getting dark. Camilla rushed down, consumed again by the thrill of the dangerous sport, the blowing wind whistling in her ears. After a few steep curves, she approached the first night lights of the ski resort below.

Shelly stood at the foothill, holding her skis and poles upright, waiting.

"What took you so long to come down?" she asked. "I'm freezing here."

A cold wind had begun to blow from the top of the mountain as dusk descended on the village. The projectors shed bright light on the twisting run as the first skiers, complaining about the freezing temperature, awaited the chairlift for night skiing.

"He followed me," explained Camilla. "The poor bastard fell. I wonder how he managed to come down with his hip so badly hurt. I helped him a bit."

"His eyes are pretty scary," Shelly remarked. "Haven't you noticed how scary his stare is?"

"It's all in your mind," Camilla said with the resolution of an experienced woman. "He has a hard stare. That's all right. That's how a man should be, but nothing is scary about that."

Grasping their swimsuit-filled bags they rushed to the building where the hotel spa and swimming pool were.

Camilla was not a bit surprised when Stanley blocked their way in the lobby.

"Nice to see you again," he said, smiling.

"How's your hip?" she asked, returning the smile.

"Very bad. I came here because I want you to take care of me." The naughty gleam in his eyes made it clear that there was nothing wrong with his hip.

"I didn't notice you limping," Camilla observed. "What do you want me to do about it?"

Shelly shot her a quick, sly glance.

"What are you doing tonight?" Stanley asked, ignoring the question, and the look. Camilla was about to say something when Shelly interrupted.

"What would you suggest?" she asked.

"I'd like to invite you to dinner. There's a very nice restaurant about ten minutes from here. The Eagle Nest. Have you heard of it?"

"You must be a rich man to be able to afford an evening there with two girls," Shelly remarked, regarding him with renewed interest. She straightened, waiting for confirmation that she was invited.

"I am," Stanley agreed.

"What do you do for a living?" Shelly asked.

"This is Shelly, by the way," Camilla laughed as she introduced her roommate. "She's a very straightforward girl."

"I can see that. Nice to meet you, Shelly." Stanley nodded. "I have a muffler shop."

"A muffler shop?" Camilla echoed. "How boring."

"Would you prefer someone with a more interesting occupation?" Stanley asked.

"As a matter of fact, I would. I like adventures. I like interesting people."

"With me, you'll have as many adventures in your life as you can handle."

"What kind of adventure do you offer us tonight?" Camilla asked mockingly.

"First, I'll impress you with the restaurant," Stanley assured her authoritatively. "Then—trust me. But I have just one small favor I would ask before we go. Will you?"

"What kind of favor?" Camilla exchanged glances with Shelly, asking silently, *Shall I go for it?*

"I have a friend here at the hotel, who is sick. He has a high fever. Would you mind taking a look at him and helping him, if you can?"

"Well . . . why don't you ask for medical help from the hotel?" Camilla frowned. "I haven't earned my degree yet. There might be legal implications."

"I see what kind of adventurous girl you are," Stanley remarked contemptuously. "You want adventures in the movies, not in real life. You're afraid of a very simple thing."

"Okay. You got me," Camilla yielded. "I'll look at him."

"Very nice of you. I have friends who can entertain Shelly while you and I are upstairs with the sick one. It won't take long. Right after that, we'll drive to the restaurant." He gave them a broad, friendly smile. "Deal?"

He made a nod toward two men, approximately his own age, who were sitting in a distant corner of the lobby. They instantly stood up and came closer. Other than their quick reaction, there was nothing weird about them. One might even say that they were handsome and friendly looking.

"Shelly, I trust you to my friends for 15 minutes," Stanley said. "They will take good care of you at the bar. Okay?"

Not really waiting for her reply, he took Camilla's hand and walked to the elevator. On the fourth floor they stepped out, turned left, and went along the narrow corridor. Once they reached the end of it, Stanley unlocked the door, threw a suspicious glance over his shoulder, and let her in.

On the king-size bed inside, a man with thick, dark hair, round face, and bushy eyebrows was lying on his left side. With his T-shirt stained with blood, his grayish pale face, and his eyes closed, he seemed dead. Suddenly his eyes opened; they glistened with unmistakable luster of high fever and pain.

"This is a nurse, Ogre," Stanley said. The man blinked. Camilla rolled up his shirt, uncovering a poorly done bandage, soaked in blood.

"What kind of wound is it?" she asked the man. He had the huge muscles of a bodybuilder.

"Knife," Stanley said.

"How long ago did it happen?"

"About an hour ago, may be more. Could you stop asking questions?"

"I ask only what's necessary," Camilla snapped. "If it was more than two hours ago, you'd better take him to the hospital."

"I won't take him to the hospital, no matter what."

Camilla carefully removed the bandage and uncovered a long, but shallow wound. Ogre groaned and clenched his teeth.

"Gosh," Camilla sighed. "He needs a surgeon. I'm not qualified to do the job."

"You're much more qualified than I am," Stanley insisted. "What should be done?"

"The wound should be cleaned and disinfected. Stitches must be put in—this wound won't heal without them—although, as I see it, the knife didn't penetrate the ribs and didn't touch any vital organs."

"What supplies do you need to fix it?"

"But . . ."

"Say it. What do you need?"

All of a sudden, fear gripped her heart. She realized that there was no way out. She would have to do the job they wanted.

"First, I need some 3 percent hydrogen peroxide to clean the wound. I need some Sofra-Tulle to cover it, and a large roll of gauze bandages to wrap around his chest. And then, if nothing better is available, I need a needle and silk thread to sew the wound. Actually, you could get all of these in any drugstore."

Stanley nodded and pointed at the bag on the table.

"Morphine, syringes, and some other things are in that bag," he said. "Someone will bring Sofra-Tulle and peroxide soon from the drugstore behind the hotel. Do whatever you can in the meantime."

Stanly flipped his cell phone and dialed.

"You are insane," Camilla objected emphatically. Stanley didn't listen; no doubt he was giving orders, but his speech was impossible to understand.

"What if I do something wrong?" insisted Camilla. "They'll throw me out of school. I might even be taken to court."

"Bullshit," Stanley grumbled, putting the phone in his pocket. He'd grown increasingly irritated, impatient, and menacing.

"I'm scared," she complained meekly, as if somebody could help her.

"Do it," Stanley demanded. "There's nothing to fear. Ogre will never be taken to any hospital, no matter what happens." He put his hand on her shoulder and smiled. "Don't worry, Camilla. Everything is gonna be okay. Do it. With me, you shouldn't fear anything."

Something clicked inside her. As her fear vanished, her mind became cold and clear. She removed everything that was inside the bag. As promised, it held a remarkable supply of syringes, bandages, and whatnot. *Where did these people get all of this?* she thought to herself.

"You'll feel better soon," she promised. Ogre nodded, and then looked at Stanley.

"Three of us were in the bar when the two jerks came in," he began speaking, hardly moving his lips. "The barman is my man, you know. They came to the bar and showed him a photograph. I saw him shrugging his shoulders. Our guys went to the washroom, too much beer, you know . . . " He sighed. "I went to the bar, like, to order a beer, and asked the barman what those two fuckheads wanted. He said . . . he said that they showed him your photograph and asked if he saw you in the bar. He said 'no.' When the barman spoke, one of the two looked at me. We recognized each other. I saw the son of a bitch two years ago in slumber. Claude's his name, if I remember right."

"Doesn't ring a bell," Stanley said.

"Please, lie back and relax," Camilla asked. "Try to stay calm. Moving your body won't do you any good."

"Tell me everything later," Stanley demanded.

There was a knock at the door, and Stanley returned with a plastic bag.

"Here's everything you needed," he said.

Elevated to the role of a surgeon, Camilla did everything with a calm, firm hand. She cleaned the wound, inserted thread into the needle, and moved the skin to close the wound's edges.

"Now, this is the unpleasant part," she said to Ogre. "I have to stitch you up, but I don't have any local anesthetic."

"Go ahead," Ogre said weakly. Camilla inserted the needle into the inflamed flesh. Ogre stiffened. She stopped for a moment, but he moaned: "Do it. Finish it."

Suddenly, Camilla felt a chilling indifference to the man's suffering. She concentrated on her job, pushing away all feelings and thoughts that could distract her. She stitched the wound, disregarding the convulsive shakes of Ogre's body; placed Sofra-Tulle on the scar; and wrapped the bandage around his chest, making sure that it was tight and firmly fixed.

"We can only pray that there's no serious infection," she said through the open door of the bathroom, while washing her hands. "Hopefully, everything will be okay. When are you going to take him from here?"

"Tomorrow morning."

"Are you leaving with him?"

"No. I'll stay another two nights. Somebody else will take care of him. Let's go to the restaurant. We'll talk there."

Ogre slowly turned onto his back, eyes closed, with a look of grim relaxation on his greenish-pale face. Camilla tidied the blanket and sheets and started to gather waste from the operation.

"He should be able to sleep now," she said gently, "and will be okay by tomorrow. Do you have somebody to stay with him?"

"He won't be alone for long," Stanley said. "Don't worry about the garbage, someone will clean everything up."

He helped her with her ski jacket, which still retained the aroma of cold, fresh mountain air, and then led her out.

"Don't tell much to Shelly," he asked.

She was quick to respond.

"Of course not. What I did may cost me my career. I'll tell her that the guy had a high fever."

They sneaked through the empty corridor and stepped into the elevator.

"How long will it take for the two of you to get ready for dinner?" Stanley asked. The elevator moved smoothly and quietly downward.

"About an hour. We have to fix our hair and get dressed. Girl's business, you know. By the way, where did you manage to get all this medical stuff that fast?"

Stanley dodged the answer.

"Where are you staying?" he asked instead of answering.

"Here."

"Let's meet in an hour downstairs."

The elevator landed like a feather, and the door opened to reveal the lobby. Two busy clerks stood behind the reception desk at the far end, while Shelly sat on a cozy sofa a few steps away, conversing leisurely with two men.

"What took you so long?" was Shelly's immediate reaction. She was pink from the drinks and the warmth of the hotel. With a sly smile, she added, "I think you were having a good time by the bed of that sick man." Her sly, mischievous but pleasant grimace was the reflection of her own intriguing suspicion.

Camilla did not respond, giving a brief glance around.

"Now, let's rush. Stanley and his friends are gonna pick us up in an hour."

Shelly leapt up. With ringing laughs, see-you-soon promises, and eyes shining, the girls departed. Shelly was excited; so was Camilla. She, however, was hiding her mood beneath a quiet demeanor.

"Weird guys," Shelly expressed her unsolicited opinion when they got to their room. "We'd better stay away from them."

"We don't have to marry them," Camilla objected. "Dinner in a restaurant is not an engagement."

She turned on the TV, trying not to listen to her friend's conversation about marriage and dinner.

According to the local news, the weather was expected to continue to be cold and overcast for another two days. However, the chairlifts at Mont Tremblant would be open. In the actual newscast, the announcer said that the local police had been informed about an Iron Ghosts biker club gathering in one of the hotels at the ski resort. In a related story, a brawl had broken out in one of the bars with a local gang, associates of the Devil's Knights. The news concluded with a warning about an approaching snowstorm.

Camilla dodged questions about the sick man, skillfully diverting the conversation to other topics, such as how good looking the guys were who had kept Shelly company. The diversion worked.

Stanley picked them up in the lobby exactly at 8 o'clock. The girls settled comfortably into the rear seat of a large jeep and looked out the windows in silence. A dense mass of trees edged the narrow road, which wound in steep curves up the hill. Occasional snowflakes swirled leisurely through the headlights. There was no traffic on this seemingly deserted road.

The car reached the top of the hill where a large building stood, its windows ablaze with bright lights from inside. Stanley pulled up close to the entrance and led the girls through the lobby and two large halls. The entire place was richly decorated and packed with well-dressed, smiling people. Elegant furniture, china, crystal glasses, and sparkling flatware added to the ambiance of this opulent place. When they entered the dining room, a huge picture window stretched from floor to ceiling like a glass wall, providing the view of a fenced courtyard, lit by outdoor lamps all around it.

"Here we are," Stanley said, pointing to a table by the window. The two men who had kept Shelly company in the hotel sat there with one vacant chair between them.

"Sit down with us, Shelly," one of them invited with a smile.

Camilla took the nicest place at the far end, where she could observe the snow-covered land outside as well as the warm aura of the dining hall. On her right sat Stanley. Shelly settled between the two men, all pink cheeks and shining eyes, happy to be the center of attention.

A large table further down the hall was apparently made up of a few smaller ones that were joined together to accommodate a party of ten men in their late thirties and early forties. Tough-looking guys, they studied everyone around with hostile suspicion.

"Some water?" Stanley asked. Camilla paid attention to his hand, which was holding a jar. She saw an interesting ring on his finger: a weird emblem surrounded by small diamonds.

"Yes, please," she said, studying the hands of the two guys across the table. They wore similar rings.

"Anything wrong?" Stanley asked, filling up her glass.

"You all have weird rings," she said. "What do they mean?"

"Anyone having a ring like that belongs to our club."

"What club?"

"A motorcycle club, the Iron Ghosts."

"Oh . . . now I understand."

Stanley raised his eyebrows, smiling with lips only; his eyes remained serious.

"What do you understand?"

"The TV news I heard. There was a brawl between two gangs in one of the bars. That's where Ogre was wounded?" She spoke in a half-whisper, making sure that Shelly would not hear anything.

"Right, you are," he said in the same tone.

"What made you chase me on the slope?"

"My guys called and told me about Ogre when I was standing behind you to take the last ride on the chairlift. They couldn't take him to the hospital because the police would have been involved. We'd had enough of that crap. We try to avoid them as much as possible. Besides, Ogre said that the wound was not serious. And then I noticed the nursing school patch on your backpack. 'That's what we need,' I thought. When I caught up with you, I noticed that you were much more than a nurse."

"What do you mean?"

"A very pretty, nice girl. Everything sweet that could be said about a girl."

"Rascal. You are gangsters," Camilla said with a frown of disapproval.

"Not exactly. Sometimes we do things that the law doesn't approve of. But we don't harm people."

"Why don't those guys have any women among them?" Camilla nodded in the direction of a large table.

"Because we're here to discuss business. I recommend you choose the seafood, although the steaks are good here, too."

Camilla glanced up only to meet the eyes of some of the club members. They regarded her with apparent interest. She diverted her eyes to the mirror on the right. Her face was a harmony of colors: natural pink spots of health on tight, smooth cheeks; large, blue eyes with a seductive gleam of joy; long, dark eyelashes; smooth, white skin on her forehead and neck; and the happy smile of a strong, healthy woman, whose full red lips parted teasingly, showing two rows of white, even teeth. A gray–white sweater stretched flawlessly over her shapely breasts and slim waist. She cast her eyes down contentedly.

"I like you as I never have any girl before," Stanley kept talking into her ear. "With me, you'll have all the excitement you could ever want. You'll have life as you've never had or dreamed of before. Say something. Why don't you speak?"

Camilla looked out the window again. The ambience of the restaurant had created a pleasant, relaxed atmosphere. In the window glass, as in the mirror, she saw Stanley, looking her up and down, his eyes glowing with lust and adoration.

"Are you a leader in this group?" she asked.

"You may say so," Stanley agreed. "But it wouldn't be entirely true. I like doing things myself. That's why I would never be a president of the club. Although I have many people working for me, that's true. Why?"

"They look at me as if I'm your property."

She turned away to avoid his piercing stare. He put his palm over her delicate fingers and caressed them. She did not object. Everyone noticed what was going on. Shelly exchanged glances and sly smiles with her companions to the right and left.

"Be with me," Camilla heard Stanley saying, his lips close to her ear. "You dream, I'll make it happen. Fair deal?"

She cast a quick glance at Stanley and his hard, sharp profile: He was her kind of man.

"So, you needed a nurse for Ogre."

"Right. But it turns out to be much more than that. When are you going home?"

"Tomorrow afternoon. Why?"

"Stay another night."

"Where?"

"With me. Stay. You will never regret it." When she said nothing, he went on. "I can do anything for you."

His presence, more than his words, excited her. She was no saint in her relationships with men, but all her affairs had been inspired by passion; they had never been about quick, casual sex.

"I can't stay," she said firmly. "But I'll give you my number. We can talk more."

Stanley nodded in consent. He observed her inch by inch, as if she were his own property, to be taken care of.

II

The cold Quebec winter turned slowly into a dull, gray spring, which was abruptly interrupted by the beginning of a hot summer. Young girls were quick to welcome the return of warm weather by wearing their new outfits. This was the time of year when everyone was making plans for vacations and travel. Even the bikers were busy, preparing to escalate their feuds with other biker gangs.

Marcel had arranged a meeting on the rooftop garden of a 25-story condominium building. The garden overlooked the twisting blue ribbon of the local river and an uneven row of tall hills to the west. A recent associate of the Devil's Knights had bought a unit here. The place was new, in mint condition, and the owner assured Marcel that it was safe—the cops had not yet installed any recording devices. Marcel agreed, but intended to observe some precautions anyway.

"Wanna glass?" the associate asked. He had brought some chairs from his apartment and arranged them around a table, on which he had placed a few bottles of beer and some pretzels.

"No. Get inside and watch the door."

The associate obeyed without uttering a sound, and Marcel walked over to the safety railing that ringed the roof. The peaceful scene of the rural community across the river soothed him for a few moments. A short rest in a quiet, distant place with his wife and cute little girl, he thought, would be a nice, refreshing change from this madhouse, but there were just too many urgent matters to attend to.

Marcel turned around, disturbed by the click of the door latch behind him. Machete and Stash came onto the rooftop, shook hands with him, and took seats at the table.

With a quick twist of his fingers, Stash unscrewed the jagged metal cap from a beer bottle and let the pressurized gas escape with a brief, protesting sound. After taking a big swig of the brew, he turned his head and looked at some of the distant hills basking in the afternoon sun.

"Nice place," he remarked. Marcel and Machete did not comment. Stash looked at Marcel with watery, tired eyes, darkened with tiny, swollen blood vessels. Marcel stared back with a disapproving grin.

"Too much coke lately?" Marcel asked. With some effort, Stash stretched his mouth into a fake, apologetic smile. His eyes, however, remained alert.

"C'mon, Marcel," he objected, but stopped short of offering any convincing argument as the door to the rooftop garden squeaked open and another guest appeared. This was a tall man about forty years old, very sporty looking. He wore a shirt, opened two buttons down from the collar, and expensive, casual pants, held up by an equally expensive belt with a designer buckle. His sturdy black walking shoes made firm, sure steps as he approached the table and sat down next to Machete.

"Hi." He did not look at anyone in particular.

"Take one, Techie." Marcel nodded toward the bottles of beer. The man reached for one, opened it with a quick twist of deft fingers, and took a tiny sip. He slowly moved his gaze, examining everyone around the table. Apparently he did not care about the spectacular view from the rooftop.

"What's up?" he asked. Marcel couldn't help but notice the difference between Techie and Machete. Machete was bulky, with a disorderly beard and long hair, and sat in his usual grim mood. Techie was clean-shaven, with neatly groomed blond hair. His suntanned face and neck radiated good health and energy. Marcel did not answer Techie's question, but turned his attention back to Stash and continued his conversation.

"You have to be alert. Stop it."

Stash was about to say something, but Marcel stretched his arm, palm out, as if pushing off any possible objection. Stash placed his bottle on the table with an angry bang and straightened his back. Marcel gave him a warning look and turned to Techie.

"There's a job for you," Marcel said. Techie was an expert in weapons and explosives, the boss of a well-trained team involved in smuggling guns from the United States, planting and detonating devices, and calibrating guns for smooth operation and precision shooting. As his nickname suggested, Techie had outstanding technical knowledge and working skill in everything related to firearms. He was the only one of the Devil's Knights who did not have a criminal record. If he had ever committed any crime, it was in the distant past. All stealing and smuggling was conducted by subordinates, and he made it clear to everyone on his team that they were not to be messed up with anything not related to weapons.

"Look . . . ," Stash began, but Marcel interrupted him.

"You wanna say something?" Marcel's voice was menacing. Techie raised his eyebrows, forming horizontal wrinkles on his forehead. Machete took a swig of beer. Stash's face hardened, his watery eyes regaining the grim energy of a gangster.

"Don't you think we've gone far enough with them?" Stash asked. "We've paid a heavy price for fighting. Twelve of our people have already been killed. Four others are missing. You and I know that they're dead. Don't you think we should talk some sort of truce with them?"

"We've killed twice as many," Machete echoed curtly. Marcel nodded in agreement.

"True. I know that you, Stash, are among those who blame me for this mess. Tell me, what else are we supposed to do? Do you know the solution? How would we look in the eyes of everyone around us if we couldn't cope with a small, independent group? How would our American brothers look upon us? Besides, you know these guys. As soon as any sort of truce was settled, they'd start to expand. Many already look at them as an alternative to us. No, Stash, forget the truce."

"They turned out to be not such a small group," Stash held his ground. "Look, they have an endless supply of candidates. You assured us at the very beginning that as soon as Jason and Stanley were out of sight, we would easily finish them off. Jason is now in jail, but Stanley is no less efficient. Do you realize what bigger mess you are getting us into? Nobody knows what could happen tomorrow."

"There is no other way," Machete interrupted angrily. "We must finish them. With or without Stanley, they won't hold out too much longer. They're in pretty bad shape. One of their full patches has left the club. After all, they do not have as much money and support as we do."

Marcel made a gesture, as if wiping dust from an invisible wall in front of him.

"Enough about the truce," he concluded. "We need to get rid of Stanley, that's for sure. Do you have your baseball team ready, Machete?"

"At a moment's notice." Machete's eyes glistened with pride.

"Send them to the bar on Pearson Street. They sell a lot of pot to yuppies there. Stanley's guy keeps it."

"Will do," nodded Machete.

"You, Techie—send your people to arrange a small display of fireworks by their clubhouse on St. Lucia Street. You'll have to—"

"I know what to do," Techie said abruptly. "It's not my first display."

"But we don't know exactly what day he's supposed to be there. You'll have to have someone watching the area."

Stash shook his head disapprovingly and interrupted.

"You know, Marcel, that they've stocked up a huge pile of dynamite. They would reciprocate. The newspapers would scream again."

"That's the point," Marcel admitted. He was about to say something else when the door opened and their host appeared, carrying a tray with sandwiches and napkins. Techie watched as their host stepped forward.

"Looks good," he commented.

"My ol' lady did it," the associate said with pride.

"Is there a washroom here?" Stash asked.

"Only in my apartment. I'll show you."

"I need to make a quick phone call," Machete said, placing a bottle of beer on the table and standing.

"Sure," nodded the associate. "Follow me."

Marcel pulled out a cigarette, lit it, and walked to the railing. Leaning on it, he took a few puffs while staring at the green hills, blind to the beauty of the landscape. Techie came up to him and, with his back against the rail, looked in the opposite direction.

"I think we should do something about Stash," he said and turned his face to Marcel.

"I know. I will talk to him."

78

"Talking has never been a cure for cokeheads," Techie insisted.

"What do you suggest?" Marcel kept staring toward the hills in front of him, but he was well aware of Techie's presence. Techie was a biker in very good standing, with an impeccable reputation. Without such members, any outlaw motorcycle organization would cease to exist.

"Let's demote him to a prospect at our next club meeting. If that doesn't help, let's take his colors and let him go. Otherwise, it might be too late and we would have to take him out. Not a good option."

"He hasn't done anything wrong yet to demote him," Marcel objected. "Don't forget, he's better than all of us in public relations. Now, when we're heading into a real mess with the Ghosts, we need him. We couldn't last long against the government, the politicians, and the media without Stash. He's well educated and knows how to speak and present things. It might be hard, but I'll fix him." He straightened up and confronted Techie. "Trust me."

"What do you think about the idea of truce with the Ghosts?" he asked, changing the discussion. The two bikers stared solemnly at each other. Their short round of silent gangster's diplomacy was interrupted as Stash and Machete returned and took their places at the table.

"Let's talk later," Techie suggested. Only Marcel heard him, but Stash and Machete looked at them intensely. Marcel took his seat and stretched out his legs.

"As you know, the situation in the Rivierre joint is not in our favor now. We did manage to grease some of the guards, but many still side with the Ghosts. I have the addresses and personal information of all jail staff." Marcel stopped, testing the impression he was making. Machete opened another bottle of beer and smiled. Techie remained calm and indifferent. A few vertical wrinkles appeared on Stash's forehead.

"I'm going to send a copy of it to the damned jail office and make sure that they know who has the original. I also have an address of Serge Gorte—he has become a pain in the ass lately. It would be nice if he goes voluntarily, as his predecessor did."

"What if they just spit on us?" asked Techie, alluding to the prison guards.

"The names of those who screw things up will be typed in bold and marked with asterisks."

"What if they're not convinced?" asked Stash.

"We'll convince them. After all, we offer them a good choice: either have money and work with us, or else . . . "

"I think you're going too far, Marcel," Stash said firmly. "Slumber office, Gorte— gosh, if it comes to that, you would provoke the government. It's the system, you know. Have you ever thought about that?"

The question was not necessary. Marcel always thought about what he was saying. He didn't respond right away, which gave Stash an opportunity to continue.

"Look at the Italians. They never touch government officials. Even Lucky Luciano was against it. He was much opposed to fighting a full-scale war with the FBI. The Italians in Canada never did it, never even thought about it. Don't you think there's a reason?"

"There is," agreed Marcel. "Our situation is different from theirs. They don't control the streets. They make money from a rather small group of people, even if it is big money. They're much smaller than us. They don't grow in numbers. Mind you, as soon as any group grows in numbers, sooner or later it'll reach the point when a political game on a large scale is inevitable. We have many more problems than the Italians. We have to control jails. We have to control streets, bars, and restaurants. We have to control the arms trade, the pot trade, across-the-border dealings, and tons of other businesses. Because of that, we have to influence politicians, the police, and jail guards. If our enemies control them, we are finished. If we can't buy them off, we have to scare the shit out of them or shut them up. This is all-out war, guys. We're still growing, and should plan to grow forever. But now, these fucking Iron Ghosts shuffle all our cards. It's the first time in our history here in Canada that another group has appeared that we can't cope with. This sets a bad example. They say to the whole world, 'Fuck you, Devil's Knights.' Just staying alive, they kick us in the ass publicly."

"We'll try to find another solution," Stash insisted. "I don't like provoking the government. They might be slow, but when they go for something, they eventually get what they want." Stash said this forcefully; he respected strength in any shape and form.

"I'll do whatever you want," said Marcel. "Just tell me what the solution is. But don't give me any bullshit that you don't know. In that case, I would do whatever I think is necessary. Okay?"

"You want Iron Ghosts to run this fuckin' jail?" Machete asked Stash, losing his temper. "What would happen to you if you got put there tomorrow? Who would defend you? You'd surely ask Marcel to do something. If you happened to be alive, of course."

Everyone was watching Stash in silence. At last he cleared his throat and looked to Marcel.

"What do you want from me?"

"You'll have more work than all of us." Marcel smiled in victory. "For sure, when everything goes down, there'll be a lot of screaming in the newspapers, on the radio, and whatnot. The politicians and police will be pretty loud; every one of them will want to get credit for fighting the bikers. Some will make a career of us."

"For sure," Stash nodded.

"We'll all support you. Now, guys, money matters. It gets costly, you know. Every member of our chapter has to contribute at least twenty grand for operations. Agreed?"

Everyone nodded. The bikers left the meeting one by one, watching each other's tails for possible undercover police.

III

The ring of the phone blew away the last clouds of a lazy sleep. Stretching and yawning in the comfortable bed, Camilla let the answering machine do the talking—who the hell would be calling on Saturday morning at 11 o'clock, anyway? Now, she lingered under the warm blanket, wasting time.

The answering machine did not deter the stubborn caller; the phone was ringing again. It was probably Nick, she decided, yet another victim of her charm. He was a teacher at the medical school and had been mad about her for the last six months.

"I'm a natural blond," she had informed him yesterday during a dance at a Latino club. "All over." A short teasing laugh had escaped her lips. This had been in response to his remarks that natural blonds were rare these days. The scene had been too much for Nick, who raised his eyes to the ceiling and moaned. Camilla gently pulled his ear.

"Why do you like me, Nick?" she had asked. "I'm serious, I'm not playing with you. The fashion today is slimmer girls. Men are obsessed with them. There are a few very pretty ones around. Why me? You can't count ribs on my body."

"I'd love to try, though." Nick had picked up the topic with enthusiasm. "Just give me a chance and I'll be busy with this counting problem in all my spare time. Considering that I am poor at math, it may take my whole life to come up with the exact number."

To look younger, he had removed his glasses and put them in his pocket. He'd made a great effort to read her reaction to his words.

"You are like the models of Renoir," he had continued, squinting, which made him look menacing and ridiculous at the same time. "Don't you think Renoir understood female beauty?"

"Renoir's tastes run against a whole new generation of men," she had advised, "and women, as well. I guess none of his models was on a vegetarian diet."

He had returned her to her apartment at 3 o'clock in the morning and stopped his car in front of the entrance to her building.

"I want to be with you the rest of my life," he had said.

"No, not with me." Camilla had replied. "I'm not ready to tie the knot. I'm too young." She had stopped short of saying, 'and too good for you—a teacher at a medical school.' What a bore to live with the rest of my life!"

Now, a bright beam of sunlight was streaming into her room through gaps in the blinds, tiny sparkling bits of dust dancing chaotically in it.

Camilla closed her eyes, trying to envision a picture of herself from above, in different positions, through the eyes of a lover, one of her choice. A burning sensation underneath the triangle of blond hair at the bottom of her stomach made her back arch and her arms stiffen above her head with clenched fists. She liked the lazy pace of her imagination in the mornings, enjoyed the fantasies of this habit. Everything was permissible in the world of fantasy— not in the real world, though, in which one had to be responsible.

Two minutes later, the telephone rang again, this time clearing her mind. Well, almost—she needed a cup of coffee to actually start a new, beautiful day. But first, she decided to pick up the phone. She sighed.

"Hello," she mewed lazily.

"Still remember me?" the voice on the other end of the line asked.

Only one man in the world could convey the strength of his character in such a short sentence. Camilla sat up and jumped off the bed.

"Y-e-e-e-s!" she screamed, bells of delight ringing in her response.

"Stanley, darling. Where are you, you rascal? Why haven't you called me for so long? Where did you disappear to?"

"I'll explain it to you soon. I'm not far from you, in the coffee shop two blocks away."

"What are you doing there?"

"I had a short meeting with someone."

"I'll be there in half an hour." She was speaking very fast, and hung up without giving him the chance to say a word. She dressed in a hurry, consulting the mirror frequently. With one final look at her reflected image, she turned around, observing herself with merciless detachment. She looked good. She smiled.

On the way out, she noticed that the door to Shelly's room was open. She wasn't there. Early bird—Camilla thought with satisfaction. Good.

The street greeted her with the joyous hustle and bustle of an early summer day. She walked briskly toward the sun, taking in its energy and warmth. It was so nice. Oh, how beautiful and happy her life was!

There he was—sitting at a table on the sidewalk. Camilla ran straight into his arms, a familiar flame rising inside her. Although an enthusiastically kissing couple was not an unusual sight in St. Michel, everything has its limits, and, even here, such behavior attracts an attention—everyone around began looking at them. Passersby smiled approvingly as Camilla impatiently pulled at Stanley's T-shirt, raising it up and out of his jeans in search of his bare skin.

"I'm so happy to see you again," she was saying, her mind racing. She ran her palms under his shirt. "Where have you been all this time?"

"In the States."

"Why didn't you let me know?"

"I didn't want you to wait for me. A guy never knows what might happen to him on such a mission. But I am here, now. Do you mind going to my place?"

"No, but let's go to mine. My roommate has gone, I hope, for the whole day. You can tell me the story there."

Holding each other, they began walking toward her apartment. While looking at his face, she almost fell, stepping off the edge of the road, but Stanley firmly caught her and lifted her into the air.

"Sorry. I'm so excited I didn't watch where I was going," she said with an apologetic note.

Alex Markman

"You don't have to," Stanley said laughing. "I'll take care of you."

They spent the next few hours in tireless, almost angry lovemaking. As dusk settled, Stanley picked up his pants from the floor, fished out a pack of cigarettes, lit one up, and took a deep drag.

"We have to go," Camilla said, looking at him with fond eyes. "My roommate may come back any minute. Shelly and I agreed to not entertain boyfriends here."

"Fair enough," nodded Stanley. "I'll find an apartment for you soon."

"I can't afford an apartment of my own. In a few months, after graduation, I'll get a job, and then I'll make enough money to pay for it."

"You don't have to," Stanley smiled. "I'll foot the bill."

"Why don't we . . . "

"What?"

"Why don't we live together? It would be cheaper."

"No, that wouldn't be as good as you think."

"Why not?"

"I can't explain it right now. You'll understand later." He noticed her disappointment. "I like you so much, Camilla. Truly. I'll do anything for you. You gave a new meaning to my life. Maybe I'll leave my club and do something else for a living. Trust me."

Camilla kissed him and smiled.

"By the way, next Thursday we're having a big party at our clubhouse. Would you like to go with me?"

"I'd love to!" She accepted the invitation quickly. "I've never been in a biker's club."

"Good. Now, let's go to my house. I can't think of spending the night without you."

86

"Me, neither!" Camilla pulled his hair in passion. "Hold your breath, rascal. It's not gonna be an easy night for you!"

They went out hand-in-hand, into the last glimmer of the day. The sun, a large red disk dropping behind a jagged line of tall buildings, shone in a futile attempt to fend off the encroaching dusk. Cars with lights on passed them by.

"Here's my car." He matter-of-factly pointed to a small Mercedes, parked near a meter by the roadside.

"Ni-i-i-ice," Camilla sang, but Stanley stopped suddenly, holding her beside him.

"Please, wait here a minute."

"Why?"

"Please." He looked around, as if trying to detect something suspicious, and then went up to the car and pressed the unlock button on the remote control. The car greeted him with flashing lights. He got in, turned the engine on, and lowered the window on the passenger side.

"Come on in," he invited, leaning back.

"What's this all about?" Camilla asked, opening the door and climbing into the passenger seat.

"Habit. Nothing else," Stanley explained. His car moved forward, like a powerful, obedient horse.

"Careful," Camilla laughed, as she was thrown against him during a sharp turn. She locked her arms around his neck.

"Tell me more about yourself, tough guy." She kissed him. "I don't know much about you. Tell me about your parents."

"Working-class people. They live in Halifax. As far as I remember, they've always been poor. I hated poverty. I finished high school, but that's all my education. I began making money when I was a student. Quite a bit, I should say."

"All in drugs?" Camilla guessed.

"Not all. As I said before, I have a muffler shop. It makes good money. I have some other businesses, too."

"Why do you need the Iron Ghosts club then?"

"It's interrelated—hard to explain. You'll understand later. Let's talk about something else. Tonight is just for us."

IV

Camilla was trembling with curiosity to see the biker's club. She had read plenty of newspaper articles lately about these almighty gangs, fearing no one, intimidating all. Journalists had been talking a lot about how their power and influence seemed to be increasing, as well as how the police department seemed unable to cope with them. Camilla had not, however, seen anything that frightening. With Stanley, she felt very safe; who, after all, would threaten such a powerful man? He seemed smart enough not to endanger his life, nor to harm anyone without a specific reason.

When he came to pick her up, she felt nothing but pleasant excitement. On the way to the club, when the car stopped at traffic lights, they exchanged smiles and occasional kisses.

"Please don't close your eyes when I kiss you," she said.

They entered a quiet street.

"Never mind, we're here," Stanley said. His sleek Mercedes rolled up to a sliding gate that was built into a fence, which ran from both sides of a weird two-story building. There was no entrance door on its front, but nothing else could be seen through the tall, brick fence. The gate began its slow slide to the right, giving way to a large parking lot. Only three cars were inside; the remaining space was taken up by shiny Harley Davidsons. A man in a biker's vest waved Stanley to a vacant spot. Camilla noticed two Rottweilers running along the inside of the fence. They were on leashes attached to a cable by a metal ring, which limited their movement to a narrow path along the fence.

Zigzagging her way between motorcycles, Camilla noticed the entrance to the building. It faced the parking lot, where a back door was supposed to be. Stanley led her inside, through a small lobby and into a spacious hall with a long bar along the opposite wall. The crowd around it sent up a roaring cheer when Stanley appeared at the entrance. A man in his middle forties, with a neatly groomed beard and short hair, blocked their way. His well-fitting blue shirt and pants emphasized his athletic shape.

"This is our president, Willy," Stanley said, and then, turning to Willy, he added, "This is Camilla."

"So, here she is," Willy nodded. "I've heard about you."

He shook Camilla's hand with a rather strange look on his face: His lips stretched in an inviting smile, but they contrasted with frozen, suspicious, piercing blue eyes. A moment later, the wrinkles on his forehead smoothed out when his eyes took a quick rollercoaster ride on the feminine curves of her body.

"Have fun," he said to her, waving his hand toward the bar. "We have plenty of everything." He gave Stanley a brief hug and winked at him in recognition of his choice of girlfriend. Stanley led Camilla through a short corridor to another spacious hall. This one held plenty of cozy chairs and coffee tables, mostly arranged along its walls. All of them had been taken, but one was vacated as soon as Stanley stopped by.

"It's a weird place," Camilla said.

"Why?"

"All windows face the parking lot; none look out on the street."

"There is another set of rooms, whose windows face the street," Stanley said. "You have to go through that door to get there. But the door is locked."

"Why?"

"Just a precaution."

"Precaution against what?"

"Never mind. What would you like to drink?"

"What do you have?"

"Everything."

"Baileys, then."

"Just a sec. I will be right back." When Stanley left for the drinks, she listened to the crowd. Splashes of laughter and agitated shouts soared from time to time above the murmur of many conversations. She decided to sit down and look around.

A few guys had the unpleasant look of hoodlums, but the majority appeared to be quite normal people. She wouldn't have singled any one of them out as a suspicious or unwelcome guest at one of her medical school parties. Four men wore formal biker vests, with patches on the back showing all the insignia of their club. Women hustled about, drinking and smiling, talking with men nearby, excited by the very fact that they were there. Some of them seemed very young, eighteen or even less, and wore vulgar, tasteless, makeup and clothes; they appeared to belong to a lower social class. On the street, Camilla would have taken them for whores.

A huge man stopped momentarily near her table, holding a bottle of beer in his hand. He wore a vest with biker gang patches. His arms, bare to his shoulders and thick with bulging muscles, had been densely decorated with bluish tattoos, which filled up all the available space. Long, untidy hair fell onto his shoulders; a beard hid his throat. He was smiling, but his unfriendly eyes made him look like a "typical" biker from a movie. He made his way toward a petite woman; the length of her miniskirt was not enough to hide her bikini underwear.

"Harry," he introduced himself. The woman giggled.

"I'd love to be taken for a ride," she said, wiggling her hips.

"I'll take you," promised the biker and put his huge hand on her buttocks to finalize their deal.

"Oh, Gary, you always cheat me," the woman said, her backside swaying in the hand of a man she was meeting for the first time in her life. She was already drunk; her lips moved slowly, as if frozen by anesthetic at a dentist's office.

"Harry. My name is Harry," corrected the biker, kneading her behind like a piece of dough.

"Right. That's what I thought."

Harry produced a pack of Marlboros and pulled out a cigarette.

"D'yah mind if I give yah something in yah mouth?" he asked, pushing the cigarette filter between her thickly painted lips.

"M-m-m-m." The woman chuckled. Her lips parted, opening for the cigarette. "Ha, ha. You're funny, Terry."

Camilla shook her head and glanced at a newspaper that was spread across the table. Large, bold letters in the headline were meant to draw the reader's attention: "Biker's War Escalates." A picture in the center of the page resembled a modern painting of a disaster—a biker bar in the aftermath of an assault. She looked more intently at the article. The assault, it said, had been conducted by masked hoodlums, who used baseball bats to break everything inside. The bar, according to the writer, was patronized by members of the Iron Ghosts and was a haven for drug sales. According to speculation, the rival Devil's Knights gang had sent one of their "baseball teams"—the author demonstrated familiarity with biker jargon—to make a mess of the place. They broke in and ordered everyone not to move. One hoodlum used his heavy bat to take care of everything behind the bar. Shards of glass flew around the room from broken bottles. Others took to beating the drug dealers. One of the clients, too drunk to understand what was happening, had tried to protest. A masked hoodlum hit his legs with a bat, sending the man unconscious to the floor. The article said that police were still looking for any traces of evidence that might lead them to identity the criminals. From there, the piece gave a short history of biker gangs in Quebec. But Camilla did not go much further because two glasses had been placed on the newspaper, making reading impossible. One glass had the whitish, brownish color of Baileys in it.

"Interesting article?' Stanley asked, taking the chair beside her. The other was half full of a golden brown liquid that smelled like cognac. "Someone must have forgotten the newspaper here. I'll tell the guy on duty to watch for these things."

"Is it a secret?"

"No. But it might give the wrong impression to someone that we're defenseless. We'll respond, that's for sure." He leaned back and took a sip from the glass. His lean face relaxed as he looked around, leisurely observing the party. Camilla watched him with a warm glow in her eyes.

Suddenly, the whole building shook like a dollhouse kicked by a monster. The sound of a rough, terrifying clap of thunder accompanied the jolt, but it was more deafening than even the strongest bolt of lightning could produce. Bits of plaster and dust jumped off the walls and fell from the ceiling, sprinkling everyone and everything. A chandelier hanging from the ceiling on a short chain began swaying and dancing. Everyone rushed to exit the room, the rowdy, commanding voices of men mingling with the piercing shrieks of women. Camilla flew off her chair toward the door but was stopped abruptly by a strong grip. She turned around, trying to free her arm. It was Stanley who held her.

"It's over," he said. "Don't rush. It's over."

"What was it?" Camilla asked, her voice shaking. "Hell, what was it?"

The exit was cleared quickly and Stanley ran out, pulling Camilla after him.

"Take my car and get out of here," he commanded, handing her the keys. "I don't want the police to see you here. Go, go! I'll come to your place later."

In the car, Camilla threw one last glance at Stanley. He and Willy were giving directions and orders to other members of the club.

"Take the dogs inside," Stanley shouted. "Open the gate. Go, go, but do not rush. There is nothing to worry about. You, stupid ass, back up. Don't block the way. Hold on, hold on."

Camilla's first sickening moment of fear had passed, its last remnants escaping through her trembling fingers and lips. She drove through the open gate and then hit the gas pedal of the powerful Mercedes. At the closest major intersection, traffic had been halted by incoming police cars, ambulances, and fire trucks, all with their sirens screaming and lights flashing. After they passed, Camilla sped toward the green light. She was out of the law's reach.

Half an hour later, she cautiously unlocked the door to her apartment. Shelly was waiting for her. After numerous failed attempts at marriage, Shelly had sworn to remain single and devote the rest of her life to her vocation. Now, pale and visibly upset, she followed Camilla into her room and began complaining about the injustice done to her on her last exam. Her agitated words were pouring over Camilla like an endless stream of water. One timid attempt to interrupt her failed. Camilla tried again.

"But—"

Shelly raised her voice to continue.

"Why," she asked like an offended child fighting the injustices of humanity, "why does mediocrity always win in the battle against genuine talent? They understand nothing in art, Camilla, I assure you. Trust me, I know what I'm talking about."

"Right," Camilla agreed and turned on the television. No method has been invented, Camilla thought, to interrupt this chirping fool, but she was wrong. The breaking news made Shelly wipe away her tears of sorrow.

"There was a huge explosion tonight near the clubhouse of the notorious biker gang, the Iron Ghosts." The female reporter was holding a microphone in one hand, the other pointing at a building, which Camilla recognized at once.

"A car loaded with explosives was parked nearby and was detonated by remote control or a timer," the journalist kept talking. "Surprisingly, not much damage was inflicted on the clubhouse. Police attribute this to the fact that the building was originally constructed as a military bunker, with strong metal and concrete walls. The outer wall was reinforced from inside by sandbags. Police suspect the rival Devil's Knights gang for arranging the explosion as retribution for the latest killing of two of their top-ranking members, who were assassinated in a parking lot on the outskirts of the city."

"Gosh," Shelly commented, " . . . unbelievable."

"Windows in neighboring houses were broken by the blast," the broadcaster said. "No casualties have been reported so far, but the neighborhood has been shaken by the event."

Shelly was quick to shower Camilla with her opinion about bikers.

"You remember that guy, Stanley?" she asked. "Have you seen him lately?"

Camilla didn't answer. She was listening to the broadcaster too intently. "The bikers were quick to react. Their lawyer prevented police and firefighters from entering the building because no formal warrants had been issued. In addition, no one from the club has agreed to cooperate with the investigation."

"You are the only one in the whole world who understands me," Shelly was saying.

The phone's ring startled Camilla. She reached for it nervously, but instead of "Hello," a croaking sound escaped her throat.

"Hi. It's Stanley," was the calm response. "Everything's okay?"

"Yes. What about you?"

"Good." She felt almost as if his voice physically conveyed his energy and surprisingly good mood to her. Like a magic elixir, his voice poured strength into her, dissolving all her fears and worries. At that moment, Shelly got up, showing signs of impatience.

"Camilla, dear, I've gotta go. I'd love to stay with you longer, but I've got a date." Shelly was speaking in an apologetic tone, sincerely believing, it seemed, that Camilla needed her company.

Camilla had an urge to yell, "Go to hell," but instead nodded in understanding and agitation.

"Bye, Camilla. See you later."

"Where are you?" Camilla asked Stanley, when Shelly was out the door.

"Not far. May I come by?"

"Yes, please."

A few minutes later, Stanley came in. He was serious but calm and self-controlled.

"Knights planted the bomb," he explained, kissing her on the lips. "Were you scared?"

"Just at first," Camilla confessed and led him into her room. "I've watched the latest news. Here, sit down." She laughed at his impatience. "Wait, Stanley," she said in a mellow voice, not wanting to yield to his passion.

"I'm too excited," Stanley said, unbuttoning her blouse and bra. "You'll soothe me."

She agreed.

"Don't rush," she whispered. "Oh, Stanley, dear."

Danger added spice to their physical intimacy.

Half an hour later, with not a stitch of clothing on, Camilla brought a tray holding two cups of coffee from the kitchen. She'd expected Stanley to watch her admiringly, but noticed that his attention was keenly focused on the television set.

"What's up?" she asked, placing the tray on the coffee table.

"Sit down," Stanley said with a smile. "Look what's going on there."

Camilla picked up her nightgown and settled down on the bed. On the TV was another interview, this time with a woman about fifty years old, dressed in a conservative black jacket. With the blank, stern face of a skillful politician, she gazed at the audience with infinite patience.

"Our guest is Monica Goddet, a member of parliament and a prominent figure in the political scene of our province," the male broadcaster said. Then, turning to Monica, he continued.

"Monica, how would you comment on the latest events, which our police have labeled an escalation of the biker's war?"

"The death toll has become staggering," Monica answered, frowning. "In the last few months, this 'war' has intensified on an unheard-of scale. Numerous assassinations have been aborted by the police. Still, as it stands now, more than forty people are dead, two of them ordinary citizens—innocent victims who happened to be in the crossfire. A few other bikers are missing and deemed dead. The bikers show extreme contempt to public opinion, law and order, police, and all our legal institutions."

"What measures would you suggest?" asked the interviewer.

"Some measures have already been taken. A special unit, assembled with members of the Royal Canadian Mounted Police, city and provincial police personnel, and other institutions involved in public security, has already begun working on this issue. A larger budget for police units dealing with biker gangs is under consideration. And, I personally feel that intensive training must be provided for police forces to improve their efficiency."

"The police have suggested that the parliament should adopt a tough new law that specifically targets biker gangs. This law is supposed to make investigations easier. What do you think?"

"Let's first consider what kind of a law was suggested. The police want to declare the outlaw biker clubs criminal organizations. The mere membership in such an organization could be the foundation for searches, arrests, investigations, or straightforward criminal charges. This would make the life of the police so easy! No hard work, no investigative skills required. If we go this way, we could, in the future, single out any group that the police or the government dislikes for any reason. I believe that this law, if adopted, would be unconstitutional and challenged successfully in the courts."

"Is there any government proposal?" the broadcaster asked.

"Yes, there is. The government intends to set up a task force to recommend measures to end the biker's war and to deal with organized crime in general. The magnitude of the biker's war demonstrates how large the criminal world has become. The public is not aware of that."

Camilla was listening with keen attention. A disturbed feeling, like a sudden ocean wave, drowned her in its chilling depth. Stanley noticed her mood and turned the set off.

"The government is dead serious about you guys," Camilla remarked.

"They'll never pass this law," Stanley said. "They're more afraid of the police having power than of us having it."

"She said that the war had escalated noticeably in the past few months. Did you have anything to do with that?"

Stanley shrugged his shoulders.

"Let's talk about something else."

"What if these Knights target your relatives, wives, girlfriends?"

"That would never happen," Stanley said. "I am quite sure about that. That would be too much. For sure, the government would do something then. The police don't care much when we kill each other. But when someone who doesn't do any business with us is hurt, it becomes a different story. The Knights are not that stupid."

"Why can't you leave the club for good?" Camilla asked. "You've mentioned that you want to do that eventually."

"Eventually, but not right now."

"Why not?"

"You don't want to turn money down if it's going to be there."

"I'm just scared," Camilla confessed.

"There's nothing to worry about," Stanley assured her. "But some measures of caution should be taken. We shouldn't live together. Like I said, I'll find you a good apartment. For now, let's go eat—someplace nice. Where would you suggest?"

Chapter 3

I

The meeting place was code number four on Marcel's list. The restaurant, owned by an Italian crime family, had been designed with its clientele in mind. It was divided into three areas—two large halls, arranged along an outer glass wall that faced the street, for ordinary visitors, and a smaller room at the back, with only ten tables inside, for those select patrons who needed privacy and wished to be hidden from unwelcome attention. The food was good, inexpensive for its quality, and served by pleasant, ever-smiling, attentive waitresses. It was a large money-laundering outlet in which illegal cash was converted into legitimate income, reported taxable, and made safe for spending. When Marcel and his two bodyguards came in, it was about 2 o'clock in the afternoon and the lunch crowd was nearly gone. One of the waitresses greeted them with genuine joy.

"Please, follow me," she said, holding large restaurant menus under her arm. In the back room, daylight from a small window mingled with electric light from a hanging chandelier. Reflected and multiplied by numerous crystals, it created an instant atmosphere of comfort, quiet, and privacy. White tablecloths; snow-white, well-ironed napkins stuffed into wine glasses; and the refreshing chill of air conditioning enhanced this feeling.

"Which table do you wish to take?" the waitress asked.

"The one in the left corner is for me," Marcel said. "That one—near the entrance—is for my friends."

"Certainly." The waitress responded with an energetic nod to emphasize her understanding.

"I'm waiting for another guest," Marcel told her, as he sat down where he could observe the entrance to the room. "He should be here any minute."

"Certainly," the waitress repeated in the same tone. "Here is the wine list."

"A bottle of my favorite," Marcel requested, not looking at the paper. "You know . . ."

"Of course, sir," she said seriously, as if on an important mission, before going to serve the bodyguards.

Raymond appeared at a quarter past two, as arranged. Settling in across the table, he asked with a smile, "Who are those two?"

"My people," Marcel responded with pressed lips.

"I don't welcome any attention other than yours." Raymond adjusted his phony eyeglasses on the bridge of his nose and started studying the menu.

"They are reliable people," Marcel growled.

"I know. But they are outside the list of the two people I trust the most."

"And who would that be?"

"You and me."

"Listen." Marcel frowned. "It's not peace and quiet now. You know as much as I do that we live in troubled times. It's not cheap to keep bodyguards these days. Besides, these guys are for your safety as well as mine."

"I know, I know." Raymond sighed, his way of expressing appreciation for Marcel's consideration. "What can I do for you?" He removed his napkin from the glass.

"Some wine?" Marcel asked, taking the bottle.

"Please."

Raymond looked in silence at the stream of red liquid pouring from the bottle.

"I need information on someone as soon as possible," Marcel said while Raymond was sipping his wine. "Stanley Mathews is his name. We know that he has a muffler shop, but we don't know what name it's registered under. The bastard is shifty like mercury; he is everywhere and nowhere. We don't know where he lives or where he hides. Besides the usual pay, I'll give you an extra two grand when we're done with him."

"I don't need the last detail," Raymond said. "Do you want me to find out where his muffler shop is?"

"Yes. Any other information about him would be a bonus."

"I'll try. Anything else?"

"I need to know the address of Serge Gorte. He's the one responsible for investigating bikers."

Raymond didn't blink. He was looking into Marcel's eyes in silence, in expectation of some explanation. The tension at the table was growing.

"Three grand," Raymond broke the silence in a low voice. "I have to share with others . . ."

Marcel smiled through tight lips, his eyes grim. In response, Raymond raised his glass and said, "Cheers."

"Something else," Marcel said.

"Sure." Raymond drank his wine in small, slow sips.

"The government is going to assemble a task force that is supposed to work on ways to deal with bikers."

Now, a genuine smile appeared on Marcel's lips. Raymond took too big a swig, made a choking sound, and coughed.

"Excuse me," he said, lifting the napkin to his lips.

"We need their addresses—if not for all the task force members, then at least for the major players."

Raymond recovered quickly. A look of respect flitted across his face, only to yield to his customary unemotional mask.

"I'll do my best," he mumbled. "As far as I know, the task force has already been assembled, but the members have not been announced yet."

The rest of the lunch passed by in meaningless small talk, with each thinking his own thoughts. Marcel pulled up his left sleeve and glanced at his watch.

"Five minutes to three," he said.

"Time to depart?" Raymond asked.

"I'm expecting someone else at three," Marcel said. Raymond produced his wallet, but Marcel stopped him with a gesture.

"On the house."

"Thank you." Having said that, Raymond left.

In a short while, another visitor came in. This was a tall, very fat man in his late forties, with short, neatly groomed hair. His round blue eyes were fixed above puffy cheeks and appeared to observe everything with constant surprise. He was dressed in a seemingly expensive dark blue suit and walked with the self-assurance and composure of someone who knew his worth and power.

Marcel exchanged quick glances with his bodyguards to signal them to relax.

"Good afternoon, Norman," Marcel greeted the newcomer and, after shaking hands, pointed at the menu. "Would you like to order something?"

"No, thanks," Norman said, rolling his eyes. "Just coffee."

"You've changed quite a bit lately," Marcel noticed with a smile. "The biker life was better for you. How far back was it? Ten years, or so?"

"Close to that." Norman returned an agreeable smile in appreciation of Marcel's fond memory. "The biker life was not for me. But you know the other reason, Marcel: I didn't want to be on the police radar screen. You can't continually be in the spotlight and outsmart the police forever."

"Right you are. But you know as well as I do that publicity is exactly what so often protects us. Anyway, you left the club as a member in good standing. There are still a few among us who recall you with respect."

Norman raised his eyebrows and looked out the small window. "How is business?" he asked.

"My traffic crew has assembled 15 units for you. You'll get them next week."

One of the gangs that Marcel controlled specialized in the car business. This was the "traffic crew." Part of their activity was theft: They stole cars in Quebec and Ontario that were sold overseas or disassembled into parts and supplied to legitimate enterprises. Their other activity was money laundering: They bought cars with cash and sold them to dealers, who in turn sold them in the U.S. market. Norman was the owner of a larger dealership to which Marcel supplied his merchandise. The two seldom met personally—only if there was a compelling reason for it.

"Good, good," Norman said, apparently in deep thought.

"Something is bothering you, I gather," Marcel remarked. "What's up?"

Norman squeezed his hands, fingers intertwined in a nervous grip.

"I have a problem with my wife. You know, the girl I married two years ago."

"Yes, I remember. She was twenty-two then. People say she's very pretty. Cheating on you?"

"If only that. No, she wants half of my assets—as a separation settlement."

"What a bitch."

Norman sat quietly for a moment.

"Do you have a man who could do a really good job, Marcel?"

"Yes, I do. When do you wish to meet him?"

"Anytime. The sooner, the better."

"Okay. Let's talk about other business for awhile. In the meantime, I'll call the waitress to bring you some coffee. Want some wine? No? Coffee, then. They make a good cup here."

II

The furniture store made her cheeks rosy. Without taking her eyes off a piece, Leila asked, "How much can we spend here?"

"Five grand," Claude said casually, as if such an expense was a matter of everyday life.

"Ouch! I want this one!"

Claude's cell phone began playing music. He raised it to his ear and said, "Hello."

"Hi. Is number seven at one okay?"

Marcel wanted him at number seven—the Golden Griddle restaurant, located downtown. Claude looked at his watch. It showed quarter past twelve. He took Leila by the waist.

"I've gotta go. Here's the money." He slipped a sizable roll of cash into her bag.

"No-o-o," was her response.

"Buy whatever you want. Arrange delivery. Take a taxi home."

At 1 o'clock, he found Marcel in a distant corner of the restaurant, sitting alone at an empty table.

"Something urgent?" Claude asked, taking a place beside him from which he could scan the whole space as well.

"Yes."

The waitress came and placed two glasses of cold water on the table.

"Ready to order, gentlemen?" she asked.

After she had taken their orders and left, Marcel turned to Claude and established eye contact with him. Marcel had done this the last time before starting a business talk. Claude already knew this meant good pay for a death sentence for someone.

"A job." Marcel diverted his attention to the glass. "Someone who was a Devil's Knight about ten years ago got into a rather big business and left the club. Not everything he does is clean and saintly. But mostly, it is a legal business."

"Uh-uh," Claude uttered, as Marcel stopped talking.

"Yah, legitimate business," continued Marcel, with a note of contempt. "Anyway, he's developed some problems with his wife. A rather easy job for you, isn't it?"

Claude nodded and raised his eyes.

"Tell me more."

"Okay. Ten grand. Mind you, it's good money, given that he'll cooperate with you."

"Sure."

"He needs someone who could do a truly clean job. No shooting, no bloody spectacle in public. Not even a tiny trace of evidence can be left for the police. I recommended you."

"How'd yah want me to do the job?" Claude asked.

"It's up to you to decide. I'm not gonna give you instructions. Discuss it with him. His name is Norman. He works downtown, so it would be convenient for him to meet you in one of the restaurants there during his lunchtime."

"Sure."

"Do you want him to bring a picture of his wife?" asked Marcel.

"Not necessary."

"Sure?" Marcel raised his eyebrows.

"Not necessary," repeated Claude.

"How do you . . . ? Never mind. It's your business."

The waitress came and placed dishes in front of each one. "Enjoy your meals."

Claude took up his knife and fork the same way Marcel did. He cut a piece of meat and noticed with satisfaction Marcel's quick glance, a mixture of surprise and approval.

"I know it's not my business, but why does he want to…? Insurance money or something?"

"There's nothing wrong with you wanting to know some details," Marcel said. "Two years ago, he married a broad much younger than he was. She is now about twenty-four. Anyway, she married for money—that was no secret. But soon after, she began fucking someone she had known before. Norman didn't want to make a big deal of it; he wasn't a saint himself. But now this bitch demands half of his property for her agreeing to a divorce. Otherwise, she's threatening to tell the police about some of his dealings. The stupid broad has no idea what she's getting into."

"Let me know where and how we should meet." Claude wiped his mouth with a napkin. "I'll take care of her."

"You must be in Movenpick restaurant tomorrow at 1 o'clock. Look for a big, fat guy in a gray suit and blue tie. You won't mistake him for anyone else. He'll be alone at a table. Ask him, 'Any seat available?' He'll respond, 'Just one.'"

The next day exactly at 1 o'clock, Claude entered the restaurant. In an instant, he noticed a big man—close to fifty years old, well dressed and groomed—sitting by the window. He seemed to recognize Claude and then turned his attention back to the menu.

"Any seat available?" Claude asked, looking at the pale blue tie. Everything on this man looked expensive: gray suit, white shirt, diamond ring, and thick, gold Rolex.

"Just one." Norman nodded to the chair at his right.

"It wasn't hard to find you here," Claude said, taking the chair.

"Yah. No problem with you, either. Marcel gave me a good description of you. I'd suggest—may I?—that you wear a long-sleeved shirt for such meetings. The tattoos on your arms make you stand out. What would you like to eat?"

Claude opened a menu, studying Norman from the corner of his eye. The man looked quite respectable, as he was supposed to, according to his status. But there was something, not explainable in words, that only people in the underworld could recognize: This was a very tough guy, a wolf dressed in sheep's clothing.

"What's your wife's name?" Claude asked, not looking at him.

"Brigitte. Why do you need her name?"

"You want a clean job, don't you? Let me take care of everything my way."

Norman shrugged his shoulders.

"As you wish."

They stopped talking when a waitress came to take their orders. After she left, Claude resumed the conversation.

"Let me do the job this-coming Saturday. On Friday, you'll tell her that you've got to go away on urgent business somewhere. Tell her that one of your business buddies whose name is Bruce—she doesn't have to know my real name—will be coming by to pay a debt. Ask her to count the money she gets before accepting it. Okay?"

Norman responded with a trace of a smile, a glow of appreciation softening his eyes.

"There's pretty tight security at the entrance to our condo," he warned.

"Let me deal with that. But give me some advance money. I'll need her to start counting."

Norman looked inquisitively at Claude, but not for long. Even for a former biker, it was not easy to contest the stare of a killer.

"Here's what we'll do," suggested Norman. "Today I'll give you five grand. In my apartment, go to the bedroom where I have my home office. In the top drawer of the desk there'll be an envelope with another five. Fair?"

"Good," nodded Claude. Indeed, he thought. After the broad is done with, I'll get the balance. Smart, good . . . Norman.

Norman plunged his hands into his large suitcase, manipulating something in its depths. Finally, he produced a thickly stuffed envelope.

"Here is the five," he said, holding the envelope under the table. "Take it."

He was glancing stealthily around. Claude quickly took the envelope and stashed it in a pocket.

"Thanks."

"Something else," Norman said. "She has some jewelry at home. Take it. It's a bonus for you. Let's make it look like a robbery. I don't need that crap anymore."

Claude couldn't wait until lunch was over.

"I've gotta go," he said, throwing his cloth napkin on the table. "Gimme your address, phone number, and a spare key from your apartment. Just in case."

Norman nodded in agreement. He produced a notebook from his suitcase, scribbled the address on a piece of paper, detached a key from a key chain, and handed it over to Claude.

"Good luck," he said.

Life is good, Claude thought on the way out, elated by a fat down payment from Norman. Driving home, he fancied Leila, her joyful surprise at the sight of the money, her smiling lips and white teeth.

The first step over the threshold of his apartment brought him from one fantasy world to another, the kind that existed, he believed, only in glossy magazines.

New furniture, affordable only to the wealthy—he had become one of them—was thoughtfully arranged in the room in a harmony of colors, convenience, and space. Leila had bought a shiny dinner table with four chairs, a dark wood and glass coffee table, and an entertainment center that included a television set, radio, and CD player. Semi-transparent curtains, hanging from the top of the window down to the floor in smooth vertical folds, dimmed the bright light of the sun. Pleasing music filled the room, and in the middle stood Leila, his beautiful Leila, in a light summer dress. If paradise ever existed, it must be this room. Never before had he had such a home. Never before had he had a woman waiting for him to share with him the joy of life.

"Wow," he growled.

"Like it?"

"Very. Who fixed the curtains?"

"The superintendent. I gave him fifty bucks. He helped me a lot. Where have you been so long?"

"Business."

"Was it good?"

Claude pulled out a thick envelope and threw it on the sofa. It opened up and money slid out. Leila giggled, jumped like a kid, and threw herself into his arms. Claude felt the irresistible urge to please this woman more.

"What would you like, what do you want?" he asked. "I can buy you anything. More money is coming."

"I need to buy some dresses. Some jewelry."

"Good. I need some good clothes, too. Next Saturday I have another business meeting, from which I'll bring more money. But for now, take off what you have on."

Leila began to undress, taking her time and demonstrating the techniques she had learned as a stripper.

III

Saturday morning arrived, and Claude looked in the mirror, observing his new clothes. Selected with Leila's discriminating taste, he thought that he looked like a decent young man from a middle-class family. His dark gray shirt, made of fine cotton, had long sleeves, concealing the tattoos on his forearms. Black, casual but dressy pants, pleated in the latest fashion, were a good fit for his tall figure. Finishing the ensemble were shiny black shoes, sturdy as well as comfortable. In addition to his new wardrobe, a friendly smile looked back at him, a final touch to his new image. Everything in the mirror was to his liking. A successful man in his trade, he thought, must be a good actor. If people took him for what he was, he would never go too far.

"You're dressed more for a date than for a business meeting," Leila said, flapping her sleepy eyelids.

"Dates never happen this early," Claude remarked, looking at his new wristwatch. "Nine o'clock. Time to go."

"Don't be too late," Leila pleaded mockingly in the tone of a small, spoiled girl. "I don't like to be alone for long."

"It won't take much time," Claude promised.

"Maybe I could help you?" she asked.

Claude laughed.

"My job is not for girls."

Leila gave him a kiss in the air.

Driving to the other end of the city, where Norman's condo was, he rolled the car windows down to let in some of the morning's fresh, crisp air. The hour was early enough; very few cars were on the road. Many people had probably left for their weekend destinations, whereas compulsive shoppers had not yet awakened. Contrary to the peaceful look of the streets, his anxiety grew. Even a tiny mistake could be fatal, or worse—for this kind of murder, he could get life in jail, with no chance of parole. He had to respond to any unexpected circumstances instantly and make the right decisions.

Claude turned into the parking lot of a plaza across the road from Norman's condo. He found many vacant spots, but chose to park his Honda in the place closest to the exit.

He walked between the cars and went inside the plaza, where it was cooler. Very few people were around. Claude went to the public phone, looked around, drew a scrap of paper from his pocket, and dialed the scribbled number. After the third ring, a gentle voice answered, "Hello."

"Hi. Is Norman at home?" His voice was unusually soft.

"No. He's in Toronto. Who's asking?"

"My name is Bruce. I have to repay a debt to him. He promised to be home at this time."

"Yes. He told me about you. He asked me to take care of this. Do you know where we live?"

Her voice was mellow and sweet, like an angel's.

"Yes, I do. Is there anyone else there?"

"No."

"Am I too early?"

"Never mind. It's time to get up. I'm a night bird, you know. Sometimes I sleep well into the afternoon."

"Good. See you soon."

"Hold on. When you come in, you'll see a phone with a display in the entrance lobby to your right. It's across from the security guard—you'll see him behind the glass. Use the arrows on the dialing pad to scroll up or down to find Norman's name, and then press the large button. I'll unlock the door and let you in. We're on the seventeenth floor, number 1703. Got it?"

"Sure," Claude said and hung up. Just then, he realized that Norman had not told him his last name.

Claude was trying to prepare as much as possible for any unforeseen circumstances. How crowded would the entrance be? Would there be video cameras in the staircases and emergency exits? Would the security guard be at his post? Claude had to sneak into the building

113

unnoticed, without exposing his face to anyone. This time he had to work without a ski mask.

The 25-story building towered like a grim, silent giant above the private houses that surrounded it. It was a very expensive condo, whose tenants did not rush around settling day-to-day matters. The entrance was at the back of the building. With no pedestrians in sight for cover, approaching the front door without being noticed would be impossible.

Luckily, there was a tiny park, which Claude could use as an observation point, farther down a side street. Sitting on a bench there, almost hidden by dense bushes, he watched for human traffic. Nobody came in or went out. A few minutes passed; tension grew inside him.

Claude couldn't afford to wait too long. When an elderly woman with a few shopping bags in her hands appeared on the sidewalk leading to the entrance, Claude saw his chance. He walked briskly and caught up with her at the door.

"May I help you, ma'am?" he asked and took one of her bags.

"Oh, thank you," said the lady, squinting her eyes as people with very poor vision do. The bag indeed might have been a bit heavy for her. Through the glass door, he caught a glimpse of the uniformed man, busy shuffling papers at his desk. Claude stepped in ahead of the old woman, positioning his back to the security guard. There was another door that the woman would have to open with her key. Between the doors, attached to the wall across from the guard, stood the useless phone system.

"It's my pleasure to help you," Claude said gallantly, letting her in. "After all, we are neighbors, aren't we?"

"Thanks a lot," the old lady said, opening the second door with her key. Claude threw a quick glance at the security guard. He was still busy with his papers. Apparently, two people chatting calmly at the entrance, who had a key to the door, did not arouse his suspicions. Claude went on, supporting his conversation as much as possible.

"It is very nice to have a neighbor like you. My name is Brian. What's yours?"

"Rosa," said the old lady. "I haven't seen you before. You are a very nice young man. Press 15, please. Thank you. What floor are you living on?"

She squinted again, trying to get a better view of him. "My vision is not as great as it used to be," she explained.

"Twentieth," Claude lied.

At the fifteenth floor, he returned her bags, said, "Goodbye," and pressed 17. When the elevator stopped, he stuck his head out and looked right and left. No one was in sight. He stepped out and knocked at the door of unit 1703. Brigitte would be allowed to see his face. The dead—as she soon would be—could not be a witness.

He stood in front of the peephole, smiling. He heard a feeble rustle in the depths of the apartment, then the click of the lock, and the door opened slowly. A petite, pretty young woman in a fluffy nightgown appeared.

"Please, come in." She returned his smile. "I am Brigitte." The woman stepped back to let him enter.

"Nice to meet, you," Claude said, searching the distant corners of his memory for a few extra nice words. Brigitte nodded and smiled again—a very sweet smile, Claude thought. She looked very tempting. Her cheeks, a bit puffy after a sound sleep, were perfectly smooth. Something childish was dancing in her large green eyes. It would be nice to fuck her, Claude thought, but no, business is business.

"Please, sit down," she invited.

"Thanks. I didn't expect to see such a beautiful woman."

Brigitte smiled again, this time with a touch of understanding and compassion. Apparently it was not much of a surprise for her to have another man making over her.

"Some coffee?" she suggested.

"No. Business first." He pulled out an envelope and placed it on the table. "Please, count."

"I trust you," she said in her gentle voice. "I couldn't care less about money."

She seemed unable to recognize danger. Claude admired her acting skills: This bitch played an innocent angel without a flaw.

"Please count it and give me a receipt. Just in case, you know. I don't want to have any complications with Norman."

She sat back in a chair and took the envelope.

"Why didn't you call from the entrance?" she asked.

"Oh, there was an old lady there who let me in. I helped her with her bags. Very nice lady."

"Sure you don't want some coffee?"

"I'd love to, but have no time at all. My wife is waiting for me downstairs in the car. We have to rush."

"Well, then," she responded, seeming slightly disappointed. She removed the money from the envelope and started counting. Claude walked behind her back, stretched on his gloves, grabbed her chin with his right hand and the top of her head with his left, and, with a powerful clockwise twist, crushed her neck vertebrae. Brigitte died instantly, without uttering a sound. Claude let her fall to the floor and went to the room where Norman's office was. He found money in the top drawer, as Norman had promised. In the bedroom he picked up some jewelry. He gathered the money that had scattered on the table, which Brigitte had had no chance of counting, and moved slowly into the hallway.

No one was in the corridor.

Claude proceeded to the fire exit door and went out, burying the lower part of his face in his half-folded right arm, as if protecting himself from the blow of a fist. A quick glance around assured him that no security cameras had been installed in the staircase. Good. Trying to make as little noise as possible, he descended to the ground floor and left the building through a side door. The short passage leading to the street was empty. With a brisk walk Claude crossed the road, went to his parking space, got into his Honda, and turned the key. A thought about Leila made him smile—she would be beside herself with delight at the sight of the pile of money and jewelry he brought her.

On the way home he stopped at a small plaza with a public phone, and dialed the pager number and then 7777, which meant to Marcel that the deal was done. Steering the car back into the slowly flowing traffic, he rolled down his windows and let some fresh warm air in. Life is good, he thought—the sun was shining; money was plentiful; and his girlfriend was really something. She was waiting for him now.

The ring of the cell phone interrupted his pleasant chain of thoughts.

"Number twelve, if you could," the voice said. It was Marcel.

"When?"

"Right now."

"Okay."

The café with the code number twelve was a half-hour drive away. *Why would Marcel want a meeting on such short notice?* Claude thought, already cruising along the streets toward the meeting place. *Did I do something wrong? By the sound of his voice, Marcel isn't angry. What's the damn rush?*

His worries were groundless. Sitting at a table on the sidewalk, Marcel greeted him from afar with a friendly smile. He stretched his arm out for a handshake.

"Everything went well?"

Claude gave him a detailed account of the events.

"I like it," Marcel nodded and took a sip from his coffee cup. "In a short while we'll have a meeting in a country home that belongs to one of our members. Big house on the lake, you know. Two boats." There was a meaningful pause. "You're invited. Mind you, mostly full patches will be there."

The joy at having such respect shown him was more than Claude could handle. He suppressed an urge to jump up, taking a cigarette, instead, and lighting it.

"Why don't you speak?" Marcel asked.

"I don't have a bike," Claude said with intonations of guilt.

"Buy one."

"I'm still short of money."

"How come? You've been paid well." Marcel frowned. "Too much up your nose?" He was hinting about cocaine use.

"No, not at all. But I've had to spend some money on furniture. I have a girl. You know. Like . . . she will be my old lady."

Marcel's eyes glowed in appreciation.

"Good girl?"

"Yah. Very pretty. But she wants to buy all the household things, and it's damn costly." Claude shrugged his shoulders, as if to say, "What could I do? A woman."

"I know, I know," agreed Marcel. "I'm convinced that having a family isn't a bad thing. It makes one responsible and careful. How much do you need for a bike?"

"Another ten grand."

"I'll lend you the money."

"Marcel," Claude said, overwhelmed with emotions. "I'll do anything for you. But . . . I don't know if I can pay you back soon."

"You can. There are a few jobs waiting for you. By the way, can you ride a bike?"

"Yes, I can. I have a friend in the car business. He has good bikes once in awhile, so I drive them. I already have a license."

"Good. One of my people will call you tomorrow and give you the ten grand. Okay?"

The whole world began a slow dance around Claude's head. It seemed that the day was an endless succession of happy events and news. This morning, he had killed a woman. It was a nice, perfect kill. He'd gotten lots of money for it and some jewelry for Leila. Marcel was going to lend him money for a beautiful Harley Davidson. And now, more jobs and money were waiting for him. Such a nice, beautiful life!

"I'm always ready," Claude said, lighting another cigarette. He drew the smoke in as if it was the elixir of life. Exhaling a thick cloud, he asked, "What are these jobs?"

"I'll give you the home address of an Iron Ghost. That's the only thing I know about him at the moment. Don't touch his wife or kid. Make it clean."

"Will do. What else?"

"Another one is a frequent visitor of the Planetarium restaurant. We have some people there who'll let us know when the Ghost is there. Our guy will be in touch with you. Be ready any minute, as time is at a premium."

"Sure. Anything else?"

"Not now. But something's cooking."

"What?" Claude sensed something interesting.

"Very soon we'll know the exact location of the muffler shop that belongs to Stanley."

A sadistic guffaw from Claude greeted the news. Marcel raised his eyebrows, which made Claude interrupt his reaction. The waiter, who stood nearby, noticed a disturbance and came over with a pot of coffee.

"Some more coffee, sir?" he asked Marcel, bowing in respect.

"Yes, please."

The waiter turned to Claude.

"Something for you, sir?"

"Only coffee."

"Certainly, sir. Here you are. Enjoy." The waiter left.

"Sorry," Claude apologized. "It was too good news for me. He's mine—don't give him to anyone else. Okay?"

"Sure. Five grand on top of the usual pay is what you'll get for him."

Claude's head began to swirl.

"I've gotta go," he said. "My ol' lady is waiting for me."

"Sure," Marcel nodded with a condescending smile.

By the time Claude got home, it was late afternoon. He found the curtains drawn to dampen the bright sunrays, Leila napping on the sofa. She was dressed in soft jogging pants and a T-shirt, and she smiled sleepily when she heard him enter the room. She spread her arms for an embrace.

Claude grabbed her and ran his palm over her back under the clothes, from shoulders to buttocks, enjoying the unique softness, smoothness, and warmth.

IV

During the next two weeks, Claude was busy executing Marcel's orders. The hunt for the first target was not simple: This Iron Ghost stayed in a different location almost every night, avoided public places, and was accompanied by a bodyguard at all times. A special crew of Devil's Knights kept his house under surveillance around the clock. Their only task was to notify Claude when the target returned to his home.

A few days passed. Claude did not take the time to indulge in any treats, except cigarettes. Finally, one afternoon, the phone rang. Claude grabbed it.

"Hi."

"Go home." The informant on the other end hung up. Claude knew the address. Without wasting time, he called Hans, who had already found a stolen car for this occasion. It wasn't long before Hans pulled up at the back entrance of the building, where Claude—dressed in a jogging suit, his professional dress for murder—was already waiting for him. When he climbed into the passenger seat, his cell phone rang. The informant, using biker's slang, delivered rather shocking news: The security guard had left the house—someone had come and picked him up. Most likely, a replacement would come shortly.

"Hit the gas, Hans!" Claude commanded, disconnecting the line. "We have only minutes, if not seconds, to get the job done. Stop very close to his house."

"Will you shoot him inside?" Hans asked. He was pale, very tense—poor Hans. The stress of this job was too much for him.

"Yes, in the house," Claude confirmed. "Keep the engine running."

Claude was tense as well. However, when the car stopped, the knot in his stomach loosened. Cold energy enveloped him, clearing his mind and sharpening his senses. He stepped down and scanned the area to assess the situation.

The sky was heavy with black, rainy clouds. Good, he thought—rain always adds to confusion on the roads. That will make a police chase more difficult. A streak of lightning flashed. After a short pause, a roar of thunder growled, its sound muffled by long distance.

In the driveway to the house, a Ford Taurus sat abandoned. Claude approached it, still not having a precise plan of action. Hiding behind the car, he feverishly wondered what to do next. His ski mask was with him, but putting it on would not make sense: If he knocked at the door, who would open it to a masked man? On the other hand, Marcel had issued a strict order not to harm relatives, but they would be able to recognize him later if he did not wear the mask. It seemed that the only solution was to get inside unseen, and quickly, because the replacement security guard could arrive at any time.

By chance, the whole family suddenly walked out the front door and headed toward the car. Claude quickly covered the lower part of his face with the mask, leaned on the hood, stood, and fired two shots at the face of the Iron Ghost. Tiny, dark spots sprung up on his right cheek, followed by a small cloud of flesh and blood that flew from the back of his head. The man fell dead.

His wife and kid screamed, terrified. The woman collapsed onto her husband's dead body, yelling through her tears. Claude laughed. At that very moment, a flash of lightning exploded, then a thunder bolt cracked—the sky, it seemed, also celebrated his success.

Smiling under the mask, Claude threw the gun on the grass and began walking toward Hans in a deliberately unhurried pace, in order to stage a great show of guts, calmness, and cruelty. Let Hans see how a true biker returns from the kill, he thought. Maybe next time he would be less scared of these things.

Devil's Knights observers said later that a replacement bodyguard had arrived at the home of the Iron Ghost just a minute after the hit, only to find his master dead.

Claude's second target was not that difficult. His favorite lunch place was a small but exquisite restaurant in a busy plaza. Killing him there was not an option, because escape through a crowded building with security surveillance would be impossible. But after some thought, he came up with a cunning plan. He bought a wig, put it on, complemented it with a phony mustache and beard, and, with a bucket of water in his hand, pretended to be a squeegee bum at the only traffic light that led into and out of the plaza. Claude's lucky card came up on the first day of the operation.

When the target left after lunch and stopped his car at the light, Claude approached the driver's side and offered to clean the windshield. The Iron Ghost behind it responded angrily and impatiently. Claude knocked at the window with the squeegee handle, and the target lowered the glass. Glowing with range, he shouted, "Fuck off, asshole!"

Claude let the bucket and squeegee fall to the ground, pulled out a gun, and fired two shots into the head of the Iron Ghost. After that, he ran. Hans, as usual, was waiting close by in a stolen car.

These two murders raised his stature enormously in the eyes of Marcel and the other club members. Now, he had enough money to buy a Harley Davidson—the beauty cost him close to $20,000—and he could repay Marcel his debt, in full. He could now attend the high-profile party on his own bike.

V

The noise of incoming motorcycles disturbed a small suburban plaza that dozed in the rays of the rising sun. Ten Harley Davidsons rolled into its small parking lot at exactly 9 o'clock. On the rear seat of each sat a woman who held the driver by his waist and leaned into his back. An elderly couple coming out of a coffee shop threw frightened glances at the noisy visitors and hurried to their car.

Marcel gave a sign. Everyone obeyed by turning off their engines, climbing off their bikes, and walking over to him. Claude knew most of them, because he had already attended a few club gatherings that had been attended by full patches. Enviously, Claude looked at their vests. He still had only a plain black leather jacket.

"Here's Claude," Marcel said, turning to a man with questioning, but friendly eyes in a cleanly shaven face. Nothing about him, except a biker's vest, suggested that he was a biker. "Claude, I don't believe you've met Techie, have you?"

"No, but I've heard a lot about him," Claude said, looking with respect at the legendary Techie, who was second in command after Marcel.

"Welcome to the party," Techie said, shaking hands with Claude. He threw a glance at Leila. "Nice girl you have."

"My ol' lady, Leila," Claude said with pride. Leila nodded at Techie with a sweet smile.

"I know." Techie returned the smile. "That's good." He did not explain what was good about that: her being a nice girl, or her being Claude's ol' lady.

Claude noticed other bikers shooting glances at Leila. No wonder—she was the prettiest of all the girls there. Claude was somewhat annoyed by the stare given Leila by a man he'd not met before. The man looked like an outlaw biker: large and fat with disorderly hair flowing everywhere. He didn't smile, but slowly rolled his eyes over Leila's body, lingering for moments on her breasts and hips. Claude didn't worry much, though: Leila's status of "old lady" would protect her from the unwelcome advances of others; it was against club rules to covet any brother's serious relationships.

"Come here, Machete," Marcel said to the man. "This is Claude."

Machete squeezed Claude's hand with all his might. Claude responded with almost as strong a grip. The exchange was not friendly.

"You did a nice job for me once," Machete said.

"I don't remember," Claude responded, in surprise.

"The Greek Delight shish-kebab house. You worked with Trasher then, remember?"

"Oh, yes, I know Trasher."

After this short introduction, Marcel mounted his bike and made a sign for everyone to follow him. The women took their rear seats and the group took off, the rattle of Harley engines disturbing the peaceful neighborhood until they merged onto a highway out of town. After an hour, they turned onto a lonely side road. As they rode past a short row of sleepy country homes, a few birds flew from the trees, frightened by the deafening sound of the mighty engines. After the last biker had disappeared around a curve and quiet had returned, the birds quickly flew back to their roosts.

Following a lengthy stretch of bush and dense forest, another row of houses appeared. Marcel stopped near the first one. It was a large bungalow with a high wooden fence built from its sides outward and around the backyard. Marcel stopped at the gate: It opened at once, as if someone inside was waiting for his arrival. The whole party drove in, past a smiling, broad-shouldered fellow with a neatly groomed beard, in shorts, a T-shirt, and sunglasses hiding his eyes. He raised a long barbeque fork in a welcoming gesture. After the last motorcycle rolled in, the guy closed the gate. The rattle of bikes died an instant later.

"Oh," Leila said. "Such a nice view." She eyed the large backyard with trees, benches, and two big tables, one on the patio and another on the grass. Beyond was an endless stretch of lake. The sails of a few boats rose in the distance.

Claude placed his hand on her narrow waist and stared at her lips. Her understanding smile touched his heart like a sweet razor. Beautiful girl, he thought.

"Claude," Marcel interrupted his fantasies. "We have to leave the girls for a short meeting." He turned around and waved his right hand. All the bikers followed him inside the house. In the large dining room, he offered everyone a seat around the table, which was loaded with glasses and uncountable bottles of wine.

"Our meeting today will be very short," he said, uncorking a bottle. "Everyone knows what we have gathered for today." He paused for attention. "We are promoting Claude to hangaround status. Congratulations, Claude."

Claude was dumbfounded. In a happy haze, he saw bikers coming to him for a handshake. Everyone smiled and raised his glass. The sharp odor of pot sprang up, irritating his nostrils. With a quick glance, he spotted the smoker—Stash, the one with a small ponytail and the bleak, wet eyes of a drunkard. Stash smiled and motioned with a sideways nod, inviting him for a talk outside. Since the group was already moving out, Claude joined him.

"Marcel says a lot of good things about you." Stash led him to a small bench under a branchy tree. "Let's sit—nice day, today."

"Right," Claude agreed, searching for Leila. She was chirping with three other women, busy eating shish kebabs. Machete went up to them and appeared to say something funny, because the women responded with laughter. Stash followed the direction of Claude's stare and produced a transparent plastic bag with marijuana inside.

"This is the best grass you can buy in Quebec," he said, offering it to Claude. "Help yourself. Here's the paper. You have a nice girl. Only you and Techie are with old ladies. The rest, including Marcel, are with mamas."

Rolling a joint, Claude continued watching the party. The wild gaiety was spreading over the backyard. Laughter and the flirtatious screams of women flew all around. At a patio table, Marcel was rolling up a $20 bill into a small tube. The mama beside him took the tightly rolled $20 bill, placed one end of it to her nostril, the other to a small stretch of white powder, and inhaled. It would take this broad, Claude thought, less than a minute to get crazy on pure coke, which was available only at the source of supply.

"I'm gonna suggest a job," Stash said. "Don't worry about Marcel," he added, answering Claude's silent question. "I've talked to him already."

"What is it?"

"Don't rush. Let me explain something. You can't make your living forever on work that you're doing for Marcel. The demand for it goes up and down. I gather that with such a beautiful old lady as you have, you need a stable income. Right?"

"Right. But I can't sell stuff. I'm not good at that."

"You don't need to. I'm thinking of something else."

"What?"

"I have a collection agency. It's a legitimate business. I need people who can influence deadbeats without resorting to force. You know how it works, don't you?"

"Yes, I do," Claude nodded. "I've done that type of work for my buddy, who's in the car business. When someone didn't pay, he asked me to talk with him. Everyone paid."

"You see!" Stash said happily. "You're the guy I need. No violence, though. That would be a last resort, and only with my permission. What do you think?"

"Sounds interesting. What's the pay?"

"Very good. We are talking about big money, Claude. Usually, our agency takes debts from $5,000 to $1,000,000. I'll teach you some tricks of the trade. I'm pretty sure, however, that after seeing you once, no one would want to see you again." He laughed, pleased with his wits. "Yes, I'm sure about that," he repeated.

"I'd think you could find plenty of tough guys out there for this job," Claude said, pleased with this joke.

"But, it's really not that simple. Most tough guys are shitheads. They can't deal with debtors who have brains, money, and connections to other tough guys. Sometimes, the job is dangerous."

"I see. I don't give a fuck how dangerous it is." Claude didn't look at Stash; he watched the party. Marcel's mama, a rather cute broad of about twenty, or maybe younger, got a boost. She laughed, threw her head back, kissed Marcel, and shouted something incomprehensible. Then, she began to undress. After the last garment fell, she ran toward the lake—a rather spicy view, she was: long, flying blond hair, firm boobs and ass, with a neatly shaped blond triangle at the bottom of her tummy. She threw herself into the water, squealing, splashing, and inviting all others to join her.

In the middle of the backyard, a petite woman was pulling two large men toward the house, inviting them at the top of her voice, "Let's do a threesome—now! C'm'on, guys."

Machete talked to Leila, who seemed agitated. He grasped her hand and held it while she attempted to free herself. Claude was about to jump up, but Stash put his hand on his shoulder.

"Don't worry," he said. "If worse comes to worst, I'll interfere. Mind you, for the next promotion you'll need 100 percent of the membership vote. Hold on."

Machete did let Leila go and looked after her as she ran to Claude.

"Let's party," she said, clutching Claude's arm. The gentle warmth of her hands soothed his rage.

"We'll talk about details later," Stash suggested. "I'll let you know how to find me."

"Gimme a puff." Leila pointed at the joint. With a melting heart, Claude saw her pink lips parting. His desire to kiss them was overwhelming.

She drew in the smoke and laughed.

"What was that joker saying to you?" Claude asked, rising to his feet.

"He told me, 'flash your boobs, babe.' He then said that I couldn't be your old lady that fast because you'd left the pen not long ago."

Leila led him to the table where Marcel sat in the company of two bikers and his mama; she now had a towel around her hips.

Claude noticed that Marcel did not drink. Leisurely smoking a cigarette, he observed the backyard from the corner of his eye.

Everyone was in a good mood, high on drugs and alcohol and the freedom from any restrictions. Agitated voices mingled into an incomprehensible chorus. Only two women were not topless: Leila and Techie's old lady. A tall and pretty brunette about thirty years old, Techie's old lady held herself with the pride of a woman who knew her worth. Drinking Coca-Cola, she talked to everyone who wanted her company in a friendly manner. All the bikers regarded her with respect.

"I wanna swim," Leila said. "Let me change. I'll be back soon."

When she left, Claude went to take a grilled steak.

"Having a good time?" somebody asked from behind his back. Claude turned around. Techie stood there, smiling.

"Yes." Claude was flattered by the fact that the legendary Techie was talking to him as an equal.

"How have my machines worked?" Techie asked. Claude new too well whose people had supplied the firearms he had used in his hits. They made sure that their stolen guns had no faults in either performance or reliability.

"Very good. I like them."

Claude could talk about guns forever. He liked these dangerous toys; they elevated him by their power and their ability to intimidate people.

Techie spoke like a polite and cultured man. He did not use foul language or take advantage of his stature or influence. But Claude felt in his gut that this was a man of iron will and a clear, powerful mind.

"You need some training, I think," Techie said, taking a bite of grilled chicken. "Marcel mentioned it."

"I can shoot," Claude remarked with pride.

"I know. But there are many circumstances when a trained hand is a must. Could you shoot with precision while you run? Would your shots be accurate when your target is moving fast? How about long-distance shots? There are some other aspects. Trust me, training would give you that extra mile in many circumstances."

Claude nodded, his eyes watching Leila in her bikini. She gave him a smile over her shoulder; then, after a moment of hesitation, she plunged into the lake with a joyous scream. It did not escape his attention that Machete, who sat with his mama on the beach, was watching Leila, too. This biker, no doubt, had snorted too much white powder. Apparently violent, he would be tough to deal with if push came to shove. Techie understood where Claude's attentions were being diverted.

"He's never gone after someone's old lady before," Techie said. "I don't have a good feeling about him lately. He takes too much blow. Sooner or later, he will lose his mind. Such people eventually become a burden, rather than an asset, to us."

This was a serious remark, just short of a death sentence, as Claude understood it. The usual way for the Devil's Knights to deal with a burden was to dispose of it.

When Leila came out of the water, Machete stood up and blocked her way in an attempt to strike up a conversation. She stepped back. Short-tempered Claude had had enough.

"Sorry," he said to Techie, and walked briskly to Leila.

"Let's sit at the table," he said, taking her hand.

"Hey, buddy," Machete objected, giving him a contemptuous look. "Can't you see that we were talking?"

His eyes weren't focused. Fighting with him, however, would be stupid: He was a full patch member, which meant a lot. Luckily, the matter didn't get that far. Techie came up and stood between them.

"Marcel's waiting for you," he said to Claude. He talked to Machete until Claude and Leila left. Marcel made an inviting gesture for them to sit nearby.

"Machete's getting into trouble," Marcel said. "I know him. When he loads up too much, it's hard to calm him down. I'm sorry to say it, Claude, but you'd better leave. Tomorrow, when he's sober, I'll give him an ultimatum. But for now, just to avoid a stupid conflict, you'd better leave with your girl."

Claude saw Techie speaking with Machete. The addict was obviously angry, but Techie remained calm, his eyes cold as ice.

Ten minutes later, in a sour mood, Claude climbed on his bike with Leila settled in behind him, and steered through the gate. Not a single car was on the road. At the first intersection, though, they bumped into a line of police cars. They were flagged over to the side.

"Driver's license," one of the police officers demanded menacingly. Claude's driver's license was in order. His answers were deliberately stupid, but polite. The police took a picture of him and copied all the data from his documents. For probably the first time in his life, Claude didn't lose his temper.

"Why have you left the party?" the officer asked with a sarcastic smile. Undoubtedly someone in the village had complained.

"Ain't no party," Claude said.

"Go," the officer commanded and turned his back on him. Luckily, he did not question Leila. She might have been in trouble if he had.

Chapter 4

I

The information technology revolution had created many new ways and methods for the police to store, organize, analyze, and present intelligence data. Serge Gorte was one of the detectives who used those new tools to the fullest. Occasionally, though, they just didn't seem to help. Like now, looking at his various flowcharts and tables, he remained at a loss—how did this murder relate to anything?

Technically, the case, which involved a car dealer's young wife, had nothing to do with bikers and therefore was the problem of another department. But something about the case piqued his interest. One thing was obvious: A professional hit man had committed the murder. No clues had been left that would help lead to the killer. Missing jewelry and money appeared to be an awkward attempt to imitate a robbery. Circumstantial evidence suggested that the victim knew the killer personally. She'd let him in, with no protest or resistance.

Too many murders in the last few months have been committed by experienced hands, Serge thought. Granted, they'd been hits on bikers or their associates and involved guns, explosives, and beatings, some in public places. This case seemed to have no similarity whatsoever to the others, but . . .

The first person he suspected was the husband of the dead woman, Norman Vincent. He had a firm alibi, though, and he didn't seem to have a police record—at least no information about him was readily available.

Serge sighed. He turned to study the pictures of ten bikers that police had taken last month on a stakeout. Someone in a country village had alerted police to their noisy arrival, and even though lawyers for the Devil's Knights club protested police harassment of bikers, the current political climate was not in their favor. Checkpoints had proven to be very valuable in the past. They often led to charges for firearms violations and to the discovery and identification of new members and associates of the gangs, which allowed their data to be gathered and recorded in police files.

No illegal substances or violations had been found, though, on any of these bikers: no drugs, no firearms, no contraband. On the other hand, only nine of them were known bikers, notorious leaders of the Devil's Knights club. One of them had not been associated with any biker gangs before. A biker wannabe, perhaps—information about him was abundant in police files and the files of various penitentiaries. He was Claude Pichette, a violent, ill-tempered psychopath who had proven to be a danger to fellow inmates and to prison guards, as well. What was he up to? What was he doing for a living? What if he was somehow connected . . . ?

Well, something was nagging at Serge, and the idea was worth a try.

He dialed the number for the security office at the Vincents' condominium building. A female officer answered abruptly, then changed her tone as soon as Serge identified himself. In a short time, she found out that the security guard who had been on duty at the time of the murder was currently working a shift. Serge picked up a few pictures from the table and put them in the breast pocket of his jacket. In his customary, unhurried pace, he went out, got into his car, and drove to the condominium.

After parking close to the building entrance, he took a walk and looked around. He noticed, first, the lonely street, which had no pedestrian traffic. Then, a small park with a few benches caught his eye. It was just off the street, and looked as if it might provide a convenient observation post for watching the entrance doors. He stepped inside the small lobby, absorbing every tiny detail.

At his left was a windowed room where a security guard was supposed to be sitting. Nobody was there. The next door was locked; naturally, only tenants of the building would have a key for it. Soon, a young woman came in. She unlocked the door and pushed it open.

"Would you like to come in?" she invited with a smile.

"Thanks," Serge said as he followed her in.

A few minutes later, a security guard—a tall, dark Indian man—came and settled in behind his desk on the other side of the window.

"What can I do for you?" he asked, leaning forward like a servant, ready to please.

"I'm Detective Gorte," Serge said, showing his badge. A look of fright crossed the guard's face.

"There have already been a few of you here asking questions," he said. "I can't really tell you anything more."

"I know. I'm not going to take much of your time." Serge forced a false grin on his lips.

"Okay." He exhaled loudly. "What can I do for you?"

"The murder happened between 10 and 12 o'clock, during your shift," Serge said. "Are you 100 percent sure that no stranger came in during that time?"

"I am positive."

"Could you remember those who came in?"

"Most of them."

"Did you see all their faces?"

"I think so. Most of them . . . I think."

"Most of them . . ." repeated Serge. "Could you give me an example of the ones you didn't see?"

"There was one guy who was helping one of our elderly tenants with some bags. They talked to each other. I supposed that they knew each other."

"How tall was the guy? How was he dressed?"

"Well . . . about six feet, I s'pose. I don't remember his dress, though—nothing that stood out."

"Never mind," Serge remarked impatiently. "Who was she, the lady he helped with the bags?"

"The old lady from the fifteenth floor. Rose is her name. She lives in 1509."

"Good. Thanks a lot. Can I have her phone number?"

"Sure." The guard opened a binder and wrote it down. "Here it is."

Serge dialed from the guard's phone. A cracking voice, undoubtedly belonging to an old woman, said, "Hello."

"Sorry to disturb you, Rose," Serge apologized. "I am Detective Gorte, investigating the murder in your building. Would you kindly agree to have a chat with me for a few minutes?"

A moment of silence followed.

"Certainly," the old lady said and hung up.

Serge took the elevator to the fifteenth floor and knocked on Rose's door. He felt that somebody was watching him through the peephole. The lock clicked and a thin woman appeared at the doorstep. She was very old, indeed: Wrinkles took up all the space on her small face. The top of her head was decorated with a crown of gray hair, light and transparent like haze, tidily arranged in waves.

"Please, come in," she invited, squinting her pale eyes at him, as if disturbed by the strong light. "This is probably regarding this terrible murder on the seventeenth floor?"

"That's right, ma'am," confirmed Serge.

"Please, sit down," she offered, pointing at a chair by her dinner table. "What can I do for you?"

Serge accepted the offer to sit down.

"On that day, the day of the murder, I believe someone helped you with your shopping bags. Is that right?"

"Yes, that is right."

"Do you remember his face?"

"Not clearly. I didn't have my glasses on."

Serge pulled out the photographs and arranged them on her table.

"Do any of the men in these pictures look like him?" Serge asked. The woman put her glasses on and bent over, moving a finger of her right hand from one face to another.

"Looked like this one, actually," she said, touching a photograph in the middle of the row. Serge felt the familiar excitement of a hunter closing in on his prey—she had pointed at Claude.

"Good," Serge said without showing emotion. "Could you identify him in person?"

The woman shrunk. With terrible fear in her eyes, she cried, "No, no! Please, I don't want to be a witness. I don't remember his face that well. You see, I have very poor vision. Please, sir—" She removed her glasses and placed them on the table.

"What makes you so worried?" Serge asked.

"They may kill me!" she exclaimed. The woman obviously was scared out of her senses. All further attempts to engage her in conversation failed miserably. When she complained about a pain in her chest, Serge stood up to go.

"Sorry, again, for the intrusion, ma'am," he said. "I do appreciate your help. Nobody will disturb you anymore. Have a nice day."

On the way back to his office, Serge thought about Rose's fear. He understood well why elderly people took such great efforts to keep themselves out of the smallest of troubles—any stress, big or small, could prove too much for their frail bodies. The puzzle, though, was why were so many of them afraid of the threat of death at their age? Was it the habit of living that made them terrified of the state of mind and body called death? Or was it because, in their older years, they had more time to think about their inevitable ends and to understand what a great value every new day has—for them to enjoy the world as it is, regardless of the successes and failures that made them so busy in the earlier stages of their lives? Even the most daring criminals, notorious for neglect or indifference to their own lives and deaths in their heydays, became cautious with the passing of years, often avoiding an even trivial risk. Why would people see a greater value in life when they had no more purpose, no goals left to achieve, and fewer things to enjoy? He shuddered at the thought that, eventually, he would have the opportunity to find answers to these questions himself.

Back in the office, Serge entered into his computer all the important points of his findings, updated a few associated files, and started to pick up the phone to call his wife to tell her he was done for the day. He was already late for the dinner his mother-in-law had arranged for them. No sooner had he touched the phone than the door opened. The boss of the special forces squad, Bertrand Tremblay, came in with firm steps, as if he owned the world. Tremblay was a tall, athletic-looking man in his fifties, with the posture and air of a noble man; thick and dark, though graying, hair; disapproving, questioning eyes; and a large nose.

"I won't keep you long," he said, taking the only chair on the other side of the table.

"My wife will either kill me or leave me," Serge growled.

Bertrand dismissed the complaint. "You know, Serge, that I've been appointed a police representative to the task force the government has assembled to tackle the biker problem. Our mission is to propose measures to 'finish,' as our smart politicians put it, with organized crime, once and for all."

They both laughed.

"I've gathered some statistics—there's plenty of data available in our information bank—to support my presentation," Bertrand resumed. "It would be helpful to have your input into our wish list of measures the government will have to adopt."

"From my perspective, Bertrand, we have to fight with our self-imposed restrictions and procedures as hard as we do with the bikers. Case in point is this murder of the car dealer's wife. Now, I know bikers did it, but I don't have plausible proof of it, yet. If my guess is correct, her husband works with car thieves. I know that the bikers control a few gangs whose activities revolve around the car business, in all forms and shapes. But it's an uphill battle to get permission to access the husband's financial information or to get any other information, for that matter, that is not internal to the police force. The flow of information throughout the government must be simplified."

Bertrand nodded in agreement.

"Another example was when some clever people in our government abolished police control over our major marine ports. I know they quickly restored it, but what was the result of that short break? About 30 tons of hash and five of coke were smuggled in. And that's just what we know. We can't even guess at what we don't know. These are mind-boggling numbers. Considering that the price of good quality stuff is $40 per gram, the street value of the coke alone is approximately $200 million! And this was only one delivery—can you guess what is going on day-to-day?" Serge paused for air.

Bertrand sighed. "Unfortunately," he said, "the bikers control our ports one way or the other. A mole alerted them to the upcoming raid. All our policing proved to be as ineffective as it was costly."

"Hah," Serge laughed with an angry burst. "That's our problem, not the government's. Our mistakes should not be the reason to cut funding or increase restrictions. I need to be able to put under surveillance any person of my choosing, without having to follow lengthy procedures. We need to tap the telephones of bikers, their relatives, their associates, and anyone we need to, even if we can't support our requests with valid arguments at the time."

"Those liberal-minded assholes would scream about breach of the constitution, violation of civil rights, and whatnot," Bertrand grumbled.

"Well, tell them that a huge amount of explosives has been stolen over the past few days from two construction sites. We don't know which gang is stockpiling them, but I suspect we won't have to wait long to witness an upswing in bombings and explosions all over the city. If I were you,

I would explain to those politicians that the biker's war is coming to their homes."

Bertrand leaned back and stretched his legs, fixing himself in what Serge noted was a too-comfortable pose. Serge frowned; he wanted to go home to enjoy this nice summer evening with his family, not to discuss the biker war.

"How are your investigations going?" Bertrand asked.

"Well, I'm pretty sure that I know one of the Devil's Knights hit men. And, I have gathered some good information on one of the prime figures in the Iron Ghosts. His name is Stanley Mathews. I suspect him of being a driving force behind many of the recent assassinations and explosions. It would be nice to put him under surveillance, but I have no evidence to support my request for that."

His telephone rang.

"This is my wife," Serge growled.

"Thanks, Serge." Bertrand stood up. "Have a nice evening. Oh, it's already 7 o'clock—I have to rush home, too."

II

The public was in fear and awe of the rampaging bikers. Gangsters killed each other in bars and restaurants—in broad daylight, blew up buildings where rivals had established their businesses, crushed bars with baseball bats to scare owners and patrons, and ousted rival drug dealers, all to expand their turf.

The police seemed helpless in their efforts to curb the violence. In a desperate attempt to save face and calm their constituents, the government had selected the best of the province's politicians, reputable police and RCMP, and respectable lawyers for a task force whose mandate was to suggest effective measures for eliminating the biker gangs. Election day was fast approaching, pushing the ruling party to its limits in an effort to regain the public's trust.

The initial meeting of the 11-member task force was to take place in a spacious 24th-floor conference room. Plenty of daylight flooded in through large windows that provided a spectacular view of the city. Nine men and two women would soon settle into comfortable armchairs around a long wooden table, its surface polished, glossy and shiny. A smaller table sat by the entrance. On it were coffeepots, a pile of napkins, sparkling teaspoons, a sugar bowl, and a few white ceramic cups.

First to arrive was Monica Godette. As a Member of Parliament she had been appointed from the government to take part in discussions. Customarily dressed in formal business clothes, today's skirt was the only touch of femininity in her outward appearance. Monica caught everyone's attention. Her long, somewhat masculine face with its small, sharp eyes made anyone looking at her feel like an accused child standing in front of an unforgiving judge who knows all secrets and is about to announce the frightening verdict. During the last election, she had supported noisy minorities such as gay rights activists, feminists, and the peace movement, but in a moderate way, never overstepping the bounds of common sense. Her latest appearances on television, interviews, and articles in newspapers had attracted enough attention to have her elevated to this panel of experts.

The chairman arrived soon after Monica. A well-known lawyer, Robert Corby took his seat at the far end of the table, from where he could observe the meeting. As soon as he was situated, he began tapping his laptop computer with the butt of his expensive Mont Blanc pen. The rest of the task force members arrived and got comfortable as quickly as possibly, perhaps moving in time with the tapping pen.

Raising the eyebrows on his very friendly face—a deceptive impression of which he was a master, as far as Monica knew—Robert asked everyone to introduce himself or herself. Monica opened up her writing pad and made notes on everyone except Robert, whom she knew too well.

"Although we are well familiar with the subject," Robert began after all the formalities had been dispensed with, "I think an overview of the current state of affairs from the police perspective would be a good starting point. I am privileged to introduce the expert on biker gangs, Detective-Captain Bertrand Tremblay." With a light nod at Bertrand, he added, "The stage is yours, sir."

Holding his head high, Bertrand opened a binder that lay in front of him but did not look in it. Instead, he exchanged glances with Monica, who held a pencil in her right hand, poised just inches above her writing pad. With vertical wrinkles on her forehead, she was ready to listen, ready to jot down all the facts and figures and matters of interest that Bertrand told them for future reference and consideration.

"Bikers now are the greatest criminal force in modern society. Forget the image they had in the sixties and seventies, or even the eighties. They are not hoodlums and brawlers, as they were in the past, disturbing the peace and committing petty crimes. No, now they are in the criminal business, and big business at that. And as all other businesses have, they have gone international. They have formed international drug cartels, international prostitution rings, and international money-laundering networks. I can't explain how or why a simple association of hoodlums changed over forty years to become one of the most powerful criminal organizations in the world. We'll have to leave that to historians."

Bertrand paused, as if he expected comments or questions or some kind of response. None came, and with a nod to his own thoughts, he continued.

"Biker gangs are not a new phenomenon in the criminal landscape. In Quebec, there are approximately 500 outlaw motorcycle gang club members and about 7,000 other bikers and associates, all of them considered criminals. Don't underestimate their wits and experience: Crime is their way of life. Many take part in direct criminal activities; others have legitimate businesses that they conduct in a criminal manner. Combined, they rival any large, legal business enterprise.

"The volume of drug sales in our province is about $1 billion a year. Because it is that large, it has become saturated with a swarm of new players who want a piece of the action. The only sure way and the quickest way to beat out the competition in the underworld is to eliminate it. The 'turf wars' that result between gangs have always been a fact of life. In most cases in the past, their outcome was the elimination of one gang by another or the absorption of one gang into another.

"The largest gang in our province so far has been the Devil's Knights. International by nature, with chapters in most developed countries, they have the largest supply and distribution networks for drugs in the world. They have also accumulated the best experience and the most expertise among organized crime organizations for assassination, intimidation, money laundering, and harassment. Recently, an unknown gang has entered the Devil's Knights turf. Though the gang is presumably small, it is evidently seen as a serious threat by some Devil's Knights who have tried to approach them.

"What has surprised the police, and has became a cause for public concern now, is the intensity of resistance this new gang, which is known as the Iron Ghosts, has shown to the Devil's Knights. In just two years, about seventy gang members on both sides have been killed, and we have averted about eighty more attempted murders. More than ten bystanders have been killed or severely injured in their crossfire or as a result of their explosions. A lot of dynamite is still not accounted for and for sure will be used soon in a larger scale as their war intensifies."

"I'd like to interrupt you, if I may," Monica cut in.

"Sure," Bertrand agreed with a welcoming glance in her direction.

"How many of those murder cases have you solved?"

"Three."

"Three out of seventy?" Monica was exasperated. "What kind of police force do we have!"

"That's exactly the point," Bertrand responded quickly. "We need more police officers. We need more funds for surveillance, logistics. And we need a tough law that would let us—for lack of better words—bypass the existing restrictions that tie our hands in fighting organized crime."

"Hold on, hold on with the law—." Monica stretched out her hand in an attempt to stop him from speaking. "One thing at a time. You want more funds from the government. Everyone wants that. Can't you just improve the quality of the police force first? Your achievements are not very impressive."

"We are trying to. Mind you, dealing with bikers is a tiresome task that requires special people. They have to have stamina, good intellectual capacity, proper training, and thorough education. How can we get such people?"

"Does our province lack people with good intellectual capacity?" The sarcastic remark came from a distant corner of the table. A brief smile stretched over Bertrand's lips.

"There are plenty. But how many of the best dream about becoming a police officer? Most, if not all of them, go where the money is. They want to become doctors, dentists, lawyers, businesspeople, corporate managers. Why? Because those occupations pay. Being a brilliant detective doesn't pay much. With the wages we have in the police force, with the workload we have, only a few elect this troublesome profession. You want to employ the best minds on a lean budget? Good luck."

After the short pause that followed, Bertrand added, "There are some among us who are proud of the jobs we do. But, we need more foot soldiers for surveillance and policing."

Monica could not wait for him finish.

"I've seen many gang members on the streets wearing biker outfits that distinctly identify them. This makes your task of surveillance easier, doesn't it?"

"Not at all. Most of them don't commit crimes. They give orders to their armies of subordinates who would do anything so they can grow in rank and status, climbing the ladder to the level of their bosses. Very often, the bosses convey their commands, not personally, but via a third person. The best we could normally expect to achieve is to capture the small fish."

Robert Corby raised his pen.

"In a nutshell, Bertrand, what do you propose?"

"We need more funds. We need simplified procedures for obtaining search warrants, tapping phone conversations, and accessing financial and personal information collected by other institutions and organizations. And last, but not least, we need a tough law against the bikers."

". . . 'A tough law' . . . ," Robert repeated, pursing his lips in a small, mocking smile. "What does that mean?" With false compassion and patience, he rested his chin on his left hand, elbow leaning on the table, ready to ridicule any stupid or weakly worded response.

Bernard did not blink.

"A law that would permit us to detain anyone who belongs to a criminal organization, such as the Devil's Knights or the Iron Ghosts, the prime troublemakers in the province. A law that imposes harsh sentences against organized crime bosses. A law . . ."

The rest of his answer was drowned out by several agitated arguments from all around the table. Some talked to him, some to each other. Simultaneous talk made further business-like discussion impossible until Robert tapped the table with his pen in a much more pronounced manner.

"Please, ladies and gentlemen." His voice, irritated, piercing, and demanding, had a calming effect. When the last arguments died under his disapproving glare, he said, "Let's express our views in an orderly manner. You want to say something, Mr. RCMP?" He smiled to a fat, balding man sitting at his left. "Please, Brian."

"I can understand the request for increased funds," the man said. "But to single out 'biker clubs' as criminal organizations is not constitutional. There are many motorcycle clubs. You have to prove which ones are the criminal organizations. Besides, even a group name, like 'Devil's Knights,' cannot be the foundation for declaring an organization criminal."

"I agree," Monica interfered. "There are many other biker clubs. Which ones are criminal organizations? And, I'm against increasing funds, as well. Better to clean up your house. The recent case of the police officer who was bribed by bikers is very disturbing. I don't believe that all depends on money. Morality—that is what should be watched in the security forces."

"We're now in very dangerous waters," Bertrand admitted, "and I'll be frank with you: There are corrupt officers cooperating with bikers and the mafia. We've already discovered one, but he managed to escape. I am pretty sure there are others. Leaks of information, failures to ambush large drug deliveries, and other illegal activities are vivid demonstrations of that. Somebody tips off the criminals and helps them escape our major actions, sometimes after months of work."

"It's appalling," Robert said in a loud, cracking voice. "I would never have suspected that the Quebec police could be so corrupt." His eyes flashed in the righteous indignation of a superior judge.

"It seems that you want to single out the Quebec police—," Bertrand seemed to be losing his patience. "What police force is better?"

"You don't have to go too far," Monica cut in. "The Ontario police are impeccable. Why don't you consult them?"

She looked around in search of admiring supporters. Whatever one might think, her arguments could not be beaten, she thought.

Bertrand did not respond right away. He stood in silence and smiled, observing the audience.

"Ontario . . . ," he said at last, as if talking to himself. And then, appealing to Robert, he asked, "Do you know, sir, that Toronto ranks third in North America in the number of narcotics sales?"

"I don't," Robert said. "So what? What about it?"

"How come there are no corrupt officers there? Can you explain it? Maybe you can, Monica? Such a big volume of narcotics sales, but no significant cases against the illegal drug trade, and no corrupt officers. . . . What are the police doing in Toronto? Please explain, don't be shy—Even your weakest arguments should be accepted seriously."

Nobody spoke. Bertrand looked around and continued to present more evidence.

"As a matter of fact, there have been a few police officers in Ontario charged for their connections with bikers. These cases simply didn't gain much publicity. When it's quiet, politicians, and I will admit, the police, tend to do little to tackle a problem. Wait until the bikers attain such financial power that we won't be able to do anything with them."

"I suggest adopting a more positive tone for our discussions." Robert was tapping his laptop. "Let's put our heads together and come up with something constructive."

"I'd rather listen, first, to the law enforcement people and how they intend to finish the biker problem once and for all," Monica said, staring at Bertrand.

"If you're asking me for a solution, I don't have an answer for you. We can only try to stop the biker wars. We can only try to diminish their power. I don't see anything beyond that."

Feeble sounds of surprise flew from different corners of the table.

"Does that mean," Monica went on, "that the police force is helpless against bikers? Then, what do you need additional funds for? I guess it's easy to spend the government's money for nothing."

In the silence that followed, Bertrand examined everyone around the table. With a feeling of contentment, Monica noticed anger in his eyes.

"Let me, for a moment, get back to what I've already said," Bertrand began. "The drug market in Quebec is about a billion dollars a year, maybe more. We don't have exact statistics, as neither vendors nor consumers are willing to participate in our survey."

This remark inspired a few relaxing chuckles.

"Do you think this market will just vanish? Do you think it will ever disappear from the radar screen of criminals? It attracts the most sophisticated and powerful criminal minds. Suppose we put all known drug dealers in our province in jail. Bingo! Do you think that the illegal drug trade would cease to exist? It would be wishful thinking to assume that it would disappear for any reason; the supply side would just be left unattended. Groups of other criminals, or non-criminals, would flood in, staging a chaotic and brutal war to take over.

"The very idea of punishing everyone in the criminal network is nothing more than a utopian idea, either. Mind you, we don't have a penitentiary system large enough to accommodate them all. And, the system itself is not much of a deterrent, as it was in the Middle Ages. For the most dangerous criminals, our prisons are more of an inconvenience than a punishment. They control the narcotics trade in the jails. They have women in there as often as they want. Some of them even have their own chefs to prepare delicious dishes. The list goes on and on.

"We need more money, that's right, but I agree with my opponents that money is not a final solution. The more

151

liberal our policies become toward our criminals, the more money the police forces need." He threw a look at Monica. She understood its meaning and hardened her face.

"Now, suppose we did magic and gathered good evidence against all the bikers and their associates," he continued. "Do you know how many people we would have to prosecute? Many thousands. We don't have enough courts, judges, juries, or lawyers to process them quickly. It would take years. I think that if this happened, we would create more problems than we solved."

"What do you expect from the politicians, then?" Monica asked. Bertrand was about to answer, but Robert spoke next.

"I agree with Bertrand that the heart of the matter is not the bikers or any other organized crime group. The problem lies with human nature in general and our society in particular. Can we do something about prostitution in our society? You could legalize it or prohibit it, or whatever your imagination suggests. But you couldn't wipe it out."

"Do you suggest legalizing it?" Monica asked Robert.

"I will come to that," Robert replied. "Take, for instance, tobacco. We don't have criminals dealing in tobacco. Politicians can regulate that industry anyway they want. Why don't we do the same by legalizing other activities, such as prostitution? Can you imagine how many lives we could save, how many abuses and violent crimes against women we could prevent?"

"This is too much," Monica interrupted. "Let's stick to our mandate."

"This is just a thought," Robert said with a smile. "But my point is, we're a society that desperately needs dreams. This is a paradox: Being the wealthiest society in the world, we still need things to take us away from reality and into

the realm of dreams. These could be drugs, alcohol—
anything else. I believe that we can fight the bikers and the
other gangs. But we have no chance to win the war against
them. Not a damn chance."

"That's not a very positive note," commented Brian.
"Let's be realistic and use some common sense in our
discussions."

"True," Bertrand agreed. "Let's be realistic. So what if I
offered to discuss ways to change the evil habits of our
society? To convince people not to use drugs, prostitutes,
and, well, even . . . alcohol. What would you say about me?
You'd say that the guy is crazy. However, some of you
probably think that ending drug distribution is a realistic
idea. I think it's not. As far as additional funds are
concerned, let me say this: The illegal drug trade makes its
lords more powerful than ever. The money they have, the
number of soldiers they command, is always increasing.
How on Earth do you expect the police to fight this ever-
expanding army with a constant-size police force? We have
to increase in numbers, too! Moreover, with our lenient
judges and a host of restrictions and stupid regulations,
criminals easily get away with serious offenses every day.
Do you want to be realistic? Let's fight first with our own
restrictions. Let's adopt and enforce some laws that will
make our jobs more productive."

"What are your concrete suggestions?" Monica asked.
Bertrand was about to answer, but Robert again demanded
attention.

"I suggest we take a break," he announced. Everyone
agreed. Monica stood up, and Bertrand saw her looking at
him as if she wanted to talk with him privately. He
accepted the silent invitation and walked over to her; she
took him by the sleeve to the doorway.

"I gather you're not receptive to the idea of passing a law against bikers," he said.

"Right you are. Forgive me for making such a tactless remark, but your agency tends to abuse the power it's given by the government. That's why it has to be so strictly regulated and controlled."

"Could you give me an example?" asked Bertrand.

"Sure. The latest case that comes to mind is when you planted evidence against the Devil's Knights. Such a scandal! Not only did the judge have to dismiss the charges, which in itself was a huge setback for you, but you also lost the public trust. Now you ask for a law that would permit you to act with no control?"

"But it's against biker clubs."

"So what?" Monica shot back, heading toward the cafeteria that was located at the corner of the floor. "There are many motorcycle clubs. Which ones would you target? Would it be up to you to decide which one is a criminal organization? Come on! What if you don't like some other minority group? Don't you understand that such a law would be unconstitutional?"

"I'm a police officer, not a politician," Bertrand pointed out proudly. "Politicians create fertile ground for criminals. The more humanely we treat them—which is a credit to you politicians, of course—the more criminals we create. You only have to wait until they come to your home. Then, I suspect you'd change your mind. I'd like to see how you'd react in your moment of need when you heard that the police couldn't do much for you because of restrictions, procedures, constitutional interpretation—whatever. I hope it doesn't happen, of course—don't get me wrong."

"Safeguarding civil rights is our fundamental principle," Monica said. "Criminal or not, each member of our society has to be duly protected."

They reached the door leading into the cafeteria where Bertrand stopped, letting Monica enter with a gallant gesture.

"Would you like to join me at my table?" Monica asked.

"Sure. I'd love to!"

She chose a table by the window, with a lot of light pouring in from outside.

"Do you mind if I ask you a few questions?" she said.

"Ask as many questions as you like. I'm here to offer my expertise to the task force."

"I understand that it's a turf war between the gangs," she started. "But all gangs are similar in structure and mentality, as I understand it. Why, then, couldn't the Iron Ghosts convert themselves into Devil's Knights?" Monica was proud of her smart question.

"Good question," Bertrand said. "Only a few of the Iron Ghosts would qualify as outlaw bikers. I won't go too deep into that. Just take my word for it. It means, however, that most of them would be thrown out of business as soon as the whole turf belonged to Devil's Knights. But business is exactly the reason for going to war with the Devil's Knights, even if it means risking their lives. Those few who choose to betray the Iron Ghosts and qualify to convert as bikers may not necessarily remain too long in the Devil's Knights ranks. Most likely, they would be killed. The war has gone too far."

"So, Iron Ghosts aren't really bikers? I gather they are more like gangsters of different sorts," Monica remarked.

155

"Right you are, Monica," Bertrand agreed with false enthusiasm. "But they took a lot from the bikers' subculture, if their way of life could be called a subculture."

"Let me ask you something else." When Bertrand nodded, Monica went on. "Why can't you plant more informants inside the gangs? I realize that it's not easy, but it's not impossible, I would guess."

Bertrand looked weary. He greeted her remark with a deprecating smile, disapproving lines running down the corners of his mouth.

"It's impossible. You see, they have a strict selection process that any organization would envy. Years of heavy involvement must pass before the gang decides to give a biker any status. To gain status in the biker's club means a lot: One has to participate in all the gang activities, even the criminal ones, which would be a no-no for an undercover law officer. But even that would not be enough. He would have to be an initiator and organizer of crimes, eventually controlling and directing the activities of other criminals, street gangs, or other biker gangs. And, I assure you—even taking part in all these activities doesn't make a biker immune from suspicion. We couldn't let anyone go into such an assignment and risk getting killed."

Monica was very impressed with what Bertrand was saying.

"But . . . couldn't you recruit from those bikers who are already under investigation?" she suggested cautiously. Noticing a trace of a sarcastic smile, she rushed to explain her stance.

"It's not that I'm advising you in the area of your expertise," she said. "It's for my understanding only."

"Sure, sure," Bertrand nodded. "But that is a topic for a separate discussion."

"Yes, yes," Monica consented. "Let's get back to it sometime later. Our talk has been very informative. Thanks a lot. But now, I think it's time to go to the next session, Bertrand."

III

The sound of a door being unlocked brought Camilla from the depths of a relaxing nap to a serene, but pleasant reality. With a deft, quick motion, she slipped into a fuzzy, soft nightgown and hurried to the living room. Stanley already stood there, closing the door behind him. She threw herself upon him with the impatience of a lover who has been waiting too long.

"You didn't come by yesterday," she reproached, but did not let him speak under the enveloping pressure of her lips. Then she stepped back and hopped onto the sofa, sitting on her crossed legs. Her eyes shone with happiness. How nice to see him again!

"Sit down," she invited. "Tea, coffee?"

"Nothing. How'd yah like it here?"

"It's lovely."

Stanley had rented this one-bedroom apartment for her just a month ago. He'd furnished it with one idea only: to please her. In the course of the shopping spree to furnish the larger space, she'd urged Stanley to consider his purchases and spend money wisely. In response, he'd produced an impressive roll of cash and asked her to mind her own business.

"Did I wake you up?" he asked, turning on the television with its remote control.

"Sort of. I have a night shift at the hospital. You can't last the whole night without an earlier nap. But never mind, I've had enough."

The black television screen flashed with the sight of a passionate French kiss, and, after a few nervous blinks and jumping horizontal stripes, it stabilized into the image of a good-looking female broadcaster.

"Our guest," she was saying, looking straight ahead with unblinking eyes, "is a well-known politician and member of a special task force that has been assigned to deal with biker gangs—Monica Godette. What are your comments on the latest development in the biker's war, Monica?"

A small square at the right top corner of the screen popped up and then grew rapidly to full size, showing a woman in no-nonsense business dress, with an air of aggressive strength that a woman was not supposed to possess.

"The latest rampage between the rival biker gangs has caused great concern in the government," Monica responded. "The bikers think that they have the world at their feet. They make shooting galleries out of our bars and restaurants. Their Hollywood-style murders terrify the public. In spite of all the police warnings to stop the war, they have intensified it, rather than terminated it. This only shows how deep this problem in our society is, how insatiable our appetites are for their illegal products and services. But punishment will come eventually, and it will be harsh. The shooting yesterday enraged both the public and the government. I can assure you . . ."

Stanley chuckled and turned the set off.

"Do you know anything about that shooting?" Camilla asked.

"Sure. I was there."

"Are you serious? You scare me."

"There's nothing to be scared about. This is my life. I can't live a different one."

"What happened there? Could you tell me?"

"Of course. You know the Black Penguin bar, don't you? That's my territory. The bar was almost full. Everyone there was ordinary nine-to-five folks, dropping by for a glass of beer or a blow of coke. I was sitting with Ogre—do you remember him? Of course, you do. He's the one with guts made of steel. He looks ugly to the girls, but he's good company. He weighs over 220 pounds—all muscle, you know. Ogre's always alert, and so am I. There was nothing to worry about. All of a sudden, Ogre says, 'I have fifty grams of coke in my car.'"

"'Not bad,' I said. I looked around, but nothing seemed suspicious. 'Who'd you bring it for?' I asked."

"'A guy from the West End is going to come and pick it up,' he says. 'I've been dealing with him a lot. So far, so good.'"

"'How'd yah call him?' I asked."

"'Shifter,' he said. 'Do you know him?'"

"'His name rings a bell,' I said. I asked Ogre to tell me what the guy looked like. Sure 'nuf, he was the one I saw once in the joint. The guy was spinning some tale about the Devil's Knights. I asked Ogre, 'Does he know that I'm supposed to be here?' And Ogre says, 'Yah. As a matter of fact, he wanted to talk to you. Why not?'"

Stanley paused, reached for a cigarette, and lit it in a seemingly calm manner. He drew in a huge puff and exhaled with force. Camilla, though impatient, did not dare to interrupt.

"'Be ready,' I said to Ogre. 'Something's cooking here. Do you have a gun?'"

"'Of course I do,' he said."

"'Then give it to me,' I said. 'I don't have one on me.'"

"But this stupid ass didn't want to part with his beloved toy. He said, 'I'm your bodyguard. I'm supposed to take care of you. Why'd you want to take this gun from me?'"

"'Because I shoot better than you do, knucklehead' I said. 'You'd better get some training sometime, yah lazy bum. For now, don't say a word until everything's over. Now, give it to me—now!'"

Stanley took another nervous puff.

"And, did he?" asked Camilla, holding her breath.

"Luckily, he did. I took it just as three jerks entered the room, one behind the other. Even if I hadn't known them, I'd have understood who they were after. With a little practice, you learn to recognize those who come to kill."

A quick thought ran through Camilla's mind: *What kind of frightening life has this man had to live to gain such experience?* Stanley noticed her strained face, but apparently mistook her fear for admiration.

"One of them I knew well: Machete is the name of this son of a bitch." Stanley kept talking, encouraged by a new look of attention on her face. "For sure, he and his buddies had killed a few of us. I knew that he was out on bail. As he stepped in, he put on a ski mask. But we'd already been moving toward the rear exit. You see, this bar is my territory. I know how to get in and out of it. Had it been anybody but me, Ogre would've been dusted; he would never have run; it's against his rules. But now, he followed me, without giving it a second thought. There were a few loud shouts behind us, someone in the bar screaming like hell."

160

Stanley stopped talking and lit another cigarette from the butt of the first.

"Do you have any whiskey?" he asked. Camilla jumped up and brought a bottle from the kitchen, with a glass. Stanley filled it halfway and drank.

"Outside, around the corner, there's a narrow passage that leads to the rear parking lot." He kept talking, his eyes grim. "We barely dodged the waiter, who was coming from the kitchen with a load of dishes. When we leapt through the rear door, we heard the rattle of broken plates—they knocked the waiter down. The commotion was good for me. I didn't have to start shooting on the run. I know too well that shooting on the run can never be accurate, no matter how much training one gets.

"The parking lot at the back was damn dark. Not a single street lamp was lit, although usually there's at least some light. I stopped about twenty meters from the rear exit and turned around. At that very moment, the door flew open and the first of them rushed out. I was already standing still, aiming at the target: the doorway. Machete— it was certainly him—was shooting very well. Bullets flew just a few inches from my right ear. But I had the advantage of being prepared for the shot, because I could stand still and take aim at him. I fired, he shrieked like a frightened woman, and fell down. Two others bolted in different directions. Machete, however, turned out to be a hard nut: He kept shooting from the ground, in pain. One of his bullets hit Ogre's left shoulder, but it wasn't serious— the bullet just scratched his skin. I fired two other shots, which calmed the shithead for good. Then I ran. Ogre followed, holding his left shoulder with his right hand."

"'What's that?' I asked."

"'I was hit,' he said. 'Don't worry; it's just a scratch. I'll drive myself.'"

"'You sure?' I asked."

"'I have the stuff in my car,' he said."

Stanley poured more whiskey into his glass and took a sip. He finally noticed that Camilla was looking at him strangely. "Why are you staring at me like that?"

"I . . . I don't know if I should tell you—," she started.

"What? You should tell me everything."

"This . . . this, Machete . . . he's at our hospital."

Stanley leaned back on the sofa, examining her as he would a complete stranger. A moment later, he stood up, took off his jacket, and, pacing to and fro in the limited space of the living room, rolled up his sleeves.

"Where in the hospital?" he asked.

"Stanley, darling."

"Where?" He threw her a no-nonsense glance, raising his voice.

"On the fourth floor. Room 419. Look, darling, let it pass. There's a police officer on guard 24 hours a day outside his room. Because the guy's out on bail, the police didn't let Devil's Knights guard the room. They want to interrogate him because the gun was found beside him."

"Will he survive?" Stanley asked.

"Yes. No vital organs were hit. He'd lost a lot of blood, but he'll survive."

"Okay," Stanley said after a silent conversation with himself. "Let's forget about that. When are you leaving for your shift?"

"In two hours."

"Good. Come here. You won't need that nightgown for awhile."

"That's better," Camilla said after her clothing fell to the floor. It was lovely to feel his warm hands running over her body. "I love you, darling."

An hour later, after glancing at her wristwatch, she placed both her hands on his cheeks in a gentle, affectionate pat and said with a sigh, "I've gotta go. Will you stay here?"

"Yes," Stanley said, his eyes half closed. She giggled happily.

"I'll sneak under the blanket with you tomorrow morning, when you're still in bed. You like it in the morning, don't you?"

"Sure do." Stanley kissed her. "Any time of the day, for that matter, any season, any weather condition."

On the way to the hospital, she smiled at the recollection of his last remark. She liked it the same way Stanley did. Anticipating the joys of the following morning, she went to the fourth floor, only to notice a police officer at the end of the corridor, sitting on a chair outside a patient room. That's where the man who'd been wounded in yesterday's shootout, a man she now knew as Machete, was recovering. Camilla walked a short distance to the nursing station, and was immediately absorbed in the busy hospital schedule. Her first priority was to check patients who were in serious condition. Machete was one of them. At the entrance to his room, the police officer was dozing in his chair, fighting desperately to stay awake. When his chin hit his chest, he threw his head back with a jerk, as if frightened by a dream. He opened his eyes for a moment, and then, after seeing Camilla in her white medical gown, let his head drop back onto his chest.

Machete was sleeping. Looking at him, she couldn't comprehend that this unconscious, bearded man, his skin pale-gray like death, had been trying to kill her lover the day before. She didn't feel any hatred toward him. With the professional compassion of a nurse, she fixed the tubes leading to his veins, measured his blood pressure, and left.

After finishing with the left wing of her floor, she went to the right wing. It was nearly 2 o'clock in the morning. On the way out of a patient's room, she noticed two men in white medical gowns coming off the elevator. Both had neatly groomed beards, mustaches, and thick hair. They turned left with the confident steps of doctors very familiar with the hospital. One of them was rather broad-shouldered and fat. He stopped at the corner while the other one kept going toward the end of the corridor, where the police officer was sleeping, his chin on his heaving chest.

At the next moment, horror make her immobile—the slim doctor had Stanley's gait; she could recognize it from among millions of others. He stopped short in front of the sleeping police officer, his right arm hidden under the white medical gown, then carefully stepped over the guard's outstretched legs. The fat doctor kept his hand under his white gown, as well; he was turning his head from side to side, looking from one end of the hall to the other.

Camilla darted around the corner to the nursing station. Aimlessly shuffling papers on her desk, she listened with pounding heart to the slightest noises, expecting a rattle of shots, a series of screams, or the noise of a chase. Nothing of that sort happened. She walked to the elevator, from which both wings could be observed. Nobody was there: only the police officer who was dozing peacefully at the entrance to Machete's room.

An interminable hour passed by. At 3 o'clock in the morning, a sickening yell from the left wing startled her. She ran in the direction of the noise, two other nurses following her. In Machete's room, they found the police officer, groaning and holding his head. Machete was lying on his back, the handle of a dagger sticking out of his throat. He was dead; his eyes were open, his sheets soaked in blood. The killer had obviously known how to make his death quick and silent.

The commotion woke up the whole hospital. The police arrived and began their investigation. The detective who questioned Camilla didn't find anything suspicious in her behavior; other nurses were shaken no less than she was.

When the shift was over, Camilla was thoroughly exhausted. She left the hospital, going out into the summer morning, holding her purse in trembling hands. The sun had just begun to rise, lingering above the horizon and throwing its blinding rays straight into her eyes. The city had started this day like any other, with traffic on the roads and anxious pedestrians on the sidewalks. Looking at the usual routine of day-to-day life, she could hardly comprehend that what had happened was real. She got into her car and steered it into the busy streets, thinking about possible consequences. A blend of excitement, guilt, and fear haunted her all the way home. At her apartment, she took off her shoes at the doorstep and walked quietly to the bedroom. She found Stanley, lying under the blankets with eyes open, smiling, and apparently in a very good mood.

"Tired?" was his first question.

"Oh, Stanley . . . ," Camilla sighed, taking off her clothes. "Gosh, I thought I would die . . . I was so terrified . . . I'm still shaking."

She lay beside him and closed her eyes, feeling his embrace.

"Stanley, darling, I can't. It's beyond me. I have to recuperate."

"I know that you like it in the morning," Stanley reminded her.

"Not this morning. Please, my dear. I can't. I have to rest a bit. Tell me, how'd yah do it?"

A proud smile appeared on Stanley's face.

"You tell me first—what happened after Ogre and I left? Lots of fuss?"

"There was. The police officer was screaming. We all rushed to the room. The biker was dead. A knife was stuck in his throat, up to the handle. It was so frightening. The poor police officer was disconsolate."

Stanley laughed heartily.

"What would happen if they discovered my role in all this mess?" Camilla asked sternly.

"Never, my sweetheart," Stanley assured her. "There were no witnesses, other than you." He caressed her hair.

"How did you do that?" she asked. Stanley sat up on the side of the bed and began to dress.

"We arrived in an ambulance. I know someone who is an ambulance driver. As you noticed, Ogre and I wore wigs, phony beards, and mustaches. A few Devil's Knights were on patrol around the hospital, but they didn't suspect us. Five other guys were waiting inside the ambulance, just in case. We had guns. I thought we'd have to take the guard into the washroom and tie him up there. I even took a roll of duct tape to seal his mouth. But the pig was sleeping like a kid. When I stepped over his legs, he moved a bit. I grasped my gun, but happily, he didn't wake up. Good for him. That saved his life. When I sneaked behind the curtain, I saw Machete sleeping. I drove my dagger into his throat. He jerked, but then died in the next instant. We left down the staircase."

"Weren't you scared?"

"C'mon, Camilla." Stanley was already dressed. He bent over and kissed her eyes. "Take a rest."

"I love you, in spite of everything," she said with her eyes closed.

"I love you, too. I promise that you'll never be involved in anything like this, again. Sleep well."

He kissed her once more and left.

When her fear subsided, Camilla had nearly regained her usual, happy state of mind. But later, she started examining Stanley not only with the care of a loving woman but also with the curiosity of a psychologist. Behind his image of a strong and tough man, she often saw glimpses of a hellhound with no human features. He claimed that his actions had always been provoked by circumstances. It was one thing, though, to have a reason, but another to act upon it it the way he did. Stanley's lack of fear and disregard for consequences were beyond her comprehension. In some way, however, she admired him even more than before. What he'd done was both terrifying and mind-boggling. One must be worth something to do that.

For a week they didn't see each other. Stanley called her every day, soothing her nerves with his confident manner of speaking, his charm, and his careful selection of words—always to the point and convincing.

"I miss you so much," he said at the end of each conversation, "but I can't come to you. Too many things I've got to do these days."

She listened to his words with a mixture of delight and fright. The newspapers, the radio, and the television were all talking about the biker's war, contract killings, staggering death tolls, and detonations of large amounts of dynamite at the businesses and social buildings of rival factions. She now had no doubt that Stanley was involved in, if not initiating, many of these events.

"I'd love to meet you tonight," he said one evening. "Come to the Dummy Eagle bar at eight. We'll have a few beers and then go to my place. I don't want yours to be under X-ray." That was what he called police surveillance.

When she arrived, he was already sitting at one of the tables with his usual welcoming, relaxed smile. Ogre was beside him, his face to the entrance, as well. Camilla couldn't understand how they could be so tranquil in the midst of such turmoil.

She threw an anxious look around the crowded bar, a rather foolish attempt to recognize gangsters that might be hunting Stanley.

"Sit down, sweetie," Stanley invited, moving a chair. "Relax. Any problems? Investigations? Tell me, what's happened since that night? I couldn't speak to you about that over the phone."

"Nothing much," Camilla said. "They just spoke briefly to all nurses who worked that shift. Since a police officer was guarding the room, there wasn't much they could ask others. Once, though, my heart stopped when the detective talked to me. He didn't ask much, but when he looked at me. . . . At first I just took him for a kind family man who had gotten his job on the police force by sheer chance."

"What was it about his look?" Ogre asked.

"I don't know. But I was as calm as a saint. I wanted to be an actress before I decided to be a nurse, you know. My acting skills have helped me a lot in my life."

"Do you, by any chance, remember the name of the detective?" Stanley asked.

"Serge Gorte. Kind of a weird name, isn't it?"

She noticed how quickly Stanley and Ogre exchanged glances.

"Forget about it," Stanley advised, leaning back in a casual manner. "What do you want to drink, my cute little actress?"

His face suddenly became hard and tight, just as she remembered it had been when she'd seen him for the first time, at the chairlift. He was looking at Ogre, but Ogre was looking intently into the murmuring crowd of beer drinkers.

"What is it, Ogre?" Stanley asked. Camilla's heart jumped in fear. These guys, she thought, don't have a minute to relax from the dangers of their busy lives. Is this the nature of an adventurous life? If it was, she wouldn't be able to live it.

"The shithead that I was supposed to meet when Machete came. You see him there at the bar counter? He's alone."

"What are you up to, guys?" Camilla asked. She looked back and saw the man at the counter. He turned his head and their eyes met. Camilla gave him a polite but meaningless smile. In the next moment, the man was staring beyond her, at Stanley and Ogre, trying to retain the last traces of his vanishing smile. She turned around, only to notice a remarkable change: Ogre was now smiling, waving at the man in a friendly manner; Stanley was not tense anymore, but had begun fiddling with his glass of beer. He touched her hip under the table.

169

"Here's the key for my Jeep, Camilla. When I give you the signal, go there and wait with the engine running."

"What are you guys up to?" she repeated in whisper.

"Don't be scared," Stanley commanded with a smile. "You've said that you're a good actress. This is your chance for a good show.

The man who sat at the bar stood up and came over to their table. By his look, he seemed a tough guy—middle height, broad shouldered, and apparently very strong.

"Hi," he said to Ogre. "Haven't seen you in ages." There was tension in the man's eyes. He was trying hard to detect the danger, but couldn't quite come to any conclusion, misled by the appearance of friendly faces.

"Sit down, Shifter," Ogre said, nodding at the remaining vacant chair. "Have a beer with us. This is my friend Stanley. You wanted to meet him—here is he."

Stanley shook hands with Shifter, who relaxed at once. He sat, accepted the offered bottle of beer, and took a large swig as he stole a glance at Camilla. Without understanding why, she took part in the game and returned the glance with a smile, that peculiar smile that only very coquettish women can master.

What am I doing? she asked herself. *Maybe they want to kill the poor man. There's nothing that they wouldn't do.* However, she felt no strength or will to say "no" and disobey Stanley.

A few minutes of meaningless small talk apparently convinced Shifter that he was safe. He even tried to pull off a few jokes, but told them in too primitive a way, typical of poorly educated people who lack sophistication and wit. While listening to one of his stupid jokes, Camilla felt Stanley's gentle kick under the table. She smiled, as if reacting to Shifter's words.

"I've gotta get home, guys," she said, rising. "It's getting late."

"Where are you going?" Shifter asked.

"I live close to Serengeti Optical," she lied. This distant store was the first landmark that came to her mind.

"I actually don't live far from there. Could you give me a ride? I don't have a car today. The busses only run once an hour that late," Shifter said. She wanted to cry "stupid ass!" but looked at Stanley instead. He smiled.

"Be careful with her," Stanley advised Shifter. "She could break a heart of steel."

Shifter responded with a condescending smile.

"Leave it to me," he said with a confidence of Don Juan.

With an incessantly pounding heart, Camilla led the way to Stanley's Jeep.

"I haven't asked your name, you beautiful filly, you," Shifter said playfully as he tried to catch her arm.

"You only need a ride, don't you?" Camilla asked, evading his advances, and pressing the remote key button. The Jeep responded from a dark corner of the parking lot.

She climbed into the driver's seat and put the key in the ignition with her shaking hand. Shifter jumped into the passenger seat, and, smiling in the dark, playfully commanded, "Let's go."

She didn't move.

"So, where exactly do you live? I know my neighborhood pretty well," he asked.

"It doesn't matter where I live," Camilla cut him off.

"Let's go, sweetie. Move along! Don't be afraid of me. You have a nice car, baby. Have a rich lover?"

"I'm a working girl," she said. "I have my own money."

"A working girl!" Shifter laughed. "I like those." He was looking at Camilla, and she was looking at him. She saw what Shifter couldn't see behind his back: two familiar figures moving briskly across the parking lot toward the car. Stanley jerked the door on the passenger side open and stepped aside. Ogre grabbed Shifter by his hair and pressed the barrel of a gun into his face.

"Be quiet," he said. Shifter froze, as if paralyzed. "You'll do whatever I say, deadbeat—Understand?"

Without waiting for a reply, Ogre took him by the collar, yanked him out, and pushed through the back door into the middle of the rear seat. Stanley went around the car and jumped in on the other side. Shifter, squeezed between two gangsters, didn't utter a sound.

"Go," Stanley commanded.

Camilla began driving, following his turn-by-turn directions. She didn't know this part of town and had no idea where Stanley wanted to go. They entered a huge new housing development that didn't yet have streetlights. Under the blinking stars the unfinished homes looked like ancient ruins.

"What do you want from me, guys?" Shifter asked at last. "What do you want? Where are we going?"

"Go a bit farther," Stanley kept saying. "To the end of this street."

"Hey, guys." Shifter's voice began trembling. "Are you crazy?" He made an attempt to move. Camilla heard a dull sound. Shifter screamed.

"Stop here," Stanley instructed when she reached an unusually large, almost finished house. She obeyed. Stanley got out and in one sweep pulled the hostage out of the car. Ogre quickly came around. They took Shifter by the arms and dragged him into the black doorway. Camilla lowered the window. As in the grip of a nightmare, she listened to the agitated, muffled voices coming from inside, probably from the basement. She recognized Stanley's angry voice, but couldn't make out what he was saying. Next, a yell of pain shuddered the walls of the house; Shifter began shrieking words, very quick words. His speech kept getting faster and faster, as if he was suddenly in a great rush to tell something very important for his life. Soon, his words became unrecognizable streams, and his screams became intolerable. Camilla had heard this kind of sound in her childhood when her mother had taken her to a farm—the farmer's son had been trying to kill a pig with his knife, but obviously lacked the skills and experience to do it quickly. At that time, she had thought it funny to listen to a desperately squealing animal with a knife in its body. This time, she covered her ears with both hands, but to no avail.

Then, the revolting sound began growing weaker and weaker.

Until it stopped.

In a strange way, the silence that followed was even more frightening than the commotion that preceded it. She heard the rustle of steps inside the house, and a few moments later she noticed Stanley and Ogre appearing on the porch.

"Give me the wheel." Stanley pulled the driver's door open as Camilla crawled over to the passenger seat. Ogre climbed into the rear. Stanley stepped on the gas.

"Did you kill him?" Camilla whispered. Her vocal cords failed to produce a sound.

"I told him that no human could tolerate torture for long. He didn't believe me. It could've been much easier for him. The stupid ass! It wasn't the best time for him to play a tough guy."

"Who was he?" Camilla asked.

"A dealer. He worked with the Devil's Knights."

"Take me back to the bar—," she reminded him, "I left my car there."

Stanley nodded. They drove in silence all the way. When they pulled up beside her car, she stepped out without looking back.

"I'll call you tomorrow," Stanley said at the last moment.

She didn't respond.

Back at home, she threw herself on the bed and closed her eyes. The terrifying, muffled shrieks of the tortured man rang in her ears. Her happy, adventurous world, saturated with love, interesting encounters, and the joy of being—all of a sudden had become a huge, horrific battleground, populated by monsters. The memory of a pig's shriek—a call for mercy from a terrified, dying animal—caused spasms in her stomach. She rushed to the bathroom and bent over the toilet, vomiting violently. Exhausted, she went back to the bed and fell on it, unable to think, unable to feel anything but angst. She was in a stupor. Seeking refuge from the world, she hid her head under the pillows, and closed her eyes, but then the endless darkness became populated by the shadows of real-world savages and terrified her even more. She spent the whole night wandering between the fright of dreams and the horrors of reality. As morning neared, just as she finally grew exhausted and distanced enough to fall asleep, she heard the familiar sound of a key opening the lock of her door. When Stanley came in, she was already sitting up on the bed.

"You didn't sleep tonight," he said gently, sitting beside her. She nodded her head in agreement and covered her face with both hands. Stanley put an arm on her shoulders.

"Don't be so upset," he said. "You're not in danger. If worse comes to worst, you won't be involved."

"I can't live like this anymore," she said. "We have to split."

"Split?" he repeated.

"Yes. I love you, Stanley, but your life isn't for me. Finish with it and come back to me. I'd be the happiest woman in the world if you did."

After a short pause, he said, "Actually, it's not a bad idea to split for awhile. There's been a lot of heat on me lately. Let the dust settle, and we'll talk later."

Stanley kissed her, but she didn't respond. He rose to his feet and left.

Chapter 5

I

"Here. Now, relax for awhile." Marcel handed him a thick stack of money as payment for the last hit. "Stay low, but be ready. You deserved a rest."

"I feel good," Claude objected. "No need to relax."

He wanted to work more so he could rent a condo in a better location and take a trip with Leila to Las Vegas. In spite of the good pay that Marcel provided, money was in short supply.

"One has to have a rest once in awhile," Marcel insisted. "Make it your habit. Stress will eventually take its toll. Don't worry so much about work: there's plenty."

A bit of rest wouldn't be that bad, Claude admitted to himself. No matter what other people might think, contract hits, in his opinion, did take nerve. The target could easily become a hunter and shoot back; if the Iron Ghosts caught wind of him, they'd be after him the rest of his life; there was no way to know what evidence the police might find after a crime—he could be locked up for good. Twenty-five years in jail without a chance for parole would be a bitter pill to swallow.

Leila welcomed the idea of a vacation with smiles and kisses.

"Let's travel on your bike," she suggested. "I've had a few such trips when I lived in B.C. They were fun!"

176

Kicking the hell out of his mighty Harley Davidson, Claude made Leila scream and squeal on the rear seat. From the driver's seat, he felt the warm air of late summer blowing in his face, smelled the aroma of the pine trees, and saw the fading freshness of the green leaves. They traveled through the rural part of the province where highways cut through dense expanses of forest. This was the area of summer cottages and vacation resorts, scattered on the shores of rivers and lakes. Sometimes it took them more than an hour to drive from one small village to another. In the rugged terrain, his bike could reach the top of a hill at 90 miles per hour. When he looked down, a breathtaking view of rivers and lakes spread out below him, with colorful dots of cottages and yachts that made him feel like he was flying in space. The unrestricted freedom to move in any direction was unreal and intoxicating.

This was the first vacation in his life. Yet, even in the midst of all this wonder, he sometimes wanted to take immediate action without thought of consequences; to release brutal force; to unleash his sadistic temper at the slightest suspicion of disrespect from a stranger. Years at the bottom of society and in jail, where he had been treated with neglect and humiliation, made his pride the sorest spot of his being. Revenge against all humanity was the feeling that stayed inside him at all times.

In the evenings though, sitting with Leila along the quiet shore of a secluded lake, he was peaceful and relaxed. They smoked pot, swam in refreshing lake waters, and enjoyed each other in their motel room. Leila knew too well how to please him to exhaustion.

"What a good life," Leila said once.

"For a short while," Claude nodded. "It's getting boring, though. I already want to be back where the action is."

"I wanna piece of the action, too. Is there anything I can do for yah?"

"Nah. Not, now. Maybe later."

"We spend your money pretty fast," Leila warned. "I could push lots of stuff in the bars, if you'd let me."

"Never."

"Did you know we have only $500 left from what we brought with us?" she asked.

"Shit. How—?"

"You don't count money when you spend it. It's that simple."

"We have lots of money back home. But you're right. Money goes fast. Let's go back tomorrow morning. Maybe a job's already waiting for me."

When they returned home, he found that nobody from the club was looking for him. Marcel had gone on vacation with his family and had left no instructions for Claude.

He decided to visit the Devil's Knights club, hoping that some of the full patches would need a gun for hire. Nobody did. In fact, a rumor was circulating that some of the bosses were secretly negotiating a truce with the Iron Ghosts. If that ever happened, Claude thought, he would be in deep shit: Contract killing was the only job he really liked to do. A truce with the Ghosts would mean fewer jobs and less money.

In the evenings, he kept busy assembling his own crew for whatever might come up. He searched for former inmate pals, and made new acquaintances, as well. Most of his meetings were in bars, where he impressed his buddies with the rolls of cash he used to pay for drinks. Flattered by their respect, Claude nonetheless kept in mind that the purpose of these expenses was to understand who was who among them: who was reliable, who was not; who was good for something, who was good for nothing.

By the end of the third week, his finances had been depleted more quickly than expected. He stared blankly out the window of their apartment, sitting at the table and drinking coffee. It was a late sunny morning at the beginning of September. The foliage was still green but had lost its luster of youth and vigor of growth. The fragrance of the approaching fall was in the air.

"You don't look happy today," Leila observed. She was sitting across the table, looking at him with the anxious attention of a loving woman.

"Very little left of my money." Claude frowned. "I have to think what to do next."

"Let's do something together," Leila suggested.

"Again this crap? Stop it. You get on my nerves."

"I can do many things," Leila insisted. "I like doing things. It's boring to do nothing."

"I've already heard that. What would you like to do? Dance?"

"What's wrong with that? If you like, I could sell coke. I'd find people who'd buy it from us."

The telephone rang. Still looking at Leila with wondering eyes, he picked up the receiver.

"Hello," he said.

"Can we meet today?" It was Stash.

"Sure. Where and when?"

"In my office," Stash said. Claude smiled. What kind of damn office did this biker have?

"Jot down the address," Stash continued in a businesslike tone. "You'll find me on the second floor."

The receiver clicked. Claude stood up and began to dress.

"It seems that I won't need your help for awhile. But we'll get back to it later."

With very little effort, he found the 2-storey building at the address Stash had given him. A small plate above the door bore a sign: Business Center. Claude pushed the handle and stepped into a small hallway that had a desk placed by the wall. On the desk, an "Information" sign had been affixed. The man sitting behind it stared at Claude with a blank face, as if requesting an explanation for his intrusion.

"May I help you?" he asked Claude, looking him up and down, as if ready to pick a fight.

"My name is Claude."

"Oh, yes." The tone of the information man changed at once. "Please proceed to the second floor, room 219."

Claude climbed the stairs and entered the corridor, which had a few doors on both sides. At the end, Stash stood waiting for him.

Took two seconds for the security man to notify him, Claude thought.

"Come in," Stash invited. Dressed in a long-sleeved white shirt and well-ironed pants, he had the appearance of an eccentric businessman.

"This is my office," he said with a note of pride, letting Claude in. After closing the door, he settled into a chair at the large wooden desk. The surface was littered with papers, stationery, and plastic cups. Two large pictures, one with a winter landscape and another with a summer one, decorated the walls to the left and right. Behind Stash was a window that overlooked a backyard.

"This building belongs to me," Stash said. The pouches under his eyes were a bit smaller than they had been at the time of the midsummer party. "Most of it is leased to different companies. I took only two rooms at this end."

"What's up?" asked Claude.

"You forgot? I told you at the party that I have a collection agency. Remember? It is called 'Comfort Collections.' Most of my clients are very happy with the job we do."

"Yes, I remember. What do you want me to do?"

"Let's go out and talk it over. I like fresh air."

He pulled open a drawer, removed a small binder, stood up, and led the way out. They passed the information man, who gave them a nod of respect, and then went out to the street. After a short walk, they turned in to a small park with a few vacant benches. Stash sat on one of them and invited Claude to take the place beside him.

"As I mentioned, you don't use your hands until I say so," he continued the interrupted conversation. "The client for whom you'll do this job is a builder. He did fairly large renovations for a guy he trusted. But the deadbeat claims he can't pay now. He's been begging to postpone payments, but this crap has been going on for more than a year."

"How much does he owe?" Claude asked.

"About eighty thousand bucks. We have fairly good information about his finances. He has about twenty-five grand in a retirement account, about ten grand in a margin account, a good car, and about a hundred grand in remaining equity in the house, if you subtract the mortgage from the average price in his area."

"How'd yah know all that?" Claude asked, raising his eyebrows in surprise. "It's none of my business, though," he rushed to add, as if apologizing for his out-of-place curiosity. Stash smiled contentedly.

"We have people everywhere, even in financial businesses. Anyway, this guy had had plenty of money in his margin account, but lost almost everything in the stock market. He's hoping that the stocks he holds will eventually appreciate in value. That's fine. But my client wants his money. Going through the legal system is a rather lengthy and in most cases a useless procedure. We have to make him pay."

"Sure," Claude nodded. "Will do."

"Now," Stash continued. "His name is Toulouse. He works for the government. Has a nice wife and two kids. Here are a few papers, your business card, and photographs of his kids and wife."

Claude couldn't help but smile.

"Like it?" Stash asked.

"Very much."

Stash spent another fifteen minutes with him, discussing some likely scenarios.

"I can see that you pretty well understand what to do. Any questions, Claude?"

"No."

"When do you want to start?"

"Tomorrow morning."

"Good luck."

II

Claude liked the assignment. Scaring the shit out of people was one of his favorite passions. Being paid for it was a bonus. That evening, he met with two former inmates from the jail. They looked like bikers in poorly produced documentaries. He knew they weren't worth anything—the stupid knuckleheads could only deal with people like themselves; they would no doubt run at any sign of real danger. But he also knew that these bums would kill their own mothers for a gram of coke. Both of them had bikes, cheap ones but good enough for his purposes.

"Don't touch the deadbeat," he instructed them in the bar as he paid for their beers. "Just show up where I tell you when I give the signal. Two grams of coke, each, for that."

They gasped and begged Claude for another beer, which he ordered at once.

"Don't be even one minute late," he warned.

The next day began with a clear sky, sunshine, and the peculiar freshness of approaching fall. At 6 o'clock in the morning, the roads were almost empty and he quickly cruised toward their rendezvous. When he turned into the neighborhood where Toulouse lived, he found the two men waiting behind the community tennis courts. They were sitting on the grass and smoking cigarettes. Their bikes stood by the curb.

"When I rub my ear, like this, pull up to where I am," he told them.

"Sure," they said together. Their faces were solemn, as if they were serious businessmen on an important errand.

Toulouse lived in a large house with a two-car garage and a driveway that could accommodate up to four cars. The Infinity Stash had described was parked there. Claude placed his Honda right behind it, lowered the window, and lit a cigarette. He knew that it would be at least an hour until Toulouse came out, but he preferred waiting to missing the client.

At 8 o'clock, a man with a leather briefcase came out of the house. Claude recognized him by the description and photograph that Stash had supplied. He was tall, with the figure of an athlete, a commanding posture, and a bossy hardness in his eyes. He noticed the shabby Honda behind his car and moved toward it with resolute steps.

"Hey," he exclaimed in a sharp voice. "What're you doing here?"

Claude opened the door and stepped out. He greeted Toulouse with the most menacing smile he was capable of.

"Are you Toulouse?" he asked, and moved so close that Toulouse had to step back to distance himself.

"Yes. What's the matter?"

Claude noticed a small sign of fear on Toulouse's large face. His look became strained but retained bits of broken self-assuredness.

"I'm from a collection agency," Claude introduced himself. "My name is Bruce."

"Oh?"

"We've sent you a few reminders to pay on a debt," Claude continued. "But it seems you didn't even care to reply."

Toulouse quickly regained control of himself. Claude had anticipated that.

"Listen, Mister Bruce," Toulouse said with poorly hidden contempt. "I can't pay right now. However, I appreciate your reminding me. I'll pay soon, I promise. Now move your car out and let me go, please."

"Mister Bruce will not move, Mister Toulouse." Claude made another step toward Toulouse and gave him his best sadistic smile.

"Don't you understand?" Toulouse asked with dwindling confidence, while stepping back. Fear grew rapidly in his face. His lips began trembling.

"I do understand," Claude growled, "But I think you don't understand what I'm here for. You owe us about $80,000. I won't move my car until I get this money. Do you understand?"

Smiling to himself, he noticed that Toulouse had gathered all his strength to withstand his stare, but failed.

"Do you understand?" Claude repeated, raising his voice. "Don't look at me like a cow. Give me money."

"I don't have the money right now," Toulouse half-whispered apologetically. "You see, I invested badly. I have to wait a bit—until the market picks up. I'll pay, I assure you . . ."

"I'll break your legs, you stupid ass," interrupted Claude. "Are they worth eighty grand, those fucking legs of yours?"

"I'll call the police," Toulouse declared with little conviction in his voice.

"You can't," Claude assured him. "I'll chop off your tongue before you can do it. I'll take care of your wife and kids after that. Give me money. Listen, don't try my patience. Nobody who's done that before has ended up very happy."

"Really, sir . . . ," Toulouse mumbled. *He's almost done,* Claude thought. He rubbed his right ear and stared at Toulouse in silence.

Seconds later, two motorcycles approached at high speed and stopped abruptly in the driveway. The hired bums stepped off the bikes. Their sleeves were rolled up, displaying muscular, tattoo-covered arms. Claude smiled inwardly again. Their faces should seem brutal and disgusting to anyone who doesn't normally deal with former cons. One of them took a position behind Toulouse; another stopped very close to him, breathing in his ear. Toulouse's face went pale.

"But I really don't have the money right now." Toulouse was begging, tears swelling in his eyes. He made an attempt to step back, but the man behind him blocked his way. "Believe me—I'd have to declare bankruptcy . . ."

"There's no time for bankruptcy," Claude said. "Better to pay up. What about the forty-five grand you have in your retirement account? What about your car? What about your house? Or your wife? You do have a pretty wife, don't you? A very good broad for fucking, I bet. We can go inside and ask her if you really have money or not."

Toulouse stared at him with terrified eyes, on the verge of fainting.

"How do you know all this?" he asked without blinking.

"You've got two kids, too, from what I hear," Claude went on "Two nice kids. If you don't want to take care of them, we can. Understand?"

"But . . . Truly, guys, how do you wish me to pay? I have no money. Even if you threaten to kill me, I will still have no money."

"Nobody has threatened to kill you—yet," Claude objected. "Tell me, how much is your car worth right now?"

"My c-car?" he stammered. "About fifteen thousand, I guess. But I can't sell it. How would I go to work?"

"That would be your problem, wouldn't it?" Claude asked. "Don't fool around with me, man. Pay the debt."

"Okay, okay," Toulouse finally agreed. "But it may take a couple of weeks before I can sell it for that price. I can't give you the money right now."

"That's okay," Claude nodded. "You can give me a post-dated check for fifteen grand. You see—we are reasonable people. We can talk business."

With pale, watery eyes, Toulouse glanced at the "reasonable" people around him and then looked beyond them, as if expecting miraculous help from somewhere. He opened his briefcase on the hood of the car, pulled out a checkbook, and scribbled a check for $15,000. His hands were shaking.

"Can I go now?" he asked. Claude put the check in his pocket.

"You must be crazy, Mister Toulouse," he said. "What about the remaining sixty-five grand?"

"But—"

"No 'but.' How much is your house worth now?"

"Please, guys," pleaded Toulouse. "I have to live somewhere." The three men laughed.

"I didn't come here to help you with your financial problems," Claude said calmly. He had no doubt that he had crushed the will of this debtor. "When are you going to put your house up for sale? I can't wait longer than a month. Mind you, this is the only help that I can offer. Otherwise, we'll not speak on friendly terms, as we are doing now."

"It's a good offer, man." The one who stood behind Toulouse tapped him on his shoulder. Claude gave him a warning look.

"Let me talk to my wife first," Toulouse said. "I'll try to sell it as soon as possible."

"How soon?"

"Within a month, as you've said."

"Good. Nice to do business with earnest people." Claude uttered a rowdy laugh. "Have a good day." He looked back over his shoulder as he opened his car door. "Good luck with your house."

He gave a look to his companions. They obediently rattled away on their noisy motorcycles as he backed up his Honda and turned back onto the street. From the rearview mirror, he saw Toulouse walking back inside, bent and limping like an old, crippled man.

III

For as far back as he could remember, Claude had had a keen interest in reading the body language and facial expressions of those he dealt with. Long years in prison had made it a necessity: Anyone there could be a possible ally, a potential foe, a traitor, or an informant. An opponent's demeanor had to be evaluated moments before the fight in order to decide whether to kill or not. The toughest ones, if they recovered, would return to even the score.

Most important of all, though, was the need to identify and understand the faults and strengths of allies and associates in crime: to determine how reliable they were, what they were capable of, and what they were up to at any given moment.

No one was at ease under his sharp stare, except perhaps for Marcel. Stash apparently did not like it at all. Listening to Claude's account about dealing with Toulouse, he stared back with an unusual mixture of contentment and irritation. Claude understood well what was going on in Stash's head. Although Stash agreed with the way he had handled the matter, Claude was still aggravated by what he considered to be too much attention to his face, which bore traces of drug abuse, sleeplessness, and chaotic indulgences—to broads.

"Do you think he'll sell the house in a month?" Stash asked. He turned his face away to observe a small kid on the playground who was under the watchful supervision of an elderly woman. The city park, rather lonely during this late weekday afternoon, could be well observed from their bench. The sun was already low and shot its blinding rays directly into their faces. Stash was squinting, too lazy and too apathetic for any effort to shield his eyes.

"I've scared the shit out of him," Claude said with a note of pride in his voice. He also uttered one of his rowdy laughs. "But it's hard to say if he'll be able to pay in a month. What am I supposed to do if he doesn't? Treat him well?"

"Wait, and let's see how it goes. In the meantime, I'll give you three grand now, for his check. You'll get the rest after his final payment."

Stash counted the money and handed it to Claude. The heavy pouches under his eyes and the premature wrinkles on his gray skin were signs of a hangover, which could be erased only by a new doping session. Claude knew the whole story. *Marcel will probably take care of him soon,* Claude thought.

"There's another deal coming in two weeks," Stash promised, pointing his bleached, watery eyes at Claude.

"Good," Claude nodded, this time casting his glance down. After all, Stash was a gangster who likely had the same, or better, ability of reading people that he did.

"See yah then," Stash promised and walked away, his legs stiff, as if lacking the strength to support his body.

Alex Markman

Claude arrived home an hour later to find Leila busy preparing dinner.

"Stop cooking!" Claude commanded, settling on the couch. "Let's go out to a restaurant tonight." He pulled some cash from a pocket and threw it on the table.

"But dinner is almost done," Leila said.

"So, stop," Claude repeated. Watching her with an apron, worn like a good, devoted housewife, he mellowed. "Take five hundred from that. Spend it on yourself. Much more is coming."

Leila's smile pierced his body from heart to groin. She had a power over him, which he was not able to resist.

"I love you, I love you," she said, and then sat on his knees, kissing him on the lips. Choking in his rough and passionate embrace, she pleaded, "Oh, let me get back to the stove. You'll squash my bones with your beastly arms. Ah-ha, that's hard . . . but I know how to handle it."

She jumped from his knees, turned the stove off, and came back to treat him to what he liked. A few minutes later, sitting beside him, she put her head on his shoulder and caressed his face with her soft, warm hands.

"We talked about going to Las Vegas," she reminded him. "I've seen an ad in the newspaper. Prices are very low right now."

"Good idea," Claude said with his eyes closed. "Could you book the trip?"

"Yup, I could. I've already called a travel agency. They have a few packages left for this-coming Thursday."

"Good. Let's go."

On Thursday, a few hours prior to departure, Claude was sitting on the small balcony of the apartment, smoking a cigarette and drinking beer. He was daydreaming about

Las Vegas, a place he had heard so much about from his fellow inmates. They had told him about high rollers placing terrific bets as bystanders watched them in awe and envy; about broads, beautiful and affordable; fabulous restaurants, shows, and blazing signs below illuminated giant buildings. Now, it was his turn to go. Today he would be there.

Leila appeared at the balcony door.

"I just saw one of your guys on a news clip. He's going to speak after the TV commercial," she said excitedly, as if announcing a great new show. Claude stood up and went inside.

"Who is it?" he asked, settling on the sofa near the television set.

"The redhead with the pony tail, remember the cottage party? I forgot his name."

"Stash. I wonder why . . ."

The commercial ended with the joyful cry of a cute kid, face smeared with greasy junk food.

A female broadcaster, experienced and confident, appeared on the screen.

"We have very unusual guests with us today," she said, looking intently at an invisible object in front of her. "A police expert on biker gangs, Bertrand Tremblay, will comment in support of the latest police actions against a huge biker gathering in the Eastern Townships. His opponent is a representative of the Devil's Knights motorcycle club, Stash Roark. My first question is to the police representative."

The face of Bertrand Tremblay appeared on the right side of the screen in a small frame.

"Bertrand, there have been numerous protests from lawyers representing the Devil's Knights about police harassment of bikers, particularly during your infamous checkpoints on the roads. They claim that the police have gone so far as to search them without warrants, confiscate their property, and take some into custody. They claim that you break the constitutional right for freedom of meetings and associations by doing so. What is your comment?"

The frame with Bertrand's face leapt forward and took the full screen. Without blinking, and hardly moving his lips, Bertrand spoke firmly, as appropriate for a tough and confident police officer.

"These checkpoints provide us with valuable information on the identity of gang members," Bertrand responded. "We have, in the past, found bikers carrying illegal firearms, drugs, and fake documents. Formal charges have been placed against some of them. In a nutshell, these checkpoints prove to be very efficient in investigating and fighting biker gangs."

The face of the female broadcaster replaced the image of the police expert.

"And, what is your comment on that, Stash?" she asked the biker. Now, Stash's face took over the screen. Traces of pouches still showing under his eyes, he didn't look as awful as he had in the park during their last meeting. His stare was firm, and he spoke with no less confidence than the policeman had. Claude took a huge swig from the beer bottle to refresh his drying mouth.

"This is typical talk from a law enforcement agency that is attempting to present its illegal actions under the guise of unfounded allegations. Without legitimate proof, they call us gangsters, our associations and clubs become gangs. Their illegal searches during the road checks are now called 'efficient ways of fighting gangs.' If you take their comments at face value, you'd think that the only troublemakers in our society are motorcycle clubs and their members.

"Don't fall into the trap of thinking that our society is made up of saints and devils. The majority are in between. By resorting to illegal procedures, you discover a lot of people breeching the law one way or another, no matter what group or association they belong to. Government agencies have no right, however, to label them using inappropriate terminology or to harass them because of their association. Single out any group, be it homosexuals, feminists, Green Peace or anti-abortion activists, you name it, and you'll find that many of them use illegal drugs, possess firearms, hide their income from the government, and many other things.

"Why don't you target them?

"Or maybe it will be their turn after the police have finished with us? Go that way, and you'll find out that our country does not have enough jails to keep them all, not enough courts, and not enough judges to deal with all the cases. With motorcycle clubs, police harassment is an easy task. On Harley Davidson and in biker vests, we become a visible minority, easy to target, easy to persecute because of bad publicity around us. But bad publicity, created by unscrupulous journalists, should not be a solid foundation for persecution and harassment. Our constitution, and only our constitution, must be the governing law for all, including law enforcement agencies."

Leila diminished the sound.

"Not bad, eh?" she asked.

"Yes. Now I understand why Marcel puts up with him."

He glanced at his expensive wristwatch. "Time to go, Leila. Shut off the box."

A few hours later they exited the Las Vegas airport and walked into the dry, pleasant heat of the desert. They rented a car and drove into the dense traffic of the Las Vegas Strip. The street swarmed with people, as if a demonstration or riot was going on, only most of them smiled. Huge hotels towered as giants, welcoming newcomers to the city of fun and sin.

Two days in Las Vegas passed as in a fairy tale. In the hottest hours, they swam in the cool water of a huge swimming pool. In the evenings, they played roulette, blackjack, craps, or walked the street past hundreds of thousands of lights, which covered some buildings from the bottom to the very top. Claude found surprises at every step: the simulation of a volcanic eruption at the Mirage, a symphony of dancing fountains at Bellagio, jumping and blinking lights of the most illuminated city in the world.

Looking at the happy crowd, Claude thought about his years in prison and how much he had missed in his life, virtually for nothing. Now, the time had come to make up for his lost years. The only disturbing factor was the nightmares, in which he was again in jail, fighting for his life or killing someone. Leila had woken him a few times, when his shouts and convulsions got too disturbing.

On the last night before their departure, Leila lost more than $1,000 at the roulette table.

"I'm sorry," she said, sipping her drink in the open bar, in the midst of the Mirage casino. "I'll make up for the loss, Claude. I wanna make money, too, as you do."

"Again, the same old shit. You don't have enough money?" Claude growled.

"It's not that. My life is just so boring sometimes. I like doing things. Do you think I left my well-to-do parents for nothing? Why can't you give me something to do for yah?"

"You can't help me with what I'm doing, I've told you more than once," Claude objected.

"What's so special in what you're doing? I'm not a coward. We can do deals together. Except, perhaps, killing. You don't kill, do you?"

He threw a sharp glance at her, but she had already turned around to look at the roulette table nearby. She didn't wait for his answer, obviously certain that he was not a killer.

"Look, Claude." She touched his hand but continued looking in the direction of her interest. Claude followed her stare and raised his eyebrows. He recognized one of the gamblers in an instant by his red ponytail. Stash was pushing tall towers of ten-dollar chips into the gaming area of the roulette table. A young, pretty woman, excited by his large bet, was commenting on his move with short applause.

"Very interesting," Claude murmured. "Let's get closer. That's a high roller's table." A quick look around showed him that several thousand dollars, easily, waited for the drop of a small ball to decide their destiny.

"Let him know that we're here," Leila suggested.

"Not now. Let him finish the game. With such bets, he'll soon be out. I'd rather stay behind and watch it."

Claude tilted his head back and let the remaining beer in his glass drip down his throat. He stood up, scanning the vast casino for other Devil's Knights or any suspicious activity. He saw only serious faces at the slot machines, staring dumbly at the rotating numbers and pictures that flashed hypnotically in front of their eyes. Claude and Leila left the bar area and moved to within three feet of Stash.

Suddenly, the roulette dealer threw a small white ball into the groove above the rotating wheel so it could begin its fast spin in the opposite direction. As the speed of the ball was diminishing, Claude observed the bets and the gamblers. On the other side of the roulette table sat a Chinese fellow, approximately his own age, frantically placing hundred-dollar chips in a rush to cover his lucky numbers before the ball fell into a slot. A Chinese woman sitting beside him was looking at her own tall towers that sat in the "dozens" area. As in a dream, Claude was taking in the steady murmur of casino sounds swallowing him: excited conversations and arguments, the silvery clinking of coins falling rapidly from slot machines, a scream at a card table across the room, a sudden roar at the craps table. At last, the small ball dropped into the rotating wheel. In a deft and rapid sweep, the dealer removed almost all the chips from the table. The woman standing beside Stash clapped her palms and laughed happily; Stash had won. The two Chinese players did not blink at their losses but began pushing another bunch of chips forward to satisfy Lady Luck.

Claude regarded the Chinese high rollers with jealousy and hatred. He wanted to be in their shoes, sitting with piles of chips, arrogantly ignorant of the admiring and envying eyes of bystanders. It would be nice to kill that bitch, he thought, looking at the rainbow of sparkles jumping off the huge diamonds on her fingers and in her ears. She must have felt his look because she raised her eyes to meet his.

Claude smiled inwardly as he saw fear flickering in the woman's eyes. She cast her glance down at the green table and then looked up again. Claude gave her his best sadistic smile. He held his stare as she took a paper napkin out of her bag and wiped large drops of sweat off her forehead and neck. No trace of arrogance or indifference remained on her face. Her fingers trembling, she did not dare to look at him again.

Stash placed his new bets. This time, however, Lady Luck knocked him down for good. He happened to notice, though, the strange look and behavior of a Chinese woman across from him and quickly looked back.

"Claude!" he exclaimed. Sudden surprise and anxiety were replaced with a contented smile. "Glad to see you. When did you get here?" His face was now even worse than it had been in the park. Undoubtedly in the sniffer's paradise, he was trying to focus his eyes on Claude's face.

"Today is our last day here, actually," Claude said. "We saw you on TV before we left home. That was one nice speech, Stash."

"Let's go for a drink," Stash suggested. "I wanna tell you something. Let the girls talk to each other. This is Merlin, by the way." He began walking toward the café that was set up in the middle of the tropical forest inside the s huge lobby of the Mirage. After passing a small bridge over the stream that ran through the dense tangle of exotic plants, he chose a table and invited Claude to sit beside him. Their women had no choice but to sit on the other side of the table. From there, they couldn't hear anything because of the loud music being played by a live band.

"Listen, Claude, I'm broke," he said. His right eyelid was twisting in a nervous tic. "Could you lend me a grand? I'll give it back to you as soon as I return."

"We have to go upstairs. I have money in my suitcase."

"Thanks." With a wry smile, Stash added, "My broad is very expensive. You have a good one, your ol' lady, that is. Expensive as well?"

Claude nodded.

"Don't you worry about money," Stash said. "There's a lot of work to do. Listen, I have something special for you. There's a deadbeat in Ontario that owes me forty grand. No, not to me. To the Vandals, you know their club, don't you? I got word that he keeps money at home. He feels safe in his territory. You have to take care of him."

"What if there's no money?" Claude asked.

"Finish him. The Vandals will pay for the deal. You'll get ten grand for it one way or the other."

Claude had a feeling that something wasn't right. But in his capacity as a contract killer, he wasn't in a position to ask too many questions besides those directly related to a job.

"I'll give you his address and telephone number," Stash continued. "He lives in a house. The trick is to sneak in when he's alone."

"Leave everything to me," Claude said.

"I like you," Stash said, a smile pushing up the pouches under his eyes. "Let's go upstairs."

IV

Claude returned home to discover that Hans was out of town. Because help would be necessary with the trip to Ontario, he agreed to take the insistent Leila with him. His only hope was that there would be no need to kill. His mood was rather grim during the seven-hour drive.

"Why aren't you talking?" Leila asked him time and time again.

"Shut up," he snapped.

The dealer had gotten a call from Stash already and was supposed to be expecting his arrival. What if his bodyguards were there, though? Should he shoot them all? Leila mustn't be involved in anything like that.

He stopped the car near the dealer's house and dialed his cell phone number.

"It's me, from Stash," Claude said.

"I'll be right out," the confident voice said.

"Watch me," Claude said to Leila. "Move to the driver's seat and wait. When I return, hit the gas. Clear?"

"Sure," Leila said.

"Do whatever I tell you to do, no questions asked. Understand?"

Claude touched the gun under his jacket and got out. Heavy clouds were coming in with the darkness of the late evening, and a windy drizzle made him wet during the short walk to the dealer's house. On the long driveway, a self-assured, tall man about thirty-five years old stood waiting.

"Hi," he said with no note of hostility. "Long drive?"

"Sort of," Claude said. "You wanna talk here, or inside?"

"Better inside. A rather nasty drizzle."

"Anyone at home?" Claude asked. As they stepped inside, he noticed the nicely furnished foyer and living room.

"No, no one. You can speak. You came for money, I gather?" He pointed to the couch. "Would you like to sit down?"

"Yes. Any bugs here?"

"No—for sure." The dealer sat back in an armchair and stretched out his legs. "I don't have the money right now. Like I told Stash, I need another two or three months. Do you want something to drink?"

"No," Claude said, squinting grimly. "I didn't drive seven hours for a drink. I was told that you keep money here, in your home. Give me whatever you have, and we'll talk about how long you need to pay off the rest."

"Excuse me?" The dealer was visibly irritated. "Didn't you understand what I said?"

"I did," Claude responded with a menacing growl. "Are you going to give me money or not?"

"Listen," the dealer narrowed his eyes, "continue with that tone of voice, and I'll throw you out. Got it?"

Claude pulled out his Magnum, walked over to the dealer, and pressed the barrel into his nose.

"You do what I say," he said with the most frightening tone he could muster. "One wrong move and you're dead. Now, put your fucking hands behind your back."

At last, the dealer understood the danger he was in and obeyed. Claude stuffed the gun back under his belt, pulled out a roll of duct tape, and began tying the dealer's arms.

"Listen, man," the dealer was growing alarmed, but began talking in a deliberately calm manner. "Listen, you're doing something stupid. Don't you know that my brother is a full-patch Devil's Knight in B.C.? Do you need that much trouble?"

Claude paused for a moment. Killing the Devil's Knights associate would certainly mean serious complications. Is this what had seemed so out-of-place when Stash was describing this job? Was it possible that Stash had sent him here, knowing that? Was Stash so crazy on drugs that he didn't understand the consequences? No— Impossible! Anyway, Stash was a full patch. He was supposed to know things like that.

"Tell me about your brother," Claude said, resuming his work. "Better yet, give me money. Then tell me about him.

Otherwise, you'll pay me in full." He began binding the dealer's legs to his chair.

The dealer was totally incapacitated and at the mercy of a rather frightening messenger.

"What're you doing, man?" he began shouting. "What're you doing? I don't have the money, I swear! I don't have any money. Just a few bucks upstairs. I'll pay the whole debt, I swear."

Claude finished and straightened up.

"I'm asking you for the last time: Will you give me money or not?"

"You, joker!" the dealer screamed. "What're you doing? Don't you understand that I have no money? Don't you understand that my brother is a full patch—"

"Stop it, you jerk," Claude interrupted him. He went to the kitchen and took a narrow, sturdy knife from one of the drawers. When he came back, he wasted no time turning its sharp point toward the left eye of the dealer.

"I don't know anyone still alive who has called me a joker," he said. "Now's your last chance. If you don't give me the money, I'll poke your left eye out. If that doesn't help you find your money, I'll poke out the right one. If that doesn't help, I'll kill you. So, where's the money?"

"I have no money . . ." whispered the dealer, scared beyond sanity. He pleaded, "I swear. I'll give you money."

Claude didn't let him finish. His rowdy laugh rang with sadistic pleasure as it mingled with the deafening shrieks from the tortured dealer.

When Claude left ten minutes later, the corpse of the dealer was still tied to the chair, a knife deep in his eye socket. Climbing into the passenger seat, Claude commanded with his customary laugh, "Full speed ahead!"

Leila smiled back and hit the gas pedal, letting the tires screech.

"You see," she said, making a sharp turn, "I can be of help to you."

When the thrill of the torture had wound down and clarity had taken its place, Claude started to play back the ordeal with the drug dealer. What if the man had been telling the truth? What if, indeed, his brother was a full-patch Devil's Knight? Was it possible that Stash had been so desperate for money that he'd demanded pay-off from a Devil's Knights associate? Would Stash make him a scapegoat when someone had to take responsibility for the kill?

"You're so quiet now," Leila interrupted. "You haven't said anything for an hour. Did something go wrong?"

"I'm in no mood to talk," Claude said curtly. "Everything's okay."

A few days later, Claude was called to perform some duties at the Devil's Knights clubhouse. Anyone who was not a full patch had to do them occasionally. Besides the task of security guard, which he didn't mind at all, he had to do cleaning, because inviting any kind of cleaning service to this most sacred place was out of the question. The very thought of cleaning up after someone else disgusted him. But the most aggravating part was the fact that anyone of higher rank could give him an order or issue him a penalty. At these moments, his mind went fuzzy with an insane urge to kill the superior. Unfortunately, the only choice for those who wished to climb the ranks of the gang was to obey without a single objection, not even a trace of disobedience or displeasure; any promotion had to be approved by 100 percent of the voters.

This evening, the clubhouse had too many visitors. The high ranks had invited a few ladies and indulged in plenty of drinking to ease the stress of intensified fighting with the Iron Ghosts, stepped-up police pressure, and an increase in media attacks. Although business discussions had been strictly prohibited in the clubhouse, some members deviated from this rule, albeit with many precautions such as gesturing, and using biker's slang and secret codes.

Stash was there, too. He took Claude by the sleeve and pulled him to the bar.

"Here's five grand for now," he said with the weak smile of an addict. Claude noticed the disapproving glance that Marcel threw their way. Claude quickly stuffed the envelope into his pocket.

"Why not all ten?" he asked.

"I'll give it to you a bit later. What's the rush? By the way, a month has passed since that chickenshit Toulouse promised to sell the house. Go kick his ass."

"Will do," Claude nodded. "Can I fiddle a bit with his furniture? That'll impress his wife."

"Go ahead. But make it when his wife and kids aren't at home. Don't overdo it, though. Make him clear that he has no choice but to pay."

When Stash left, Marcel took his place.

"Let's go out," he suggested. "I need to talk to you."

The parking lot was empty, but Marcel threw a quick glance around, more from habit than necessity. A bit tipsy, he drew his unusually grim face close to Claude's ear.

"We found out where Stanley's muffler shop is. It's time to take care of your friend."

Claude uttered his rowdy laugh. He even went so far as to impulsively embrace Marcel. His gesture was not well received.

"This son of a bitch is like mercury," Marcel continued when the distance between them had grown to an appropriate space for his rank. "Mind you, it's not going to be an easy task. But I won't give you any instructions. After you've done with him, I'll propose to promote you to Prospect."

"Thanks, Marcel. I'll do it. I couldn't die in peace if he were still alive. His death will be a good lesson for all the others."

Marcel's grim face relaxed at last in an agreeable smile.

"I trust you. You're my messenger."

Chapter 6

I

Monica threw an anxious glance at the face of the clock on the table and saw that its hands pointed at 4:30—almost the end of another workweek. But on Friday nights, when everyone else rushed home to begin a weekend, she was one of a few workaholics who usually remained in the building. Not in the least concerned with having leisure time anyway, tonight she had a special reason for staying: She was mentally rehearsing her speech for a television interview scheduled at 8 o'clock.

As a politician, and a very active one at that, she had to respond to the media outcry about the escalating biker's war. Particularly troublesome for her constituents were the deaths of innocent bystanders who had had the bad luck of being in the crossfire. The public at large was concerned that the streets of the city were no longer safe. Explosions and shootings in this time of peace were more frightening than in times of war.

Monica was sure that a few questions would be about her stance on the proposed laws. Inevitably, the interviewer would ask her: "Why are you against a law declaring the outlaw motorcycle clubs criminal organizations?" "Why do you oppose giving the police special powers to detain and interrogate their members who are under suspicion?"

"Why do you oppose giving police the authority necessary to curb the biker's war?"

Indeed, her arguments against the proposed measures, which she saw as contradicting Canada's constitution, were becoming less and less convincing in light of the recent numbers of deaths, amount of destroyed properties, and threats to businesses, journalists, police, and government officials. Tension was reaching the point at which politicians had to do something to ease public rage and fear.

At the far end of her desk was a large tray, filled with mail that she had intended to read at the end of the day. With her mind already far away on the television show, she eyed the first few pieces. It was probably just the usual crap, she figured. She unfolded the first one, which was typed on a very fine paper with watermarks. Its content quickly cleared her mind. She read it twice, still not believing her eyes. It had only a few lines:

Dear Monica,
Happy birthday!
We appreciate your position on any proposed law against motorcycle clubs. We praise your efforts to defend the constitutional rights of minorities. Without people like you, our democracy would plunge into a dictatorship.
We wish you success in all your endeavors.
With warmest regards,
The Devil's Knights

Under the load of her busy schedule, she had completely forgotten her birthday, coming up next Sunday. And the first to remind her about it were the Devil's Knights!

The last thing she wanted was praise of her work coming from these professional criminals, whose very existence she deplored. Their short note, however, was quite a vivid reflection of how complicated the situation had become. It would certainly be easy to single out the Devil's Knights or the Iron Ghosts as criminal organizations and put their members in prison. However, such a law would be a clear breach of the constitution.

History had many examples of arbitrary rules that had been successful with picking out and locking up criminals. Mussolini, for one, Italy's dictator during World War II, put all members of the mafia in prison. There hadn't been a problem with identifying them because the police had created good files on everyone. Nobody else before or after Mussolini had been able to cope with this organized crime structure. But the people of Italy did not have a good memory of that dictator, nor did they praise anything he did. They'd rather live in a democracy that tolerated occasional inevitable evils than adopt a dictatorship that was an evil for all. As soon as the presumption of innocence until proven guilty was discarded, the road would be open to all excesses of undemocratic governance under the guise of constitutional laws.

The constitution, in her firm belief, must be respected by all, no matter how inconvenient it sometimes becomes for those who rule the country or have judicial powers. Its current structure must be the foundation of a democratic society.

Her thoughts began to wander. She recalled Bertrand saying that bikers wielded too much power and money and that their activities would soon reach a point when coping with them would become an impossible mission. "In our society, with its widespread notion that money is the only measure of success," he had said, "corruption could leap beyond control. It all depends on the amount. If the offer were tens or hundreds of thousands of dollars—how many in the police force or the government would hold onto their moral grounds against a bribe that might change their lives? Mind you, Monica, we're fighting with our hands tied by laws, rules, and restrictions, whereas organized crime has nothing to slow them down at all. With unrestricted flexibility and plenty of money, they could do anything with our society." The stream of her recollection was interrupted by the ring of her telephone. Startled by the contrast to the quiet of after-work hours and the concentration of her deep thoughts, she reached for the phone with a nervous jerk.

"Hello?" she said, trying to compose herself. Crunching the receiver between her ear and her shoulder, she started gathering all the papers she might need into her elegant briefcase.

"Hi, Aunt Monica," the voice on the other end said. "This is Toulouse."

"Oh, it's you, darling." Monica smiled into the space of the empty office. "How nice of you to remember your aunt on the eve of this weekend. What are you planning to do?"

"To hell with the weekend," the nephew said abruptly. She caught the unusual notes of desperation and sadness in his voice. "I'm in trouble. I need your help."

"Anything you want, Toulouse," Monica responded. "Let's meet tomorrow."

"Could we meet . . . now?" Toulouse asked rather meekly.

"What's the rush? Frankly, it's not the best time for me. Where are you?"

"A few steps from your office. Just outside the building."

"Hmm. Could we make it short? Say, ten minutes or so?"

"I'll try," Toulouse promised. "May I come up now?"

"Yes," Monica consented. "I'll make arrangements with security. Come ahead."

She liked her nephew and often treated him as her own son. Good looking, always in a merry mood, gentle, and invariably optimistic, he had a strong sense of family and tried to be of help to her whenever he could. Regretfully, she hadn't seen much of him in the last two months, being too busy with political matters and the approaching elections.

Five minutes later, the door of her office opened slowly and Toulouse stepped in. At his appearance, her welcoming smile transformed to a look of frightened surprise.

"My dear, what's happened to you?" she cried, rushing to him. His face bore traces of the recent brawl: a large bruise under his left eye painted half his cheek dark blue; his lower lip on the same side was cut, dried blood already forming a crusty red patch over the wound. His right cheek, in its usual shape and smaller than the swollen left one, caused his lips to be positioned at an angle to his nose instead of being perpendicular to it. This deformity would have prompted laughter if not for the gloom in his eyes.

"Please, sit down . . . ," she said, pulling him by the sleeve to a chair. "Where have you been?" She couldn't help but notice that Toulouse was dressed with his customary attention to detail: a dark suit without a single wrinkle, a well-ironed white shirt, and an elegant tie hanging down from a perfect knot. It was odd to see such a well-dressed gentleman as Toulouse with the beaten face of a hoodlum.

"I was beaten in my own home," he explained.

"Beaten? What are you talking about?"

"Yes, beaten. You see . . . I owe money to the contractor who renovated our house. I was sure that I'd be able to pay him, because, at the time, I had sufficient money in the stock market. But then, my shares went south. The contractor has now transferred the debt to a collection agency. They sent their people to me—Aunt Monica, those guys were typical gangsters. They made me sell my car in two weeks to pay part of the debt. They demanded that I sell my house in one month to pay the balance, but I wasn't able to. Then they came to my home and trashed it inside . . ." Toulouse began sobbing.

"Oh, my God," Monica half-whispered. It was so unusual to see this strong man in such grief. "I'm speechless . . ." She walked around the room, pressed her temples with the tips of her fingers, then returned to her chair.

"I'm speechless. But it's largely your own fault." Her questioning eyes did not blink as they fixed on him with a blend of disapproval and fright.

"Monica, I came to you for help, not for a reprimand. As I've said, I lost my money in the stock market. Anyway, I'll be able to pay my debt, but not all at once, and not now, as they demand. How can I sell my house in a month? In such a rush, it could be done only for a price much below its value."

"Oh, such a mess," Monica said, crossing her arms. "What're we supposed to do?"

"How can you not know what to do?" Toulouse asked. "You're known as an organized crime expert. You speak with such authority on TV about biker's matters. You certainly have lots of good connections—"

"Bikers!" Monica interrupted him with a trace of contempt. "Not every crime is committed by bikers. What makes you think that these people from the collection agency were bikers?"

"Two of them were on motorcycles. They looked like bikers. They scared me to death."

Rather confused, Monica did not comment.

"I don't know what to do," Toulouse complained.

"Did you call the police?"

"No." Toulouse looked up at Monica. Answering her silent question he said, "I'm scared."

"I understand." Monica leaned back in her chair, forcing herself out of emotional chaos. The deep vertical wrinkles on her forehead were in grim harmony with the toughness in her eyes. With a clear mind and a cool voice, she told him, "Relax, dear. Tell me some more details."

"Like I said, he told me to sell the house in a month."

"Who is he?"

"The one from the collection agency. You can't imagine how frightening this fellow was."

"What was so particularly frightening about him?"

"I can't explain, really. It was just a feeling—I was scared out of my wits. Even his laugh . . . it made my stomach turn over."

"How did they manage to get into your house?"

"Yesterday, I came in from work around six. Without a car, it takes more than an hour to get back and forth between the office and my home. Luckily, Valerie and the kids weren't there. I didn't see anybody around when I approached the door, I swear. But when I opened it, three men jumped on the porch as if from nowhere and forced me into the house. One of them had on a ski mask; the two others didn't. Large, hairy fellows, you know, like actors from a biker movie. I thought that they wanted to kill me. But the one in the mask just punched me a few times as the others took out baseball bats and smashed the furniture in the living room. The whole episode must have been a warning, a prelude, so to speak, to more serious actions. The one in the mask was the fellow from the collection agency, I'm pretty sure about that."

"What makes you think so?" Monica asked.

"He left with that peculiar, sadistic laugh. I couldn't mistake that laugh for anyone else's."

"Let me talk to someone," Monica said, reaching for the phone. She dialed and leaned into the receiver, looking through Toulouse as if he were transparent.

"Hello—Bertrand," she said. "This is Monica."

"Good evening, Monica. What can I do for you?"

"Could you spare a few minutes for me?"

"Certainly. Go ahead."

"My nephew is here and he's in trouble. Briefly, he didn't pay a debt in time to a renovation company. A collection agency, apparently run by criminals, is now stepping on his heels. They went so far as to beat him and destroy some furniture in his house. My nephew thinks the attackers were bikers. Do you know any collection agency that's run by bikers?"

"Yes, there's one," Bertrand confirmed. "We know that he's very successful at it, too, mostly because his guys intimidate the debtors. So far, no one has been willing to be a witness against the agency in court. If you wish to know more, I suggest you talk to our biker expert, Serge Gorte. I'll give you his direct number."

"That's fine. I certainly will. But for now, what can be done?"

"That's rather a tough call." Bertrand made a long pause. "He could file a formal complaint to the police, of course, but . . . consider the situation, Monica. Your nephew does have the debt to repay, right? What would his complaint be about? Their methods? He would have to admit to several acts in public. And, everyone is scared to be a witness against bikers. Is your nephew interested in being a witness?"

"Of course not," Monica answered quickly. "After so many unsolved murders, who'd have the guts to stand up against their threats?"

He chose to ignore her retort and pursued another line of thinking. "So, tell me, Monica, what would you like me to do? Close down their agency?"

"Why not?"

"What a good suggestion, Monica. But aren't you the most ardent proponent of protecting bikers' constitutional rights? If you and the like-minded members of the task force had listened to us, we could have gathered up these crooks and locked them away long ago. Give us a law that makes membership in criminal gangs illegal, and we'll be able to shut down this agency and all the other businesses that operate using criminal methods."

"But—Bertrand—you're talking about suspending the constitutional rights of people."

"Not people, Monica—criminals."

"Stop it. We can't suspend the freedom-of-association provisions . . ."

"C'mon, Monica," Bertrand interrupted. "Criminals are already in your own backyard. I think you've stretched your liberal sentiments far enough."

"Let's discuss that at the next meeting," Monica suggested. "Going back to the subject at hand: My nephew needs more time to sell his house, but they won't let him have it. What do you think he should do?"

"I'd advise him to call this agency and ask for some more time. When they see that he's serious about paying his debt, they might soften their stance. In the meantime, talk to Serge Gorte. I'll talk to him, as well. Maybe we'll find a way to close this agency your way. Still, just between us, it would be easier and quicker if we could use methods that do not agree with the existing laws, regulations, and constitutional rights."

"I see your point. Perhaps your arguments do make more sense than I originally thought."

"In a week or so, I'll let you know what our options are."

"But . . . for now, could you provide some protection for my nephew?"

"I'm surprised that you asked for that, Monica. We don't have sufficient funds to protect even primary witnesses against gangs. And, honestly, we don't have any formal cause to spend money on his protection."

Monica sighed as she realized she was stuck.

"Our final meeting is in two weeks. If we approve the draft that the police and the RCMP have proposed, what would you be able to do in such cases?"

"We could obtain financial records. We could get lists of clients and victims. In the course of investigations, we would likely find enough evidence to close such businesses. I'm pretty sure that we'd be able to lay formal charges, and it's quite possible that we would find someone who would cross over and become an informant. Many things might happen . . ."

"Thanks, Bertrand. See you in two weeks." She hung up and glanced back at Toulouse.

"Try to talk to the agency," she said, answering his silent question. "Ask them to let you have some more time."

"And if they don't agree?"

"In any event, you and your family move into my house. There's plenty of space. I'd be happy to have you with me. It's distressing to be alone in such a big house."

"That wouldn't solve the problem."

"It wouldn't," agreed Monica. "You'd still have to repay your debt. You'll have to start building your fortune all over again. But you'll have a safe place to live while you're doing that."

"Thanks. Your birthday is soon—"

"We'll celebrate it together in my home. Now, I've got to go, Toulouse. I have a live television interview at eight. I can take you home, if you wish. Don't be so depressed, darling. It's not the end of the world."

II

Cruising at a deliberately slow speed to the television station, Monica mentally ran through questions the interviewer would likely ask. Even a short delay with an answer could diminish the value of her argument, no matter how clever and convincing the response was. Unfortunately, she knew that the general public trusts appearance over substance, a confident look over an outstanding mind. Her frequent appearances on television and radio had prepared her well for the unexpected. Yet, she was a tiny bit nervous this evening: Her interviewer was a quick-witted journalist, notorious for putting the sharpest interviewees into a tough corner during his shows. She had learned that the best thing she could do in such circumstances was to stay cool and alert. That was another reason for her concern: A rage against bikers was boiling in her heart and head. The fear for Toulouse and his family made her frown. But the time for meditation and soul-pacifying exercises had run out. Whatever will be, will be, she thought.

She arrived at the studio just in time, and the interview started almost immediately.

"You're among the few members of the Provincial Parliament who still stand against adopting the new measures that law enforcement agencies have proposed," he began.

Monica judged by his relaxed appearance that he didn't have anything nasty up his sleeve. This would probably be just another question-and-answer session to entertain and pacify the public, she concluded. If only her previous answers to those questions could remain the same tonight. If only her own circumstances had not changed.

"Actually, in light of some late developments and some recent considerations, I tend to think that, with the removal of some extreme language, much of this law could be adopted."

"Isn't this a different stance than what you've been saying?" The interviewer was fast thinking, she admitted, and knew his stuff. "How would you single out biker's clubs from other organizations? There is no proof that their clubs have any purpose other than to provide places for social gatherings. They publish their rules and even the minutes of their meetings, which can be obtained—granted, with some effort—by the media. How could you call an organization 'criminal' if its formal goal is not crime and if they have neither structure for nor rules governing criminal activity?"

"Circumstantial evidence exists, in abundance, to prove otherwise," Monica said, for she had been thinking about this point. "The club members help each other in crimes, in prisons, and in all sorts of conflicts with the law. Each member has to provide unconditional help to the organization in all its activities and its troubles, be it the war with other gangsters, the intimidation of our institutions, the disruption of our public lives, whatever. Their organization is obligated to provide help for its members no matter how hideous the crime they commit. The issue of biker gangs has to be addressed as soon as possible. I tend to think that a tough new law, with a few temporary compromises to the constitution, has to be adopted, rendering our police agencies the proper instruments to fight this new form of organized crime."

The eyes of the interviewer got sharper. He asked a question that Monica had not foreseen.

"But any association renders help to its members, including legal and financial help," the interviewer said with a malicious flicker in his eyes. "Take a look at religious institutions, professional or political associations, trade or financial organizations, you name it. Do you think that motorcycle clubs should be denied the rights so common to other organizations?"

It took only a moment for Monica to find her answer.

"There is no generality that could be a common denominator in this issue," she said with a frown. "From coast to coast, bikers need legal help of only one nature: criminal defense. Murders, drug trafficking, money laundering, intimidation—that's what all their chapters need help for. I don't know any religion whose communities need legal help like that regardless of where they establish themselves. The same with associations of professional engineers, architects, writers, or nonprofessional groups with political orientation—they might need occasional legal help for a civil dispute. But it would not be fair to compare any of these organizations to outlaw biker clubs whose cases are, with few exceptions, criminal in nature, and related to their 'profession.' I don't know any non-criminal organization that actively and consistently helps its members when criminal charges are laid against them."

The eyes of the interviewer glowed with apparent delight. A good answer for the public could be an even better achievement for him than embarrassing a prominent politician. Monica was pleased with herself as well. Her experience in public speaking and her habit of thinking with a cool head while heat raked her nerves had helped her in another pinch.

III

For the next two weeks Monica was busy preparing for the last meeting, at which the final version of the bill would have to be adopted. Although the draft stopped short of declaring the outlaw motorcycle clubs criminal organizations, it did contain numerous provisions that compromised the constitution to make investigation and prosecution of bikers a much easier task for police.

In the late evenings, she enjoyed the company of her nephew and his family, who had moved in with her temporarily, until their problems could be solved. One day before the final session of the task force, she returned from work earlier than usual. The sun was already throwing long shadows across the street, but dusk was still an hour away. Monica was thinking about her husband and how nice it would be if he was still alive. It had been three years ago . . . she had arranged a small barbeque at home, and he had called and asked if she needed any last-minute shopping.

"Some whiskey," Monica advised. "Don't be too late, though, darling."

Crossing a large intersection with the yellow light, he had been hit by a heavy truck and died instantly. *How fragile human life is,* she thought. How stupid and premature death could sometimes be. *Bikers have no respect for life or for death,* she thought, be it their own or others. What makes them so fearless, so thoughtless, and so disrespectful of all that governs the rest of humanity? Why did even the most sophisticated of them choose this terrible way of life and its inevitable outcome of a premature and painful death? What a puzzle.

She pulled her car up to her house and stepped out. Only then did she notice a man stashing an envelope into her mailbox on the porch.

"What are you doing here?" Monica asked. Her voice had a menacing tone, a tone that could have intimidated a tiger. The man turned slowly, as if he had more business to do. As his face came into view, she was stunned with what she saw: The man's face was hidden behind a mask suitable for Halloween—the distorted face of a woman, mouth opened wide in a cry of despair, and red tears of blood painted under the eyes, running down one after another until they reached the bottom of the mask.

"Happy Halloween," the man said and passed by.

"It's not October yet. What kind of Halloween is it?" Monica yelled after him.

The man uttered an ugly, rowdy laugh and hopped onto his motorcycle.

"Who are you?" shouted Monica. The man had already fired the engine of his bike.

"A messenger," he shouted back, raising his voice above the noise of the roaring engine. "Read the message."

The motorcycle jumped forward and disappeared with an angry rattle. Monica removed the envelope from her mailbox, opened it up with trembling fingers, and read the short note:

Death Certificate:
Name of Deceased: Monica Godette
Occupation: Political Prostitute
Date of Birth: July 3, 1953
Date of Death: October 1997
Delivered by: Messenger of Death

With a huge knot in her stomach, she glanced around. No one was on the street, but its very emptiness was more frightening than a crowd would have been. She ran up the short flight of porch steps, unlocked the door, and sneaked inside. Toulouse and his family were already waiting for her, peacefully sitting at the table.

"Anything wrong?" Toulouse asked anxiously. Monica made an effort to smile.

"Everything is okay, dear. Oh, dinner is ready. How nice. Give me five minutes, though."

She climbed to the second floor and went into the bathroom to wash her hands. The nauseating spasms in her stomach did not go away. Monica splashed her face with cold water, but it didn't help.

Back in her bedroom, she pulled out the biker's note and read it again. It seemed even more frightening than it had the first time. They had issued her a death certificate! How terrifying. Despicable. What kind of a sick mind does one have to have to intimidate this way?

Monica went downstairs to the dining room and said in the calmest possible way, "I'm sorry, but I don't feel well. I can't join you for dinner. Please, excuse me."

An outcry of sympathy and regrets was the response.

"I have a very important meeting tomorrow morning," Monica continued. "I'd better retire early tonight. Enjoy your dinner, darlings."

Lying in the bed, she leafed through some papers that were pertinent to the proposed change in legislation, but she was not able to concentrate on anything. Exhausted, she fell asleep. In a dream, she saw a tall man with the face of a very ugly, tormented woman. Under her eyes were large tears of blood. The man chased her, crying like a woman. She woke up, terrified, disoriented. Listening to the feeble sounds and cracks of the house, she fancied that somebody was walking in it with the cautious steps of an assassin. She was expecting a sudden bang on the door, after which the killer would appear in the opening, pointing his gun at her. Nothing happened, though, but in the morning, she left the bed tired, as if she had already worked a full day.

The final meeting of the task force was scheduled for 10 o'clock, but coffee and a continental breakfast were supposed to be ready by 9:30. Some task force members took advantage of it, having neither the time nor the desire to cook at home. Monica had never shown up for it, but she did arrive early, not for breakfast, but with the hope of meeting Bertrand. Luckily, he was there, sitting at the table alone, enthusiastically devouring a large doughnut. He noticed her at once: *This man would not miss an ant under the table,* Monica thought. Chewing with an enviable appetite, he waved his hand at her in genuine welcome, inviting her to join him for breakfast.

"What brought you in so early?" he asked.

"To tell the truth, I wanted to see you," she responded.

"Me?"

"Why not? I need your advice, possibly your help."

She produced two papers: one, the letter of appreciation from the Devil's Knights; the other, her death certificate.

"I got these two notes within a short time period," she said. "This one was brought to me yesterday by a biker wearing a terrible mask. It was rather frightening, Bertrand."

Bertrand read the notes and shook his head.

"They went too far," he said.

"It's beyond my comprehension how these people have the guts to fight against the government."

"It's very simple—they believe in our democracy."

"Don't be so cynical, Bertrand. Anyway, what do you think about this death certificate? Is it serious?"

"Everything the bikers do must be considered seriously. However, I don't think you're in any immediate danger, but some precautions must be taken."

"What precautions?"

Bertrand shrugged his shoulders.

"Move temporarily to another location. If you have relatives, move into their home for awhile, until everything is settled. I'm sure that after the bill is adopted, they won't be a threat. Why would they need to hurt you after that?"

"That's the advice of a policeman?" Monica asked more loudly than she had intended, which attracted unwelcome attention from different corners of the cafeteria.

"What else could you do?" Bertrand raised his eyebrows in sincere surprise.

"I can't do much. You should do something."

"For instance?" Bertrand asked.

"For instance, provide protection for me and possibly the other members of this task force."

"Protection?" Bertrand echoed in a disapproving note. "Where could we find the funds to provide protection for everyone who's scared of criminals? Somebody has to foot that bill, don't you know? Give us the budget, madam, and we will do whatever you want."

He picked up another doughnut and began eating it, a gleam of appreciation in his eyes. Monica saw that the last one was still on the plate, and she felt a great temptation to throw it in Bertrand's face. He had called her "madam" instead of "Monica." She was no longer a prominent politician to him, but simply one of those citizens whom the criminals had threatened—madam.

"A week ago there was an article in one of the newspapers that the police had aborted the assassination of Marcel, leader of the Devil's Knights." Monica was speaking in a stern voice, which she hoped would precede a devastating argument. "This tells me that you have the means to know what gangsters intend to do. With the information I've given you, could you provide protection for us?"

"Not for us. For you, Monica. Your understanding of the subject matter, though, is not correct. We don't have information of any kind about what bikers intend to do. We just arranged to have around-the-clock surveillance for the most notorious leaders of both gangs. We know some of the places they frequent. Our people happened to notice the preparations for Marcel's assassination and aborted it. What else were we supposed to do?"

"Nice!" Monica uttered in a sarcastic cry. "The most dangerous leader of one of the notorious biker gangs is in fact under police protection. You've found funds to protect his life, but not mine!"

"Good gosh, Monica, what are you talking about? Don't you think I would single-handedly arrange around-the-clock surveillance for you?" Bertrand wanted to say something else, but a voice from the meeting hall made him stop.

"Please, take your seats, ladies and gentlemen," Robert said, appearing at the doorstep.

"Let's continue during the break," Monica suggested, rising to her feet.

"The draft of the bill, along with some supporting materials, has been distributed around the table for everyone. There's no need to study the papers—every paragraph of this important document has long been under the scrutiny of each member in this room," Robert told them. The current version had a rather loose definition of a criminal organization, one that could easily be interpreted as needed, or desired, by a judge or the police. Monica knew that every member of the task force sincerely thought that common sense and honest integrity would prevail when application of the law became necessary. After all, the final verdict of guilt or innocence would still rest upon a judge and a jury.

There were also provisions that allowed for the confiscation of the property of criminals and criminal organizations, for the gathering of information from civil organizations and agencies, and for conducting covert searches, as well as the use of telephone wiretaps and listening devices.

Monica knew that in any other circumstance, she would have voted against such a law. She also knew, for sure, that a few other members of the task force shared her concerns about the law and its implications.

Still, the bill was adopted—unanimously.

Chapter 7

I

Claude spent almost a week in painstaking reconnaissance, trying to plot his attack.

The muffler shop was located in a business–industrial area of town, off a street that was almost desolate, with few pedestrians and hardly any traffic. He quickly realized that parking a car there without it being noticed is not an option. The one possible place for it to blend in was a parking lot between the muffler shop and a furniture factory next door. But it was always full and likely under the surveillance of Iron Ghosts. A neighborhood grocery store down the road would not provide much cover or distraction either, because its visitors were very occasional, as well—workers from the area or residents from a row of single-family houses that ran along one side of the street, further south. The opposite side of the street had no buildings, only a small park.

Hans suggested using the park—a small Japanese motorcycle, he told Claude, could be easily hidden behind one of the benches. From there, it would take him less than half a minute to get to Claude, pick him up, and escape. Claude agreed that the suggestion was a good idea and they began to finalize plans for the hit.

A few days later, Claude received the secret combination of numbers on his pager. The message was from Marcel and the display on the screen meant one thing: Ready. Claude called Hans, who arrived on a stolen bike ten minutes later. He was not as nervous as he had been in previous hits. Practice and Claude's exemplary behavior had slowly made him more confident in his skills and in the existence of Lady Luck.

They traveled to the park's rear entrance as planned, via a twisting side road. Nobody was there, as the time was only 10 o'clock in the morning. Blue-collar workers would not be arriving until later, during their lunch breaks to eat, drink, and chat. Hans turned the engine off and rolled the bike inside the park. Holding the handlebars as if they were a stubborn goat's horns, he pushed the bike toward the nearest bench, which was littered with remnants of food and paper bags.

For the end of September, the weather was still warm but the trees, tired of making new blooms and fresh leaves all summer, had begun to fade. Their dry, gray branches were shedding an amazing number of tired lifeless leaves, dropping them to the ground, one upon another, to create a rustling, red–yellow carpet with all the beautiful colors of death. Some of the tree branches were almost bare, which enabled Claude to peer between them to observe the muffler shop, from which Stanley must eventually appear.

"I still don't know exactly who we're after," Hans reminded Claude.

"As I said, it's a muffler shop owner," Claude said. "Five grand in two hours—not bad, eh? That's all you've got to worry about." If Hans had known who they were actually after, he might have refused to take part in such a dangerous hit.

Now, sitting behind the thinning veil of yellow foliage, Claude was beginning to realize that the success of the task was almost entirely in the capricious hands of fate. If Stanley exited the building unaccompanied by his bodyguards; and if there were no pedestrians on the street, in the line of fire at that one, specific moment; and if there was sufficient time to approach him without being noticed so Claude could reach a distance short enough for an accurate shot; and if Stanley was not armed . . .

So many if's.

Of course, Claude could allow Stanley to get into his car and then shoot him at the first stop sign or traffic light. The option of killing Stanley inside the muffler shop was definitely out of the question as Marcel had told him that the Iron Ghosts inside would be armed. Considering everything, the best decision would probably be to cancel the ambush altogether and tell Marcel the reasons. That, however, would require another team to find out exactly when Stanley was visiting his muffler shop again. And, who knew if, and when, such a chance might come along?

On the other hand, the success of this hit would make Claude one of the most respected of the Devil's Knights. The road to the gang's higher circle was over Stanley's dead body.

Watching the entrance into the muffler shop, Claude felt sweat gathering in his palms and under his armpits. Staying cool when one's death might be a few minutes away was not that easy even for the toughest guys. Having a steady arm and fast, precise reactions at such moments was the ability of a select few. He was sure of being one of them.

"Anything wrong?" Hans asked, giving Claude a sharp look.

"Not at all," Claude responded in his usual confident tone. "It's just taking a bit longer than I had thought."

At last, a man about thirty years old, with hair receding from his forehead, came out of the main entrance of the muffler shop. He was dressed in a business suit; holding a briefcase in one hand, he adjusted large glasses on his nose with the other, and walked briskly to the parking lot, where he climbed into his car, and drove away. A minute later, an old woman appeared on the sidewalk as if from nowhere, pushing a stroller with a baby inside toward the grocery store. Suddenly, Stanley came out of the building and headed toward the grocery store, a few steps ahead of the woman with the baby. Claude touched the gun that was stashed beneath his belt and stood up.

Stanley briskly crossed the road. Claude followed closely and moved up to hide behind the woman. He sped up, shortening the distance between himself and Stanley, and then pushed his mask up to cover the lower part of his face in case the old bitch might recognize him later. He passed her, his hand still on the hidden gun. Stanley was about twenty yards from the grocery store when he looked back. In an instant, he darted forward and disappeared behind the corner of the building.

Roll the dice, Claude said to himself, rushing into a deadly game with Lady Luck. Whatever comes . . .

His gun ready, he turned the corner.

The hand of Providence, though, did not throw the dice in his favor.

He saw Stanley—standing still, his outstretched arms steady, holding a gun. Stanley fired. Claude pulled the trigger, too, but he was on the run and well aware that the accuracy of his shot, even at point-blank range, would never match that of his stationary adversary. The mingled sounds of gunshots reverberated along the narrow street, and Claude saw a flash of fire coming out of Stanley's barrel. At the same moment a crushing blow hit his chest below the left shoulder. It seemed to him that a huge, red-hot boulder had been thrown by a powerful force, knocking him down and incapacitating his body and mind.

Claude collapsed onto the pavement, face down, hands stretched forward. He was suddenly disoriented, his body in the tight grips of pain. By sheer effort, he managed to raise his head and look forward, hoping to find his gun and take another shot at his target before passing out. But his gun was three feet away—it had fallen from his hand when the bullet slammed into his body—and Stanley was nowhere in sight. Claude let his head drop—the right side of his face hitting the coarse surface of the sidewalk. Somewhere in the distance, he heard the growling sound of a motorcycle engine approaching. His first thought was that Stanley had come back to finish him off. But when the bike stopped nearby, he saw that it was Hans, not Stanley. Hans jumped off, the engine still running, picked up the gun, tore away Claude's mask, hopped back on the bike, and raced away.

Claude closed his eyes, and in his mind, he saw a long, red band flying into eternity. *Good, clever Hans,* he thought. *Now there will be no evidence against me. I will be a victim, not a hit man.*

Pity, I never got trained by Techie's guys.

That was his last thought before his mind plunged into darkness.

Claude regained consciousness with the frightening feeling that he was on the verge of passing away. Through his weakness and numbness, he saw Leila's face, with tears and hope in her eyes, looking at him from above. He rolled his eyes toward her and blinked while his body remained still, too weak for any physical effort. The loveliest words of all surfaced in his mind: He was alive. For the first time in his life, he thought about God. He was grateful to the Creator. He was alive.

He looked beyond Leila's face and saw clean, white curtains covering large windows. Strange display screens showed green pulsating waves and had ever-changing numbers running across them, the meanings of which he had no idea. Undoubtedly, he was in a hospital room. He smiled at Leila, and she smiled back. A tear from her cheek dropped onto his face.

"You will live, darling," she said and shook, sobbing. "The surgeon said that. No vital organs were damaged." Claude, in spite of his weakness, was overwhelmed with emotions. No one in his whole life had had any compassion for his suffering. No one had cared about his well-being. But this girl, his dear, dear girl, did. With some effort, he took her hand and squeezed it lightly.

"I will live—for sure." His voice was hoarse, hardly audible. She kissed him and stepped back. Stash appeared in her place.

"Hey, buddy," he said in a theatrically cheerful tone. "Hold onto it. We've arranged security, around the clock. The police won't guard you, since you weren't the one they could lay charges against. No witness was there to tell the story."

An authoritative voice of a nurse interfered.

"Please don't talk to him," she demanded. "He's too weak. Let him sleep."

The next day, he was still very weak and in much pain, but he felt stronger. He even exchanged a few frivolous words with a middle-aged nurse, to show off his bravery. He didn't know what else to do. Claude was uncomfortable in the hospital—its atmosphere was so unusual to him.

Everyone was being so kind. For as far back as he could remember, any stranger had been a potential enemy with malicious intentions. How was he supposed to react to nurses, doctors, and others who genuinely cared for his life? Why didn't he have to threaten beating the hell out of them?

At noon, he fell asleep, but an hour later he was awakened by an angry quarrel. Stash was arguing with someone, his voice irritated and aggressive.

"What the hell do you want from him?" Stash was growling. "He's sleeping. Give him some time to recuperate."

"Don't block my way," the cold, bossy voice responded. In no time, Claude realized the police had come to question him. In the next moment, the curtain slid abruptly to the wall and a man in civilian clothes appeared, a man with nasty but calm eyes in a round puffy face.

"I am Serge Gorte." The man showed his identification card as he introduced himself. Claude didn't look at it. He knew too well that this was the man who Marcel had mentioned more than once. Serge unbuttoned his brown jacket, which seemed larger than he needed for a good fit, and took a photograph from the inside pocket.

"I wonder if you could recognize one of your clients," Serge said, placing the photograph in front of Claude's eyes and watching intently what kind of effect it might produce. Claude didn't blink. It was a picture of Norman, whose wife he had killed. Claude had almost forgotten about that job.

"Never saw him." Claude was on the verge of fainting, but his mind was clear. *The bastard knows that I killed Norman's little bitch,* Claude was pondering with surprising speed. *How? Better to think about it later, when everything's quiet. One thing is clear: The police have no solid evidence yet; otherwise, they'd have already arrested me. This pig Serge must have another card up his sleeve, I'm pretty sure.*

Serge nodded in consent, but Claude knew what Serge wanted to convey. "I know the truth," the gesture meant.

"Maybe you know this one?" Serge asked, producing another photograph. He showed Claude the smiling face of Stanley. "Old buddy, eh?"

Now Claude understood the game. The investigator was interested in Stanley more than in him. He was after the leaders of the gangs, those who instigated and ran the gang's business and the biker's war. After Claude's recovery, he would likely be taken to a police station where Serge would offer him a deal: Testify against Stanley and you won't get the maximum sentence of life in prison for killing Norman's wife. Stanley would then be charged later with attempted murder, possession of firearms, and whatever else they had on him by that time, without a doubt enough to isolate him for ten years or more. For a biker, though, to cooperate with the police was worse than suicide. Under no circumstance would he help the police against anyone, even the gang's—or his—worst enemy. Even if death was unavoidable, no biker would call the police for help. Breaking that biker rule could be worse for Claude than losing his life.

"We found an empty cartridge beside you on the pavement," the detective continued. "There was another cartridge, of course, fifty feet away. From the bullet that hit you."

"Fuck off," Claude growled.

"I don't need your answers right now." The photographs were returned to their inside pocket. "Take your time."

Alex Markman

"Get the fuck out of here," Claude said.

Serge Gorte sighed.

"I know that my words fall on deaf ears. Lots of troubles are waiting for you around the corner. We'll see each other soon. Think about this, Claude."

"Fuck off," Claude repeated with his eyes closed. Gorte left. Stash came in and sat on the bed.

"What did he want?"

"He showed me Stanley's photograph," Claude said.

"Get it out of your mind," Stash advised. "Let's solve problems as they come."

Claude closed his eyes. What if . . .

He shivered.

What if the cop wasn't bluffing? More long years in jail, this time perhaps for the rest of his life. Dark cells, disgusting smells, slow-moving, depressing days.

And, good-bye Leila—what woman in her right mind would wait for someone with a life sentence?

His thoughts began drifting to the past. His youth had been wasted behind bars, lost—the best years of his life. He was beating inmates, getting beaten, many times with the sadistic cruelty of lifelong cons, and watching grim, boring days drag on in unremarkable succession. Would this be his way of life until his death?

It would have to be different now, wouldn't it? Claude was trying to soothe himself. At least, I might be a Prospect by then. In jail, that would put me at the top. There would be lots of broads, pot, cocaine, hash. It depended, he knew, in what joint he got placed. If it was one controlled by the Iron Ghosts, or any group besides the Devil's Knights, there would be the same rough zoo.

And now, too, he had a life with Leila to lose—

The voice of a nurse dragged him back to the real world.

234

"How do you feel today?" she asked. The woman was looking at him with compassionate eyes. "I have to give you some shots," she told him. "If you're still in pain, I can give you painkillers."

"Can you give me some morphine?" he asked.

"Yes, of course. I'll be back in a minute."

Should I tell Marcel about Norman's photograph? Probably not. Marcel might decide to get rid of all potential witnesses. It wouldn't be easy for him, though. The destiny of a club member is supposed to rest in the hands of a collective gang decision, not the whims of an individual leader. But Marcel had his authority and a host of servants, and could make anything happen when his life was at stake. Well, well. I should listen to Stash. He may have been right: We should solve the problems as they come.

II

By his fifth day in the hospital, Claude was fit enough to sit on the bed. With envious eyes he looked out his window at the routine, day-to-day life outside. An endless stretch of bumper-to-bumper traffic was converting the highway into a huge parking lot; pedestrians on the street were rushing to get somewhere special; a clear, cloudless sky overlooked them all. *The air must be fresh and crisp,* he thought. It would be nice to ride on his bike with Leila on such a day. But it might also be nice to simply walk, or to sit on their balcony, smoking pot and drinking beer. A simple, uneventful, wonderful life, it might now be beyond his reach. He had never felt such a nostalgic desire to be outside, even when he was in jail looking at the world through iron bars.

235

"It's nice out there," he said, pointing at the window. Leila, who sat beside him, put her arm around his waist.

"The doctor promised to release you in two days," she said. "At home you'll recover quickly. I'll take care of you."

A huge wave of warm feelings almost drowned him. He had never thought she would stay with him so faithfully at a time of such a misery. Women like strong, rich men, he believed. Such a beauty as Leila could easily find another man who had tons of money.

"Why don't you just drop me?" he asked.

"I can't. I love you." These frighteningly gentle words sounded like music from her lips. Claude had to lie down to calm his racing heart.

On the seventh day, Leila came to pick him up. Two club members accompanied them all the way home to their parking lot, where they found Hans waiting.

"You'll out-survive all of us, old buddy," Hans said. "How d'yah feel today?"

"Okay."

"Wanna smoke a bit, or do some blow? I brought everything."

"Smoke will do. And some beer."

"Anything you like," Leila said.

Hans offered him his hand for help, but Claude dismissed it with an angry gesture. In the apartment, he walked straight to the balcony and sat down in an easy chair. He leaned back and stretched his legs. Hans was soon at his side. Leila, happy and moving around the apartment gracefully, was busy fixing and serving them whatever they wanted.

"I jumped on the bike right after you crossed the street." Hans was talking rapidly, almost in a whisper, leaning forward, impatient to share the thoughts and feelings he had accumulated since the day of the near-fatal shooting. "You know, everything went so fast. I heard the shots. When I turned the corner, this guy was still there. He was about to sneak into the small alley between the houses when I pulled up near to you. His gun was still in his hand. He stood and watched me. I took your mask off and picked up the gun you dropped. He could've killed me, anytime, if he'd wanted to. But he just kept watching me. I got back on the bike, and sped past him. I threw your gun and the mask into a dumpster near a large apartment building, and then I called Leila. She said that she knew how to contact your club. I couldn't have done much more at that time."

During the speech he rolled a joint and offered it to Claude.

"All the newspapers printed stories about us." Hans was beaming with pride. "I've saved a few with photos. The police contacted the newspaper reporters. They said it was, for sure, a fight between two bikers, but they had no clue who shot at you. They all said that no gun was found on or near you, only an empty cartridge." Hans moved closer, staring at Claude with the intensity of an accomplice contemplating a multimillion-dollar deal. He was swelling with self-esteem and self-importance.

"The police suspect that there was another biker who helped you. Everyone was stunned—yes, they said exactly that, stunned—at how fast all the material evidence disappeared. They said that the bikers staged a great show, only with real bullets and blood."

Hans smiled at last and took a huge, nervous puff. Claude understood Hans well, if only because they shared fully their feelings and egos. Although this was not the first time newspapers had printed articles about their hits, all the previous ones had been about anonymous, unknown killers. Now, Claude's name was at the center of attention. Hans probably thought he would be famous soon, as well.

Claude was happy, too, in spite of his pain and weakness. Any criminal worth something wants to be famous. When his actions, no matter how dreadful they might seem to the public, became the subject of media attention, the respect for him in the underworld would grow beyond all proportions of the crime. Nothing makes a gangster happier than fame.

"You did a good job, Hans. I'll pay you for it as soon as I can."

"Forget it," Hans said. "Money's nothing. You don't owe me a penny."

"We'll have plenty of money, Hans."

"I know. Forget about it, though. Tell me something—can I join your club? I can get a Harley anytime—" He looked around and changed the subject quickly. "Here's a beer. She's a nice girl, your Leila."

"Don't you even look at her. I'd kill anyone for her."

"Enough killings for today," Leila said, looking back over the threshold to the balcony. "You'd better go, Hans. He has to rest."

"Let's talk a bit longer," Claude protested.

"No."

"C'mon, Leila."

"I said no," Leila insisted. Her tone was firm and uncompromising. Claude was surprised, but said nothing.

"I've gotta go, anyway." Hans stood up. "Be well, Claude."

When he left, Leila took Claude by the arm and led him inside.

"Take a rest, honey," she said. "I with you."

III

The wound in his body was healing well. In less than a month, he had recuperated a great deal and was able to return to all his usual activities, except for his work as a contract killer: That demanded much better physical and mental fitness. His other wounds were not recovering so well or so quickly, however. The bullet had dealt a devastating blow to his spirit, his mood, and his gut. These invisible wounds were bleeding day and night, their torture eased only when he could lose himself in a haze of cocaine or marijuana. Never before had he been scared of death, even in those brief moments before the deadly fights in jail. He hadn't given a damn what life was about and figured that hell would probably not be much worse than Earth. Now, he was afraid of dying at the hands of an Iron Ghost, and gruesome nightmares woke him and forced him to peek into the dark corners of his bedroom in desperate attempts to make out a hidden assassin.

Swarms of thoughts, annoying and biting like large mosquitoes, attacked his mind. Life in the past had been stupid, useless, meaningless. But what was in his past? Only an ugly childhood and a youth as a hoodlum, for which he had been awarded a total of eight years in jail. If he died now, would it have been worth living such a short and stupid, worthless life? Was there any way out of it? Any way to turn to another life? Certainly not. So, what was next, then? Damn the bullet that had made him realize what death was about.

Or was it Leila who had brought these new thoughts into his mind?

Alex Markman

He visited the club a few times, claiming to all his buddies that more time was needed for a full recovery. He bumped into Marcel once, but all he got was the cold shoulder. Marcel no doubt noticed the effect that drugs were taking on Claude's face, because after this encounter, the Devil's Knights terminated their financial support.

The cold days of winter were saturated with the intensified heat of the biker's war. The number of deaths on both sides had grown far beyond one hundred, with others missing and deemed dead by police. Hundreds of explosions shook the city and provided huge headlines for the media.

Marcel was growing impatient. He called Claude a few times, hinting that he needed his services. But Claude still insisted that he needed more time to recuperate.

When the last of his money had disappeared like the smoke from a joint, Leila told him that she couldn't pay the rent for the next month.

"Don't worry, Claude." She ran her palm over his head, trying to soothe him. "We'll survive. I'll just dance for awhile. I'll make good money there until you're well. I could even sell stuff there, too."

In the past, the very thought of Leila dancing naked in front of other men would have driven him mad. But now, his mind was so clouded with the effect of the drugs that he only nodded in consent after a brief moment of hesitation.

"I'll place you in one of our bars," was all he said. "Nobody there will hit on you. And if they do dare, I'll take care of 'em."

He arranged Leila's job rather easily as the owner of the bar looked Leila over with glowing eyes.

Claude never attended a performance. He only came at the end of the shows to pick her up. Successful as expected, she soon began selling pot and coke, which was supplied by Devil's Knights dealers. Claude resumed paying his club membership fees, but he still declined Marcel's business offers.

After the government adopted its tough new law against organized crime, both gangs began feeling some heat. Many gang members were arrested, and the gang leaders had to ease their selection rules to recruit new members and maintain their counts.

As spring began wiping away the remnants of winter and replacing snow with an assault of chaotic, violent colors, Claude's mood finally began to improve. Although his dependency on drugs continued to grow, his fears and fits of depression began to subside. Shy at first, an urge for violent distraction was growing stronger and stronger, taking the place of his mental fatigue. A decisive wake-up call came one day from Marcel, who invited him to a meeting.

"I'll let you know where and when we'll meet," Marcel said. "Be ready, anytime. Got it?"

"Okay . . ."

"Anytime," Marcel repeated. Something unusual was in his tone, and Claude sensed trouble. Marcel had never made a habit of repeating his words.

"No problem, Marcel."

An hour later, an unexpected knock at the door made him reach for his gun. He had the nasty feeling that something was fundamentally wrong, and the feeling grew stronger as he opened the door. Beyond the threshold stood a typical biker: a leather riding suit—but without any insignia, Claude noticed—and high leather boots. He wore a band around his head and sported a disorderly beard, mustache, and long hair. Claude remembered him at once. They had been in the same jail at one point in time. The guy had belonged to a biker gang that had been controlled by Marcel. He handed Claude a folded piece of paper and left, not uttering a sound.

Claude spread the paper on the table and studied it with a frown. It was a map, drawn by a very practiced and firm hand, with arrows pointing to a destination and instructions detailing how to get there and what landmarks to look for. A note from Marcel demanded that he be there at 4 o'clock, sharp, that afternoon. Claude glanced at his wristwatch. It was already two. What the hell was going on? He couldn't have done anything wrong. He hadn't done anything.

The obvious choice for the drive was his beloved Harley Davidson. The warm day, the cloudless sky, and the light breeze were very inviting. Claude put on jeans, hopped on the bike, and drove away. Once outside the city, the rural scenery of the country, the air blowing in his face, and the feeling of freedom known only to motorcycle riders and flying birds eased his anxiety. With no cars or humans in sight, he let the engine roar with its full might. The sun glowed directly above his head, throwing no shadows from the trees on either side of the road. Brightly lit pastures, stables, and farmhouses, scattered great distances one from another, flew past him in pleasant but monotonous succession. He arrived at the meeting point fifteen minutes early and found it to be a farm, plunged into a state of afternoon drowsiness. A gravel road led him through a collection of retired and dirty farm machinery, scattered like a rusty scrap yard, and up to a farmhouse. Farther, behind the house, was a big barn, its large doors looming open. Claude pulled up close to them and turned his engine off. The sudden silence of this remote, uninhabited place alerted him—this would be a perfect place for murder, he thought. Nobody would hear any cry for help.

With cautious steps, he walked slowly toward the barn entrance, the gravel under his feet protesting with grinding crunches. Inside, he stopped and listened. It was pleasantly cool, and the afternoon sunlight slanted through the opening behind him, making the shady space beyond seem darker than it really was. A voice from the depth of the barn startled him.

"Come in."

Claude nervously reached for the gun stashed under his jacket, but withdrew an empty hand with the same impulsive jerk. Turning to where the voice had come from, he saw Marcel sitting on a long wooden box, dressed in a leather suit, but with no club insignia. He was rolling a joint.

"Sit down." Marcel nodded to the place beside him.

"Some work to do?" Claude asked, settling on the box and smiling. Marcel stretched his lips tight in a contemptuous grimace.

"Last fall, a dealer in Ontario was killed." Marcel fixed his eyes upon Claude.

Claude's heart began pounding, defying any effort to control its beat.

"We found out that Stash wanted to collect on the guy's debt to the Vandals. You killed him?"

Lying to Marcel meant a certain death penalty.

"Yes."

"Did you know that the brother of this dealer was a full patch in B.C.?"

"Gosh," Claude exclaimed, pretending great surprise. "I had no idea."

243

He quickly reran the events of the hit in his memory. Only the dealer had told him about his brother being a full patch Devil's Knight. There was no witness to that.

"I've been watching Stash for the last year or so," Marcel continued. "He puts all his money up his nose. Often, he couldn't even pay his membership fees. I never thought, however, that he'd go so far as to collect debts from our own people. Enough is enough."

A silent exchange of sharp looks followed. Claude nodded, waiting for instructions—on how to execute the death sentence.

"You've been friends lately, the two of you," Marcel started.

"I don't give a fuck," Claude growled. "If I'd known the truth, I'd have told you right away. Son of a bitch wanted me to be a scapegoat."

Marcel shrugged his shoulders.

"It's hard to keep a tight leash on a pack of wild wolves. Anyone's free to leave the club. There's nothing wrong with that. But one cannot be in the club and not obey its rules."

It was unusual for Marcel to explain his point of view.

"I agree with you," Claude told him.

"The dealer's brother is in an active search for the killer," Marcel kept talking. "It's better to finish with Stash before they find you out. Stash, in his current state of mind, would spill the beans. I don't want to lose you."

"But Stash has a brother who is a Prospect in Nova Scotia," Claude cautiously remarked. He was sure that there were other reasons to get rid of Stash.

"That's right. We'll let him know everything after the fact. He'll understand. Once a Devil's Knight, one has to remain so 'til death."

"How d'yah wanna do this?" Claude asked.

"I'll arrange it for next Thursday, here, in this barn. Just between you and me, I've suggested promoting you to Prospect. This is supposed to be a surprise to you, but I have a reason for telling you sooner. Everyone approved your candidacy, Stash included. At the meeting next week, we'll discuss a few things, full patches and selected Prospects only. I know that Stash is planning to play golf that day, so he'll have his clubs with him. We will use them for teaching him, and reminding all others, a lesson. Everyone has to take part in it. You'll start."

Claude nodded. Killing a full patch needed to be a collective decision and had to be carried out as a group responsibility. Apparently all the high-profile members had agreed about the action that would be taken. By participating in the execution with them, even leading it off, he would be admitted into their circle.

"The shovel's over there." Marcel pointed his finger to the wall where a few manual tools were arranged.

"The cornfield behind the barn would be a good place for his grave. You won't have time to dig it next week, so go and do it now. No one from the farm is around. I have to go. See you next Thursday."

Marcel went outside. The roar of his bike thundered from somewhere behind the barn where Marcel had hidden it before Claude arrived. As the bike moved past, the sound of its engine grew weaker and weaker, until it died in the distance. The peace and quiet returned. Claude took the shovel and went to dig the grave for his friend, the one man who had guarded him so faithfully in the hospital.

IV

The following Thursday was an ideal day for outdoor activities. Around the farm, where the meeting was about to take place, nature seemed ready for an afternoon nap. Without the gentlest breeze blowing, fresh green leaves hung on their trees in drowsy immobility.

Even inside the barn, where the bikers were gathering, it seemed everyone was in a good mood. The place bustled with the sounds of friendly greetings and lively conversations. The rattles of motorcycles rose from the distance, growing louder and louder until they arrived and settled into their own resting places. Only three members did not ride their bikes: two came in cars, one in a pickup truck. A few of them wore the club's colors.

Stash came on a bike, his golf bag attached to the rear seat as expected. Half a day on a golf course, exposed to sun and fresh air, had brought a trace of color to his wrinkled, swollen face.

"Glad to see you," he said to Claude, firmly shaking hands. "How are you these days?"

"Getting better."

"I have a deal for you, Claude. Could we meet next week?"

"Of course. No sweat."

Claude found himself enjoying the unusual fun of having a friendly talk with this high-ranking Devil's Knight—who would be beaten into a bloody mess with his own golf clubs within the hour.

"I had to shut down my collection agency," Stash was still talking. "The new laws have given the police too much power. They came to me demanding that I give them the list of my clients and debtors—since the inception of the

246

company! Lawyers would have cost me a fortune. I'm thinking of running back to the States."

"Good idea," Claude absently agreed. "It is getting pretty hot here."

"Exactly. See how many of us are missing? Dead or in jail . . . The police are closing in on us. I was against this war with the Ghosts from the outset. See how many new members we've taken in, in a rather short time? We're paying a heavy price."

"Marcel said that there was no way back."

"He said," Stash nodded. "There's more than one solution to this, I think. What would be the good of a truce with the Ghosts after all of us are wiped out? That's what will happen eventually, believe me. Well, most of us think that Marcel's doing the right things. So, be it. There will be no winners in this war, Claude, you'll see. But, enough of this crap. Marcel is calling everyone. Let's go."

Claude shrugged his shoulders. There wasn't much sense in arguing with a dead man.

Inside the barn, everyone settled down in a circle, sitting on whatever was handy: wooden boxes, blocks of wood, or armfuls of hay spread on the ground. The mob, it seemed, was in a relaxed, friendly mood. The last splashes of conversations died when Marcel took the stage and introduced the topics of discussion.

His main concern was the amount of money that they needed to maintain pressure on the Iron Ghosts. He requested, in fact, demanded, that everyone contribute more than he had before, as all expenses pertinent to the planning and executing of explosions and killings—as well as the gathering of information on enemies, police officials, businesses, and politicians—were growing faster than anyone could have expected. Nobody objected, although a few bikers complained that because of pressure from the Ghosts, their business had shrunk, leaving them with almost nothing to live on.

Next, Marcel suggested that they promote one of the biker's gangs in northern Quebec to Prospect status. They were doing very well, he maintained, contributing money and soldiers to support the Devil's Knights in fighting the Iron Ghosts. He also suggested easing restrictions for admission to the club, as they had recently seen significant losses, some through deaths, some through incarceration.

Claude looked around the barn. He saw Techie sitting next to Marcel. Techie had regarded every speaker with his cold, inquisitive eyes staring from his unemotional, stony face. A few seats down was Stash, who had apparently begun sensing that something was going to happen before the meeting was done. He wiped sweat off his forehead with a sleeve, his eyes jumping from face to face, looking in search of an answer to his gruesome suspicions. But all the discussions were conducted in a businesslike manner, nothing really stood out as being unusual, and the meeting concluded within an hour, as planned. A short break was announced, and a purr of conversations filled the barn.

"Now . . ." Marcel raised his voice above the noise of the crowd. "I have an announcement to make—Good news. Claude is promoted to Prospect status."

The uproar of congratulations pleased Claude immensely. Status in the gang was very important to him. It meant he would have the companionship of high-ranking members and the friendship of like-minded people united by common goals, rules, and mentality. It meant recognition of his wits, guts, and achievements. It meant business and money. Everyone shook hands with him, gave him strong, manly hugs on the shoulder, and spared a few words of praise.

"We'll celebrate this event at the Speaking Parrot bar tonight," Marcel added. "I've booked it until morning. Everything will be paid for: broads, drinks, and food."

Another uproar of appreciation.

"One more thing, before we go . . ." Marcel paused, allowing a feeling of apprehension to descend over the mob.

"A question to you, Stash—," he paused again.

"We've discovered that you helped to collect a debt from one of our own people—a debt payable to the Vandals." He was looking directly into Stash's eyes, waiting for a look of fear or panic to fill them.

"It seems that you've even gone so far as to kill the Ontario dealer, whose brother is one of our own full patches."

Claude turned his attention to a biker standing at the entrance to the barn. He held the bag full of golf clubs.

"Debts must be paid, Marcel, you know that. Our people shouldn't be exempt." Stash wiped some sweat off his neck and looked around in search of Claude. He didn't see the biker at the entrance put the bag on the ground and remove one of the clubs from it.

"So far as this dealer is concerned . . . ," Stash began, stopping mid-thought when he found Claude, already standing behind him holding one of his golf clubs in both hands.

When their eyes met, Claude swept the club around, using the full force of his body and arms. The air whistled under the pressure of the fast-moving metal rod until the heavy end of the club landed on flesh with a dull, somewhat wet sound. Stash collapsed, yelling in pain.

Bikers snatched up the remaining clubs and joined Claude in the execution. Marcel and Techie did not participate: They only watched.

Stash was dead in a few minutes, his head smashed. Claude produced a large garbage bag, spread it on the ground, and, with the help of a few others, slid the body inside it. Several of them carried Stash to his grave, the grave that Claude had dug the week before. They threw the corpse in, followed by the bag of golf clubs, and the grave was quickly filled with soil, which was then smoothed level with the surface around it. Someone loaded Stash's bike onto the pickup truck as bike engines roared to life. Soon, not a biker was left, and the place returned to its native stillness and quiet.

Claude was high, as if he had enjoyed a snort of cocaine, all the way back to town in anticipation of being the center of attention through a whole night of wild binging.

There was nothing, he thought, that he would not do for the gang.

Chapter 8

I

Serge glanced one last time at the photographs that were spread over his table. He picked one up and placed it into a black leather binder he held. As he did so, he looked over and noticed the hands on the clock were pointing to 12:30. The door to his office opened just then and Patrick came in.

"Time to go?" he asked. His tone suggested both a question and a reminder.

Serge nodded, closed the binder to place it under his arm, and stood up. As he moved away from his desk, Patrick raised an eyebrow. Serge had not picked up the jacket and holster that were hanging on the back of his chair.

"You're not taking your piece?"

"You have one," Serge replied. "That'll suffice. Let me enjoy summer once in awhile. I hate wearing a jacket all the time." Without a jacket, it was impossible to conceal a gun. But he didn't really expect a violent response from the man they were going to meet. And if a problem arose, he would simply use his experience in psychological warfare.

Outside the office, Serge fully appreciated the warm, sunny day. The air was dry and crisp, typical for the first week of July. A light breeze gently touched his skin as he opened the car door and climbed into the passenger seat. He quickly rolled down the window to let some fresh air inside.

Serge found it convenient that Patrick didn't talk much during the drive so his thoughts could flow without interruption. Today he chose to reflect on the recent successes they had had. Their fight against the biker gangs had become so much more efficient after the new anti-gang legislation had passed and increases in police funding had gone into effect. Taped phone conversations, evidence from raids on clubhouses and biker residences, reports from undercover police agents who had penetrated low-level dealer networks, and information from other sources were flying into the central police database like numerous rivers flowing into a large sea. The police were finally able to start bringing charges against bikers from rival gangs, their puppet clubs, and many associated businesses.

But Serge had to admit the gangs were demonstrating remarkable resilience and were fighting back with vicious determination. The bikers were quick to recruit new members, to restore destroyed drug networks, and to continue pushing narcotics to the public with no noticeable change in availability or price. They had managed to identify and eliminate a number of police informants. And several prison authorities had received accurate lists of their own prison guards with details such as home addresses and a variety of personal information. Some of the lists also contained unexplained asterisks that made a few wardens panic. One arrest had even uncovered a similar list of all the anti-biker squad personnel and their addresses.

With that, he had to acknowledge the one major setback that had recently been discovered: A mole obviously existed inside the police department. That was the only possible explanation for where that privileged information was coming from and also for why so many important raids had resulted in nothing more than biker's laughs.

Another obstacle was those damned gang lawyers—they made so much noise about the constitutionality of the new legislation, the reliability of evidence gathered from informants, and the validity of taped conversations, as well as the importance being placed on circumstantial evidence.

But most frustrating of all was the fact that for the top-ranking gang members business went on as usual; they gave orders, but did not commit crimes. They were immune to prosecution because there was no way for the police to prove they had participated in any crimes, save minor offenses or perhaps possession of small quantities of drugs. Serge knew that only the arrests of these gang leaders could substantially damage the biker organizations and possibly end the turf war. His primary target was now Marcel, the undisputed leader of the Devil's Knights. Marcel's arrest would be possible only with the testimonies of many witnesses. But who in their right mind would testify against Marcel?

"Here we are." Patrick nodded his head toward an office building positioned in the distant corner of a large lot full of newer model cars. Patrick parked close to the entrance, in the place reserved for management.

"Business is booming," Serge said sarcastically as he stepped out of the car. "So many cars for sale, but no buyers. Weird, isn't it?"

Patrick nodded. He threw a sharp look around and followed Serge into the building. It was cool inside, and only the hum of an air conditioner disturbed the quiet of the place. A few sales desks had been arranged along the windows, but nobody sat at any of them. Two doors in the wall to the right were closed. With resolute steps, Serge approached one of them, the one with the sign, "Norman Vincent, Manager" on it. His knock was too loud for a casual visitor, and a muffled voice from inside responded quickly.

"Come in."

Serge pushed on the door, walked through it, and showed his badge to the fat man sitting at the desk.

"Police," he said curtly. "My name is Serge Gorte. Do you mind talking to us, Norman?"

"No, sure," Norman said, raising his eyebrows in surprise. "Please, sit down."

Serge took a chair with a cursory glance around the room. The office was a typical one for an average car dealership. It had a sizable desk littered with papers and brochures, a computer terminal, and a small calculator. A few chairs around the desk and a small table in one corner with a coffee machine on it took up the rest of the space.

"What can I do for you?" Norman asked. His fat face did not show any sign of fear, but a mix of curiosity and displeasure. He shifted his eyes from one policeman to the other and finally fixed them on Serge.

"Business is booming?" Serge asked with a friendly smile.

"Business isn't bad," Norman agreed with indifferent politeness. "Anything wrong with that?"

"Yes, there is. There are many things wrong with your business. We've arrested a few car thieves who worked for a man named Marcel. It turns out that a lot of the cars they stole passed through your dealership. We know that you intentionally bought some of the cars for cash and then sold them in the U.S. market. A very simple money-laundering transaction." Norman raised his shoulders in surprise. "But this isn't the sole purpose for my visit."

"What're you talking about?" Norman directed his stare sideways, away from the detectives, to the point where the wall met the ceiling.

"You'll know, you'll know soon," Serge said in confidence. He pulled out a photograph from the leather binder and placed it in front of Norman. Norman regarded the photograph with a blank face.

"You must know him," Serge said. Norman leaned back in his chair, his face expressing nothing.

"Who is it?"

"This is Claude Pichette, the hit man who killed your wife."

"Oh?" Norman did not blink. "Is that right?" He looked at Serge in anticipation of additional details.

"You don't recognize him?"

"How the hell could I recognize him?" Norman raised his voice in indignation. "What are you getting at?"

During a deliberate pause, Serge studied Norman as an entomologist would examine a rare insect. Norman was the first to break the silence.

"What're you talking about?"

"I'm talking about the murder of your wife. You paid for it. You know what you'll be getting for such a crime, don't you?"

"I think I'll call my lawyer," Norman said, stretching his arm toward the telephone.

"That's your right. Do you want to call him right now? Or would you rather listen to the deal I'm going to propose?"

Norman withdrew his hand and hid it beneath the table.

"You'd better leave," he advised.

Serge picked up the photograph and stashed it back in his binder.

"For the money-laundering operation and selling stolen cars, you would normally get a pretty long term. The evidence that we have couldn't be contested in any court. For plotting and ordering the murder of your wife, though, you'd get life. However, with our help . . ."

Norman's left eyelid began to tic, but his lips remained tight.

"We know Marcel recommended that you contact this hit man about killing your wife," Serge continued. "If you agree to testify against Marcel, we'd take you into the witness protection program. You'd get a substantially reduced sentence because of your cooperation with us."

Norman took a deep breath.

"Fuck you, gentlemen." Norman didn't change his tone a bit. He seemed neither irritated nor scared. "I don't know what you're talking about. You may continue your bullshit in the presence of my lawyer."

Serge smiled. Being a realist, he hadn't expected a quick victory. This was just a preliminary move in an ongoing, complicated game, the outcome of which he'd calculated far in advance.

"We'll talk soon, when you're behind bars. With the lawyer, of course—if you still wish." He stood up and shoved the leather binder back under his armpit. "Maybe there you'd be more cooperative, Mister Norman Vincent. For now, here's my business card—just in case you change your mind."

As they approached the car, Patrick asked him, "Why didn't we lay charges against him for money laundering and trading stolen cars?"

"We could have," Serge said, taking his place in the passenger seat. "But that would be only one small victory. I need him to testify against Marcel. That's the target: the gang leader."

"You've already arranged around-the-clock surveillance of Marcel," Patrick said. "Don't we need to do the same for the other leaders?"

"Don't we need . . . ?" Serge repeated, and then sighed.

"We need to do many things. But we don't have enough people to do everything. Mind you, it's not that easy to pick the right target for surveillance. The Iron Ghosts have turned out to be even more secretive than the Devil's Knights. By the way, Patrick, we need to watch one of them. Stanley Mathews is his name. Take care of him. It won't be easy, though."

"Do we know his address?" Patrick asked.

"He has a house. But he seldom stays anywhere longer than a week at a time. He's very close to the gang's president, but tries to keep a low profile. I know for sure that he's very active and efficient. It's not for nothing that the Devil's Knights sent one of their best hit men to kill him. Arrange surveillance around his house and proceed from there."

II

Ominous clouds had been thickening over Marcel. Damage to the gang had been enormous—almost all the money from their drug trafficking revenue went to fund the ever-expanding war with the Iron Ghosts. The police force was tightening its grip around all full patches. And at the last meeting, the top-ranking members of his club had begun questioning his policies, many among them coming out in favor of a truce with the enemy in order to calm the public, the government, and the media. Worst of all, even

Techie had raised his voice against him, giving much weight to these specific arguments.

"The police get funding only when the public screams," Techie had said in his chilling, self-controlled manner. "And they did. You remember that our lawyers assured us that the government would never pass the anti-gang law because it was unconstitutional. They passed it. Now the lawyers claim that this law will not be applied and could be contested successfully in the courts. Just watch, Marcel. The court will apply this law. They are letting the cops do whatever they want, even things that are against the law, when nothing else works. We can fight the Iron Ghosts, but we cannot fight the government. They will tire us out, no matter what the law or constitution says."

After that, the discussion had gotten rather jumpy. Marcel had at his disposal only his same old arsenal of arguments: the Devil's Knights would lose respect in all the underworld; a truce with the Iron Ghosts would not last long because low ranks and street dealers, having little brains, would never adhere to the strict rules of it; a truce would give the Iron Ghosts time to regroup and recruit more foot soldiers.

"That might be true," Techie argued, "but in the meantime the public would forget about the whole thing, the politicians would again cut funds to the police, because they always need money for their own use, and we would have time to restore our own trade networks."

At that moment, Marcel lost his customary confidence and strength. With clenched fists, he defended his position. He vowed to avenge those who had been killed. He would not betray those who were still committed to the fight.

"Even if we wanted to," he argued, showing his teeth, "how would we do it? Invite the Ghosts to the negotiating table? After so many deaths? Mind you, they are very weak now. Most of their strong people are in jail. As soon as their remaining top ranks are wiped out, no negotiations will be needed. Trust me, another few months, half a year at most, and they will come to terms with us."

In the end, no decision was made, but a change in attitude toward the whole mess was in the air.

A few days after that meeting, Raymond called. He said that he needed to discuss something urgent and important. It was not easy for Marcel to lose the tail following him, but he did lose it far in advance of the meeting, which had been set up at a family restaurant in a suburban area. Raymond was sitting at a table when Marcel arrived, with a cup of coffee. The customary smile that was usually on his face was gone. He wore no glasses.

"I won't take much of your time," he told Marcel, fumbling with a teaspoon. "I felt, however, obligated to meet you and explain everything personally, so you'd understand what I'm doing. I'm going to take a break."

"A break?" Marcel repeated, as if questioning his understanding.

"Exactly. I'm going to leave Canada in a few days."

"Why?"

"This is a troublesome time."

"What troubles do you expect?"

"The police are after leaders of both gangs now. They believe that when the top ranks are in jail, peace and quiet will be restored in the province. They're after you, Marcel. They'll lock you up, one way or another."

"They couldn't. They'd never be able to bring any evidence against me in court. I've never done anything wrong, not in the last ten years. The only way to get me is to find a witness that would testify against me, which would be a pretty tough thing to do. Do you think that there are many who'd volunteer for that?"

"Not many," Raymond agreed. "But there's always a chance, and it might only take one. I wouldn't take anything for granted in this game."

"You don't know the people I'm dealing with. They'd rather die than roll over."

Raymond smiled sardonically and dabbed his lips with a napkin.

"I wouldn't bet on anyone except you and me," he said. "That's why I'm leaving."

"For how long?"

"Until the dust settles."

"How long is that?"

"As long as it takes to get you in jail, I would guess. I assure you, Marcel, I won't be among the witnesses. I don't want to be anywhere near this mess. I have enough money to withstand the storm in remote places. But I'm glad that I've dealt only with you."

He stood and threw a five-dollar bill on the table.

"Good luck, Marcel."

Raymond left, but the conversation rang in Marcel's ears long after. The warning was impossible to ignore. He became even more jumpy after receiving a note from Norman, begging Marcel to meet. To be as safe as possible, Norman suggested a cafeteria in an office building in the crowded downtown area.

Marcel agreed. He drove to a big plaza on the outskirts of town, parked his car in the back of the parking lot, and walked into the shopping mall. Dodging shoppers, he quickly reached the front entrance at the far end of the building, and rushed out. Norman's man was waiting for him a few steps away, sitting on a motorcycle with the engine running. Marcel hopped onto the back seat, and the driver, an experienced biker, rushed out of the lot, dodged cars stuck in traffic, and in ten minutes delivered Marcel downtown. There was no chance for a tail to follow him. Nonetheless, Marcel got off the bike two blocks away from the meeting place and walked slowly toward it, scanning the area to make sure he was not being followed.

Norman was already in the cafeteria. Looking at Marcel, he went straight to the heart of the matter, telling the details of his conversation with Serge Gorte.

"How the hell do they know about Claude?" Norman kept asking. "Did he roll over?"

"You must be crazy," Marcel said. "Gorte probably just wanted to scare the shit out of you. If Claude had rolled, I'd already be in stir. Just forget about it. Claude is one of my most trusted men. Besides, he's done so much . . ."

"But how do they know?" Norman insisted. "You know what this means? If the cops get me for my car business, I could live with that. I've discussed that option already with my lawyer. He's told me that five, seven years at the most—that's what's in the cards. In four years I'd be out. But for the little bitch I can get life."

"You won't."

"Look, Marcel. We've known each other for a long time. The only witness against you and me is Claude." When Marcel started to say something, Norman made a protesting gesture.

"I know, I know," Norman cut in quickly. "You trust him. But just for peace of mind . . . Once he's out of the way, we wouldn't have to worry. Do you know how much money you're getting through our outlets? Millions. Do you need troubles like this?"

"Look, Norman," Marcel said, "I'll meet Claude soon. I'll think about what you've said, and—"

"Don't think, Marcel. Do—and do it quickly."

Money speaks, Marcel thought. He nodded reluctantly in agreement.

This was the second meeting to leave a bad taste in Marcel's mouth. Could he rely fully on anyone when the stake was his own life? Norman was a very tough guy, but he'd grown too accustomed to everything big money could buy. If given the choice of life in prison or testifying against Marcel, what would he choose? Killing him would be easy, but not expedient. Norman had made him a shitload of cash with the car business. And, he was not a penny pincher: He contributed once in awhile directly to the war with the Iron Ghosts. This was a good gesture for one who was no longer a member of the club.

But Marcel clearly saw where the danger could come from. If Norman cracked, Claude would be arrested.

In the midst of the gang war, the cops, desperate to arrest gang leaders, might offer Claude a good deal, one that they wouldn't have contemplated in earlier times. A life sentence without parole in a high-security prison would be a tough break for anyone. Claude was a tough guy—no doubt. He was one of those who would accept the blows of Lady Luck without complaint, Marcel believed. But he was in love with his girl—possibly too much in love. Marcel wondered if she might mean even more to him than the gang. When offered a reduced sentence, during which he could have access to his girl, Claude might turn. Nobody could predict how many other hits the police would discover then.

Removing him would solve the problem.

A way to be rid of Claude had to be found.

Disposing of hit men was not an unusual practice for the Devil's Knights, but the reason for such a decision had always been more solid than just a safeguard against likely defection. It was usually because they made unforgiving mistakes. Most professional killers were not clever people. Inevitably, successful hit men developed a feeling of infallibility, sometimes killing the wrong people for trifling reasons. Sooner or later they did other stupid things or started bragging about their heroic acts. Former cons usually cannot keep their mouths shut for long, and when a killer cannot keep his mouth shut, tracks eventually lead back to full patches, which endangers the well-being of the whole gang. Claude, though, had not done anything stupid or wrong so far, which was quite remarkable.

Marcel knew he would not have a chance to get the approval of other members of the gang. So, how could he arrange a hit? What if Claude could be killed by an Iron Ghost?

Marcel recalled a strip bar that had recently fallen into the hands of the Iron Ghosts. Stanley was a frequent guest there. His people, surely armed, were usually around, expecting retaliation from the Devil's Knights baseball team. Why not ask Claude to kill Stanley there? No doubt Claude would take the risk without thinking twice. There was a tiny chance of his success in killing Stanley. But there would be no chance for him to dodge bullets in an escape from the Iron Ghosts.

III

Leila and Claude were having a good time on the balcony, taking advantage of a warm evening. They

263

watched the brightness of the day give way to the spotty glow of streetlights. After snorting a few lines of pure, uncut coke, they exchanged smiles and stupid remarks, and then laughed as if they had made some very witty jokes.

"I gotta go to the bathroom," Claude said, rising drunkenly to his feet. Leila giggled; this triggered Claude to burst into laughter, too. He did his best to aim his finger at her, and then stumbled gracefully into the room. A casual glance at the pager, which he had left at the dinner table before their snorting session, dragged him down from dreamland to harsh reality: The pager displayed the secret code number that meant to meet Marcel at a designated park outside of town, where they would be out of reach of any police surveillance gadgets. When Claude returned from the bathroom, Leila was still laughing.

"Wan' another snort?" she asked.

"Nah. I've got a meeting tonight."

"A meeting?" Leila laughed again.

"With Marcel," Claude whispered. She stopped laughing.

"Anything happened?" she asked.

"I don't know. For sure, I've got a job to do."

"Maybe I could help you with something?"

"Nah. Stop it."

A few minutes later, he was on his Harley. On it, he could lose any tail, take dangerous shortcuts, or dodge cars if need be. It was easier to escape at night, anyway, when the headlights of a car behind him could trigger his suspicions. Before he knew it, he was on the final leg of his journey to the park, a rural country road with no cars anywhere in the darkness.

A nice place to kill, he thought, steering his bike toward the entrance. Nobody would dare come to this place at night. What was Marcel up to now?

As he approached the end of the road, the bike's headlights captured the black bulk of a Jeep. He pulled up beside it, turned the ignition off, and sat motionless for a few moments, disoriented by sudden darkness and silence. The jeep door flew open and the light inside went on. Marcel stepped down and walked up to him. The bikers shook hands and exchanged greetings.

"Let's stretch our legs a bit," Marcel suggested. "Just in case my car's bugged."

"What's up?" Claude asked, walking alongside.

"There's a very big fish to fry." Marcel stopped, staring fixedly into Claude's eyes.

Claude responded with one of his best tough-guy looks, but said nothing, preferring to listen.

"You know the Madrid bar in the South End?" Marcel asked.

"Sure. It's in the industrial area. Lot's of truckers stop there."

"Right. The Iron Ghosts have taken it over. For now we can't do much about that. It's the Ghost's territory, and we don't have enough manpower to take it back, let alone keep it for long."

"What's the deal, then?" Claude asked.

"Hold on—Listen. To keep our baseball teams out, they've posted guards inside and outside the bar. I'd guess that all of them have guns. It wouldn't make sense for us to turn that place into a shooting gallery at this time. I wouldn't mention this to you for nothing," Marcel paused, "but your old friend visits this place very often. A stripper working there told us that."

Claude's muscles stiffened. His hand moved instinctively to his gun, but it wasn't there. His eyes had adjusted to the feeble light of the night, and he could now see Marcel's face, with its appreciative smile.

"Our hit teams are busy elsewhere," Marcel continued. "I can't provide you with much help, other than to let you know when he's there. The stripper will send me a signal."

"I don't need any help," Claude growled. "Leave it up to me."

"If you're going to shoot him inside, make it fast. Two, three seconds at the most, then rush out and fire away."

"I don't need your instructions," Claude responded rudely.

Marcel smiled.

"It's a risky job, Claude."

Claude uttered his customary rowdy laugh.

"I don't give a fuck."

"Here's five grand for now. I'll give you twenty more after the hit."

"Thanks." Claude was impressed. He took the thick roll of cash and stashed it in his breast pocket, smiling contentedly.

"That's all for now," Marcel said. "I'll leave first. You leave in a little while. Good night." He stretched out his hand and after a brief, firm handshake walked back to his car. The door of the Jeep slammed, and its engine roared to life. As its lights swept across the road and the vehicle rolled off, Claude climbed aboard his bike and sat, waiting until the hum of the Jeep engine died and quiet returned to the park. A rustle in the forest behind him grabbed his attention—the throaty cry of an animal, probably fighting a predator and pleading for mercy and help. From the depths of the forest, a bird responded with an agitated shriek, and then silence was restored. Claude turned the ignition on. The Harley obediently drowned all sounds of the night forest. Claude steered the bike to the road and took off with such powerful force that the front wheel jumped into the air, a foot above the surface. A few seconds of maddening acceleration, with only the rear wheel touching the ground, gave him the feeling of riding a wild, bucking horse.

The excitement of the risk associated with this hit and the chance of revenge against Stanley was overwhelming. His mind, like the bike's engine, was firing on all cylinders. Making dangerous turns on the dark roads, he fancied different scenarios for the kill. His first impulse was to enter the bar quickly, shoot Stanley, and then run back out, trusting his life to Lady Luck once more. But his last meeting with Stanley had taught him to appreciate life a little more. The chance of escaping the bullets of so many Iron Ghosts on their own turf simply did not exist. Even if those inside didn't react quickly, the guards at the door, who observe customers coming in and going out, would kill him. And if not them, then those on duty outside the bar would. So, what about waiting for Stanley outside? This might not be easy, either, as observing the site to make preparations for the shooting and escape would not pass unnoticed by the Iron Ghosts. All of a sudden, a more sophisticated and practical scheme began taking shape in his mind. Baring his teeth in a wolf's smile, he lifted the front wheel of the bike again, speeding up as if for a takeoff.

"We'll settle the score, Stanley," he said out loud. "I promise."

Back at home, he found Leila still in cocaine haze.

"I took another snort," she said with a stupid giggle. "Wan' some?"

"Yes," Claude answered excitedly. He stepped up to the table, unbuttoned his jacket, and threw the roll of bills down in front of her.

"Wow!" Leila cried. She glanced up at him, a look of surprise and curiosity on her face.

"An advance on a job," Claude explained, throwing his leather jacket and pants on the sofa.

"What job?" Leila asked as she lazily picked up his clothes.

"A very interesting job," he said. "And . . . there'll be something for you to do, as well."

He took her in his arms, a move that made her think he wanted sex. She leaned forward submissively. Instead of the expected, though, he whispered in her ear: "This fuckhead Stanley, the one who shot me . . . Remember?" Leila nodded. "I found out what bar he frequents. You'll dance there and take him out to our place."

Leila's head jerked back as she realized what Claude was saying. She stared at him with round, scared eyes.

"You wanna kill him?" she asked.

"Sure."

"What if someone at the bar hits on me? It's hard to dodge those guys if they want a girl, you know."

"Don't you worry. Hans will take you there and tell the owner that you're his old lady," Claude kept whispering. "I'm sure that it won't take long until Stanley zeroes in on you. You've gotta tell him he'll get to fuck only at your place. That's it."

"And," she nodded toward the money on the table, "that's the payment for the hit?"

"This is only an advance. Much more is coming."

"They'll be after us for the rest of our lives," she said. She pressed her cheek against his.

268

"They'll never know who did it," Claude said with confidence. "Right after that, we'll move away, to another place. Maybe we'll travel for a few months. Our club will arrange us a place in B.C.—we have a chapter there."

"What's next, then?"

"I'll talk to Hans tomorrow morning. We need a big car for this. Hans will help." Claude tightened his embrace. "Don't worry, Leila. This is the last job that you'll ever do. I'm back on my feet. We'll have lots of fun together."

"I've never taken part in a murder," she whispered.

"This is the last job, Leila. Trust me. Nobody will ever know who did it. We'll live in B.C. or another province. Nobody will ever recognize you."

IV

They sat in darkness; the only light in the room came from some streetlights outside. It was close to 1 o'clock in the morning, and Leila would soon finish her last dance and come back with Stanley. Claude took his metal rod out of the closet and wrapped it in a kitchen towel. When he returned to the sofa, Hans was fumbling with a pack of cigarettes. Even in the dark, Claude could see his fingers trembling.

"What do you need a sleeping bag for?" Hans asked, drawing in the smoke.

"We'll wrap him up in it. I don't want to kill him here— just knock him out. We must quickly put him into the sleeping bag and tie him up tight. I have some good strong rope. In the sleeping bag, we can keep an eye on him and make sure that he won't be able to move. We have to take him out and make him talk. This guy must have lots of money."

269

"Something feels wrong," Hans said and cleared his throat.

"C'mon, Hans. Everything's going well. You see, he hit on Leila the very first night he saw her. He wanted to fuck her right there in the owner's office. But she told him, 'Not here, Stanley. Only in my place, nowhere else. And not tonight, 'cause my boyfriend is gonna take me home tonight. Let's do it tomorrow.'"

Claude laughed. "Clever girl, she is. He believed every single word."

"You threw a shovel into the car. What's that for?"

"We have to bury him, Hans. I know a nice place. It's a farm, not that far of a drive away."

Hans grumbled.

"Something's just not to my liking," he said, shaking his head.

"Look, everything's going smoothly," Claude went on, "even better than I expected."

"That's what worries me," Hans said. "My old buddy, the one I used to take care of cars for, always told me that if something goes too well at the outset, expect trouble in the future. He was always right. He's dead now."

The pager on the table beeped. Claude rushed to grab it.

"I can't believe it," he said in a low voice, looking at the code. "They're coming, Hans. Now, take this sleeping bag. We'll pack him in it nicely." Claude stashed the rod under his belt. "Turn the light off in the staircase. Hold the flashlight, just in case. Let's go."

He stood up and led the way out. Hans followed with the sleeping bag, to the staircase and then to the ground floor, where they took their positions on both sides of the rear entrance.

After Hans turned the light off, almost nothing could be seen inside.

"I wanna smoke," Hans said. "Just a few puffs."

"No," Claude said with irritation in his voice. "He'd be able to smell the smoke. This fuckhead is too fast and could have a gun."

No single mistake could be made with Stanley. Not one tiny error. Claude knew too well how dangerous this Ghost was.

Twenty minutes passed—for Claude, it seemed an eternity. *How does Hans feel?* he thought. *Poor devil is scared to death. Not good.*

At last they heard a car coming into the parking lot, and then they heard approaching voices.

"Please come in." It was Leila.

"It's damn dark here," Claude heard Stanley saying.

As soon as he crossed the threshold, Claude hit the back of Stanley's head with the wrapped metal rod. Stanley fell down, not uttering a sound.

"Go home, Leila," Claude demanded in a low voice. "Fast—now."

She disappeared in an instant. Claude turned on the dim staircase light and began spreading the sleeping bag on the floor. Hans, it seemed, had revived. He helped with spreading the bag and putting Stanley inside it. They pulled up the zipper, quickly wrapped their prisoner with the nylon rope, and threw the package in the back of a stolen Jeep.

"Is he alive?" Hans asked, jumping into the driver's seat.

Claude studied Stanley's face, which was sticking out above the top of the sleeping bag.

"Yah, he is. Let him relax a bit. He'll be having a tough time tonight."

Hans started the car and drove out of the parking lot.

"This was a good one," Claude said with a contented smile. "Smooth and easy. I told you so, Hans, I told you so. This is the first time that I've ever liked Stanley. Good chap, he is, isn't he?"

"Let's kill him and throw him into a lake somewhere," suggested Hans. "Let's just finish him as soon as possible."

"What's the rush?" Claude was in a good mood. "I can't let my friend Stanley go that quick." He laughed heartily.

Stanley groaned.

"You see, he's alive. I told you." Claude was addressing Hans, but had turned his head to make sure that Stanley heard him.

"What the fuck is going on?" shouted Stanley in a somewhat muffled voice. He began twisting, kicking, and shaking, trying to free himself from the tight rope.

"Hi, Stanley," Claude turned in the seat and greeted him. "Did you sleep well? Do you remember me?"

"What the fuck you are doing?" Stanley shouted again. "What do you want?"

"I wanna kill you, my friend." Claude couldn't help but laugh. "I love killing my old friends."

"You'll pay for this, " Stanley said. "You'd better let me go."

Claude uttered his rowdy laugh.

"It's too late for making bargains," he said in mocking regret. "How'd yah prefer me to kill yah?"

"Stop it," shouted Stanley again. "Stop it."

"He doesn't want us to kill him." Now Claude was pretending to address Hans. "What should we do?"

"Forget it. Let's finish him as soon as possible." Hans was angry and nervous, but Claude dismissed it.

"Actually, I know what we can do . . . ," Claude said slowly, as if in thought. "He doesn't want us to kill him, so let's not kill him. Let's bury him alive. Eh?" Claude leaned back, roaring with laugher.

"Are you serious?" Hans asked.

"You know me, Hans. And you know me, Stanley, don't you?" He turned back again, as if to make sure that Stanley heard him.

"Let me go!" Stanley sounded nearly crazy. "Let me the hell go!"

Claude uttered his rowdy laugh again. He was very excited with this opportunity for an easy kill.

"Drop it, Claude," Hans insisted. "Let's finish this. My rule is, the quicker, the better. Let's not take a chance."

"You fucking idiots!" Stanley resumed his shouting. "What do you want? Tell me what you want. Maybe we could make a deal."

Claude turned back.

"You can't bargain your way out of your grave," he said. "But if you tell me where you keep your money, I'll shoot you in the head—a nice, quick death for such a pig as yourself."

"At home. In the basement. Let me go, guys, and I'll give you all my money."

"Where in the basement?" Claude asked. To his surprise, the response was silence.

"I'll make him talk," Claude announced, as if speaking to himself. "He'll talk. Stop the car."

"Hold it!" Stanley resumed talking. "In the right corner of the basement. The last three tiles cover a metal case. The money's there."

Hans uttered a gurgling sound, as if rinsing his throat.

"How much is there?" Claude asked.

273

"Four-hundred thousand and something."

Claude and Hans fell silent.

"Where do you live?" Claude asked. This time there was no sadistic note in his voice.

"187 Parkdale Crescent. But you couldn't get in there. It's a tricky system. Take me there and I'll get you the money."

Claude looked back at the rear seat, where Stanley was wrapped in the sleeping bag. Hans drove in silence. In the meantime, Claude was thinking hard and fast. A new, completely different game had started. He had no doubt that Stanley was telling the truth. The punishment for such a lie would be horrific. It was unlikely that Stanley would want to complicate his predicament further. What Stanley was probably hoping was that once Claude and Hans had their hands on his money, they would kill him quickly and painlessly, a much better end than going through the horrors of being buried alive.

On the other hand, Stanley might also be hoping that with such temptation, Claude and Hans would fight with each other for the treasure.

"Go that way." Claude pointed a finger to the left.

"Why?" asked Hans in surprise. "I know where Parkdale Crescent is, and it's not that way."

"Go that way," Claude repeated, irritated. "We're going to bury this jerk first."

Looking back at Stanley, he warned: "We will bury you—alive."

Stanley began shouting again; this time the shouts were desperate and incomprehensible.

"I can't stand it," Hans said. "I can't."

"I'll calm him down," Claude growled. "I know what to do. I'll break his nose." Claude looked back with a hoarse laugh.

"Shut up, corpse." Claude was delighted with his joke. "Corpse. Ha, ha! Shut up!"

He opened the toolbox between the seats and fished out a dirty rag, probably used by the owner to wipe his greasy hands.

"Stop the car," he commanded. When the Jeep stopped, Claude stepped down, opened the rear door, and began stuffing the dirty cloth into Stanley's mouth. Stanley vigorously resisted, turning his head quickly and forcefully from one side to the other and trying to shift himself back and forth.

"He doesn't want this rag in his mouth," Claude said with mocking notes of regret. He went back to the front seat, took the biggest wrench from the toolbox, returned to the back door, and raised it, preparing to crush Stanley's left eye and nose. The wrench landed with remarkable accuracy; blood splashed all over the rear of the car. His terrified shrieks made Stanley's jaws opened wide enough to accommodate the rag. Claude used all his force to stuff it inside his mouth, as far as it would go. Now Stanley was only able to utter muffled sounds through his broken nose.

"You see," Claude said, returning to his seat, "I know how to deal with the Ghosts." There was tremendous pride in his tone.

On the way to the farm, Hans didn't utter a single word. Claude glanced at him once in awhile with a smile: The guy was terrified.

When they arrived, the farm seemed to have been deserted by its owners. Claude took the shovel and began digging a grave behind the barn, not far from the place

275

where Stash was buried. The soil was soft and yielded easily to his shovel. Not accustomed to this kind of work, he soon grew tired and gave the shovel to Hans. Hans worked in silence. When the grave was deep enough, they went to the car, lifted Stanley out, and carried his twisting, shaking body toward it. After throwing him into the grave, Claude began pushing earth back into the hole. Stanley worked desperately to get out; he moved frantically, turning from side to side and trying to get to his feet. His silent, determined struggle was unreal and terrifying. His face, distorted by horror and hatred and covered with blood, looked yellow and pale in the moonlight.

"Son of a bitch," Claude growled. He jumped into the grave, stamping his feet on Stanley's face.

"Push it," he commanded to Hans. "Push as much earth as you can. That's good. A bit more." When the soil covered Stanley's face, Claude jumped a few more times to make sure that the surface was hard enough to sustain the last agonizing resistance of the living corpse below it. Claude stepped up and out, picked up the shovel, and pushed the rest of the soil into the grave. Hans was not much help anymore. His hands were shaking. It seemed that he had lost all his strength.

"I have some pot," Claude said. He sat down on the grave and put his hand in his breast pocket. "Let's smoke a bit."

Hans crouched nearby and took the weed from the small metal box that Claude held in his outstretched hand.

"Let's get out of here," Hans said, his voice trembling. "Let's fuckin' get out of here, Claude. I don't like it at all."

"We did a good job, Hans." Claude slapped his back with appreciative laughter. He lit a joint and gave the lighter to Hans. "Just a few tokes, Hans, then off we go. Just a few tokes." He took a deep drag himself.

On the way back, they didn't speak. Silence filled the car like black, choking tar. Claude wasn't laughing anymore. He realized that he had pushed Hans too far. Hans was visibly shaken; his pale face looked dead even in the darkness of the car.

"Here," Hans said, bringing the car to a complete stop. His voice was coarse and broken. He stepped out of the car, leaving the engine running. Bending over, he grasped the open door with both hands, his body shaking while he vomited.

"We have to go a few blocks more," Claude said.

"No. I ain't going anywhere, Claude. You go yourself." He straightened up, wiping his mouth.

"What the fuck you are talking about?" Claude had lost his temper. "Help me unlock the door in the house."

"I won't. You don't need me there. Just break the window and get in. For sure, there's no alarm system. It's a biker's house."

Hans began walking down a side street.

"Motherfucker!" Claude shouted at his back. Hans vanished into the night.

Claude got behind the wheel and continued toward Stanley's house. He pulled up on the opposite side of the road and walked across the street, scanning the neighborhood for any suspicious activity. Nobody was in sight. Stanley's house seemed uninhabited. Its windows, like large black eyes, were staring at him in menacing silence. Claude went behind the house, holding the wrench in his hand. There, he knocked out a basement window and crawled in, careful not to scratch his skin on the glass shards that remained in the window frame.

Stretching his hands ahead of him in the total darkness, he made his way through the basement, until by pure chance he touched a wall and found a light switch. The light was too bright for him at first, and he squinted as he looked around. The space was nicely finished, with a bar, cozy chairs, and some coffee tables. In the corner, where the money was supposed to be, stood a huge vase with artificial flowers in it.

Claude went upstairs first, trying to make as little noise as possible. If anybody was there, he would have to be killed. The staircase squeaked under his feet, loud unnerving sounds in the dead silence of the house. Claude turned the lights on in each bedroom, three of them. Nobody was there. Even in such a stressful moment, Claude managed to notice that the furniture was very expensive. The owner must have lived a good life, no doubt. Then he rushed to the basement again. Only now, he realized that there were no tiles on the floor. It was covered by a gray carpet. Claude moved the vase, tore the edge of the carpet up, and saw bare concrete under it.

Stanley had cheated him.

"No damned money," he whispered, fuming. "Sucker."

He got up and went upstairs to the ground floor, without looking back. When he unlocked the front door and stepped out, he saw a police car on the street, parked directly in front of him.

"Hands up," shouted someone from behind the car. "Don't move. Police."

Claude obeyed the command. Now, he understood what Stanley had hoped for. His house was under surveillance. That was why it had taken so little time for a squad car to arrive. Two huge policemen jumped on him, twisted his arms behind this back, put handcuffs on them, and then dragged him to the police car, pushing him inside.

The game was over. Now, he was back to square one.

V

Claude couldn't sleep. His cell, built like a concrete box, didn't have a single piece of furniture, or even a rug, to rest on. His face was swollen from the punches the policemen had given him in response to some abusive words he had offered while he was being handcuffed. He was the only one in the cell. Sitting on the cold floor, he thought about his situation.

It was clear to him that long years in jail were in the cards now. Lady Luck had not been kind to him tonight. The question was, What would the cops be able to find out about the hit? Had Hans been arrested? If not, they would never know about Stanley's death. Even having a wrench with Stanley's blood on it, they would not be able to lay charges against him. Claude had worn gloves during the ordeal with Stanley and had instructed Hans to do the same. As far as his other hits were concerned, they didn't know anything about them, that's for sure. For breaking into a house with the wrench . . . Well, if it hadn't had blood on it, the only charge against him would have been breaking into the house. It wasn't even a robbery, since he had taken nothing.

At 7 o'clock in the morning, two policemen unlocked his cell. They took him to a room where a detective in civilian clothes sat at a desk, his face bearing traces of little sleep. Claude recognized him at once as Serge Gorte, the one who had talked to him in the hospital. Naturally, Claude thought, he'd been awakened early because of this important event: A biker had been arrested during an attempted robbery. One cop took a position at the entrance, the other sat beside Claude. Both of them carried guns.

"My old acquaintance," Serge said with a smile. Claude shrugged his shoulders.

"Tell me, how'd you do it? How'd you kill Stanley? Who was your accomplice?"

"I ain't killed nobody. What are you talking about?"

"I'm talking about murder. You've been after him for quite awhile. And, now you've done it. We have all the evidence."

"What fuckin' evidence do you have?" Claude asked in a rough voice.

"A wrench with his blood on it. Your arrest in his house. Where did you bury him?"

"You shove your fuckin' evidence up your fuckin' ass," Claude barked. "No court would find that good enough to lock me up. You have to move your ass to find more." He uttered his usual rowdy laugh.

Serge remained calm and composed. He even smiled in false sympathy with Claude's arguments.

"Funny," Serge said, "you're right. We don't have sufficient evidence at this moment. Mind you, it's only half past seven in the morning. Suppose we just give the court our insufficient evidence. The court would charge you with the attempted robbery. But the Iron Ghosts would quickly figure out two plus two. They have far better methods than we do for discovering the truth."

Serge paused for a few moments, enjoying the effects of his words. Claude ground his teeth. He knew how the Ghosts would find the truth.

"Exactly!" Serge continued with the same air of understanding and sympathy, as if he had read what was going on in Claude's mind. "Your guess is correct. They'd find you and do the same to you. I doubt that you would be able to escape their revenge. There are too many of them, these Iron Ghosts. What would happen to you in jail? Stanley wasn't just an ordinary guy. They'll hunt you the rest of your life."

Claude stared at Serge, trying to cool himself down. With the handcuffs on his wrists, he contemplated jumping forward and biting Serge in the throat.

"Actually, it won't be that hard for the Iron Ghosts to find the missing evidence," Serge interrupted Claude's train of thought. "You had an accomplice. We'll find him. They'll find him, too." Serge's stare became intense. "He'll talk."

Claude nodded.

"Fuck you."

Serge sighed.

"You remember, I showed you the photograph of Norman and his wife, the woman you killed. He's now in our custody. He's prepared to testify against you, and Marcel. Life without parole—that's what's waiting for you around the corner."

Is he bluffing? Claude thought.

"By the way, the Devil's Knights will be after you, as well. You probably think that we'll put you in a jail where they hold the upper hand. Not necessarily so, Claude. But even if we didn't, they'd kill you eventually anyway. You know too much. Marcel wouldn't take the risk of having a potential witness against him serving a life sentence. Your gang, or the other, it doesn't make much difference when you consider your future."

He's not bluffing; it would be better to commit suicide than face any of those choices, Claude thought.

"That's not all. You have a girlfriend. She'll talk. Most likely, she'll be in jail, too. You'll never see her again."

That thought caused Claude to blink. He cleared his throat.

"What's your point?" he croaked.

"We want your cooperation. Putting you in jail isn't a big deal for us. We're after top-ranking Devil's Knights. Particularly, your boss, Marcel. We need you as a witness against him."

"What would you offer for that?" Claude asked. Serge straightened up with a jolt, fixing a gimlet-eyed stare on Claude.

"We'll put you in the witness protection program. We'll change your identity . . ." he started. The two policemen guarding Claude exchanged nervous, excited glances with Serge. Serge flapped his eyelashes, as if tasting a good cognac. Claude felt a powerful urge to vomit.

"Take off his handcuffs," Serge commanded.

The policemen rushed to unlock them. Claude rubbed his wrists.

"I wanna go to the bathroom."

"Take him." Serge nodded to the policemen. In the bathroom, Claude vomited into filthy toilet. It seemed to him that his guts were coming out through his throat. His negotiations for survival had begun.

Chapter 9

I

The flood of information from Claude's confession made huge headlines in all the newspapers, magazines, and television shows. But in the midst of the hoopla about police success in fighting the biker gangs, Serge Gorte remained calm and as busy as ever. He actually worked even longer hours than before, collecting material facts, supervising autopsies, analyzing lab results, and then assembling all this information into logical order to prove without any doubt the guilt of those accused.

As soon as Claude told the story of Stanley's death, Serge sent a team to the farm. The bodies of Stanley and Stash were exhumed and autopsied. Stanley's body was later released to the Iron Ghosts, and a lavishly grand funeral was announced.

A police patrol was placed on guard outside the graveyard that day to stave off any possible disturbance from the Devil's Knights or one of their puppet gangs. The last thing the police wanted was a skirmish in the graveyard, which would result in the police being blamed for not being able to maintain order.

Out of professional curiosity, Serge arrived at the cemetery one hour before the motorcade arrived to observe the funeral. He could have obtained reports about the event from officers in the lower ranks, but preferred to rely on his own observations, which he felt were far superior to those of anyone else. From his vantage point, which was behind a huge gravestone located little more than a hundred yards from the fresh grave, he recalled the events of that unforgettable morning when Claude had agreed to cooperate with the police. Although Serge had prepared himself well for the interrogation, he had never expected it to be such a huge success. If only Claude had known that most of his taunts and accusations had been bluffs, or near bluffs. . . . First of all, at that time, Norman had not been under arrest. Second, although Serge had felt sure that Claude had killed Stanley and that there had been an accomplice, he'd had no proof of either.

Serge's threats about the inevitable revenge of the Iron Ghosts and the possibility of Claude being killed by the Devil's Knights were real concerns, worries that Claude understood, and that put him off balance. But none of those had been the reason that Claude had rolled over. This biker was so obsessed with his status and image in the underworld that in all likelihood he would have accepted his death as part and parcel of his gruesome profession. That's why Serge began talking about the girlfriend, the one he didn't know existed.

This was another sheer bluff on his side. He had recalled the girl only that morning, on the way to the police station. She had been at Claude's bedside in the hospital. She was too beautiful to have been an occasional broad. Serge then remembered his thoughts about the rather strange makeup of the human mind. Very often, even the most despicable criminals fell in love with a woman only to behave like an inexperienced schoolboy, losing all commanding attitude and gangster pride for a weak, helpless object of love.

So, Serge concluded then, she must have been his old lady, the girl he was likely in love with. If that was the case, Claude's feelings might outweigh all other considerations. Serge had guessed right. After his remarks about the girlfriend, Claude's face had grown deadly pale. Serge clearly saw that he was devastated. That was when the tough demeanor of this contract killer had cracked.

A lot of work had yet to be done to lay formal charges against Marcel. The only proof of his participation in crimes was Claude's testimony. As expected, the gang's lawyers unleashed a vicious campaign that questioned the validity of such testimonies. They were right in a way, Serge admitted to himself. The benefits for the informer were enormous: Along with significantly reduced sentences for all the horrendous crimes he had committed, he would get huge financial rewards, witness protection, and a comparatively comfortable life in prison. However, the testimony of this one witness would take them further than any investigation had gone before; no other proof of participation in criminal activity had been found, or would be found, because the gang leaders did not commit any crimes themselves. And then Norman. For sure, he'll be arrested. Once in the custody . . .

At last, the funeral procession arrived. A long, impressive escort of motorcycles rolled along the streets to the cemetery—the place where the spirits of the dead live on in the good memories of the living.

A few speeches were made. Serge stood far away, watching the bikers, trying not to be too conspicuous but mingling with the occasional visitor. Soon the place was deserted. Serge waited a few minutes longer, after the last biker had left, just to make sure that nothing else was going to happen. A large crow flew over his head and settled on a tree branch. Folding its black wings, the bird uttered a furious cry, after which silence enveloped the beautiful and sad land of death.

Serge was about to leave when he noticed a lone figure, dressed in black, approaching Stanley's grave. It was a woman, apparently pregnant, hiding her head under a hood. She walked up to the grave, threw a single rose on it, and wiped silent tears from her eyes. For a few minutes, she stood almost motionless, slightly nodding her head as if talking to the one under the ground. And then she left, stumbling and staring forward, as if blind. Serge followed her with curiosity and very little compassion. This was his profession: Every day he dealt with a river filled with human blood, filth, tears, and despair, with no beginning and no end in sight. For him, this woman was just a potential witness or source of information on bikers. Although he couldn't see her face, he had a strange feeling that he had seen her somewhere before. But at that moment, he couldn't remember exactly under what circumstances they had met. When she climbed into the driver's seat of her car, he pulled out a notebook and wrote down her license plate number.

Strangely enough, he thought, a lot of the information he collected would be about those who were already dead and therefore out of reach of the law or revenge. For some reason, though, it was important for his investigation to find the truth, to discover the victims and those who had committed the crimes against them, even if they had ceased to exist. *All human sins are recorded in heaven,* he thought; *their crimes are recorded in police files.*

II

The election campaign turned out to be a fierce struggle among savvy politicians, many of them new to the political landscape. Monica expected an easy victory on the huge wave of her achievements against organized crime. Instead, she had been forced to defend herself and her government for the poor handling of the biker's war, for an inability to stop the bloodshed sooner, for negligence, incompetence, and lack of ingenuity—all the failures demonstrated by politicians and the police in dealing with gangs and the illegal drug trade. Her sharpest opponents accused her of compromising the truth and public interest in favor of political correctness.

In an article in one of the largest newspapers, a journalist called her a chameleon. "She defends vocal minorities regardless of how just or fair their requests are," the journalist claimed. "Initially she was against the anti-gang law on the grounds of its unconstitutionality but changed her stand later, perhaps for personal reasons." Now, according to the journalist, she wanted to get credit for her activity, which was more like a public relations campaign than a show of the productive work of a politician guarding her constituents.

Still, Monica did get reelected—by a very thin margin. After all the noisy celebrations, congratulations, and speeches, she decided to relax and gladly accepted an invitation to attend a concert of a famous pianist from Europe. She entered the theater lobby, following a crowd of people who had already gone inside to wait for the concert hall doors to open.

Many in the crowd recognized her, some with appreciative smiles, others with intense curiosity in their eyes. Throwing casual, sideways glances, Monica noticed people talking while staring at her, likely gossiping and exchanging views about her. She recalled how, in her younger years, she had been sitting on a bench with a schoolgirl friend when they saw a prominent person—she had forgotten her name by now—walking by. No tiny detail escaped their attention then: not the dress of that woman, not her gait, her looks, or her hair. Now, Monica thought, it was her turn to be the center of attention and to feel, sometimes, not very welcome.

Finally, the doors opened and people began pouring into the concert hall. As Monica took her place in one of the front rows, she had a strange feeling that she was being watched by someone. When the pianist came out and bowed to the public, her attention turned to the stage. After a short round of welcoming applause, the European sat at his stool and ran his fingers over the keyboard of the grand piano. The magical sounds of Beethoven, magnified by the outstanding performance of this musician, took her mind to a place of pleasure and fantasy, a place that only true art can create, in the way only true art can.

During intermission, she went to the lobby for a glass of wine. Gently pushing her way through the crowd, she heard a soft voice behind her right shoulder.

"Good evening, Monica."

She turned around. A short, stocky man stood there. His round face and cold blue eyes seemed familiar. A blonde woman was holding his hand, shy admiration on her face.

"Have you forgotten me?" The man smiled, as if hoping Monica would more easily recognize him that way. Indeed, in the next instant, she smiled in apologetic, pleasant surprise.

"Oh—Serge Gorte!" Monica stretched both arms towards him for a handshake. "How could I possibly forget you? You're the expert on biker gangs in Canada. How nice to see you."

"That's very flattering," Serge bowed. "This is my wife, Miriam." He nodded toward the lady beside him. "She must be given a great deal of credit for my career. Without her patience, understanding, and help I wouldn't have done much."

"Come on, Serge," Miriam said. She was slightly embarrassed and threw him a loving, happy glance.

"How is Toulouse doing these days?" Serge asked.

"Actually, very well. The collection agency stopped threatening him—perhaps after your interference. They sent him a few reminder letters but didn't bother him much. He's returned their money to them. Do you know what happened to the agency?"

"Its owner was killed," Serge said. "He was one of the high-ranking members of the Devil's Knights gang. His own gang killed him."

"How awful those people are," Monica remarked. "I've been busy with other matters, particularly so after you arrested so many of them in both gangs. But I know that there is much less violence lately, thanks to your efforts."

"I'm just a small cog in a huge machine," Serge said. Monica noticed that something distracted his attention from her. She followed Serge's stare and saw a man passing by with a delicate woman clutching his arm. Monica remembered his neck—big and thick like a wrestler's—and was trying to recall where she had seen him. His face radiated strength and confidence.

"Hi," Serge said as the couple was passing by. "What a surprise."

"It's better to meet here than at your place," the man responded sharply, obviously stopping only out of courtesy. His stare and posture were a weird mix of animosity, ridicule, and mocking obedience.

Monica raised her eyebrows. The man had appropriate manners, but should not have spoken or acted that way.

"This is my wife, Kathy," the man continued more casually, looking directly at Serge. The woman beside him smiled amiably to Monica and Serge.

"How do you like the concert?" Serge asked.

"I'm not fond of classical music, but my wife is," the man said. "I have to treat her, once in awhile." He bowed slightly toward Serge, and turned, ready to depart without another word.

"See you later," Serge bowed in return.

"I hope not," the man was quick to respond, with a feigned friendly smile. He left, his wife following him.

"He looks like a decent man," Monica remarked, her bewildered face turned to Serge. "How could he speak that way? I'm surprised that you talked to him."

"That man," Serge informed her, "is president of the Devil's Knights, Marcel Barette. I've talked to him a few times in my office. He has a good reason for not wanting to see me there later."

Monica was astonished.

"Unbelievable!" she exclaimed. "I'd never have taken him for a hoodlum."

"So far as a 'hoodlum' is concerned, he isn't. If he was one, it would have been a long time ago. As to why he's here, I've noticed a few other members of their club strolling in the foyer. Nobody would suspect bikers would gather at a symphony music performance. They can discuss urgent business matters here without worrying about surveillance. My guess is something important is cooking."

"There was a lot of ballyhoo in the newspapers about a former biker who turned informant. Is it true—that at last you have a live witness against Marcel? Yet he's still a free man, walking around and probably getting along with his hideous crimes."

"Well, you see," Serge began, "lawyers are fairly vocal about how trustworthy such testimonies are. 'How could the judge trust the informant?' they ask. 'Look how many benefits the collaborator gets,' they say. 'He gets off the hook with his crimes; he gets money. For a criminal with no virtues, it's an easy escape from punishment at the expense of others. Why wouldn't he testify against everyone?'"

"But . . . the confession this man gave makes it obvious that this . . . Marcel . . . is the one who masterminded many assassinations. You can't, you mustn't let him off the hook. I don't believe that whoever the judge is, he or she could be that stupid."

Serge smiled.

"It's not a matter of stupidity, Monica. The case is gaining publicity. The judge must now enter into the political game—from now on, he'll be dealing not only with the jury, but also with the general public. The public now becomes the jury. You see? He has to make a political decision. You know better than I do what that means. By the way, that's where publicity helps the bikers. They challenge our adherence to the constitution, specifically to the principle of being innocent until proven guilty."

"I understand that," Monica said firmly. In her area of expertise, she spoke with great authority. "I assure you that the public would support the judge against the Devil's

Knights. The political climate is ripe for such a decision, even in the absence of material evidence."

Serge was nodding as she spoke. His eyes got shiny and kind, as if he had just finished a good dinner with a bottle of excellent French wine.

"I'm not so sure. Mind you, publicity and public opinion are no substitutes for each other. The most vocal groups get the most attention. Who are the noisiest ones? Different kinds of leftists, libertarians, feminists, lawyers, you name it. They would kick-off a screaming campaign about the abuse of civil rights and freedoms. They would inform the public that the presumption of innocence has been trumped. No one, they would say, including the Devil's Knights, should be denied fair justice."

Monica's stare hardened. She happened to lean toward all the groups Serge had mentioned. She was a civil rights activist, a feminist, and a prominent supporter of minority group rights.

"I appreciate your comments, Serge," she said, grimacing in displeasure. "I suspect we should be getting back inside. Have a nice evening."

III

Claude was kept in a cell at the police station, under the watchful eyes of police guards. He was too valuable a witness to risk his life in jail, where both the Devil's Knights and the Iron Ghosts would be able to carry out numerous ways to kill him. To allow Claude to feel better about his new position as a traitor, a rat despised by all in the criminal world, he was allowed privileges far beyond the normal limits.

For example, Leila was allowed to visit him in his room—a depressing, confined space with bare walls, dirty stains of unidentifiable origin, a filthy floor, a small bed, a toilet, and a single plastic chair, which was not strong enough to withstand the abuse of two sex-obsessed lovers. Claude used the furniture to its fullest: He turned Leila this way and that on it, arranging the parts of her body into positions that could have been used in a textbook for a yoga class. His love for this girl, his physical intimacy with her, became more blissful and thrilling than all the adventures of his brutal life.

She smuggled in some pot for him—thoughtful girl that she was. He enjoyed it immensely because it sharpened all his senses. When she left, he felt the pain of separation and loneliness. This feeling grew stronger from visit to visit. There was a period of a week or more—he lost track of the passing days because they were dull and uneventful— when, for some reason, the police did not grant them their date. One of those nights, she came to him in his dreams. She was sweet, as usual, but did not yield to his passion, or speak. In fact, she slipped out of his hands, like a snake. The following morning, he fancied himself in the future, at the end of his fifteen-year sentence, as agreed upon in his deal with the justice system. That future was wonderful, and Leila was an integral part of it.

It may not be that bad, after all, to spend only fifteen years, he pondered. Of course, there was a risk of being killed by bikers, but who cares? Death had been his everyday reality. The dead feel nothing. Life, that's what counts. He would come out of the system almost a millionaire, a rich man, with a different identity, and, perhaps, a different mentality. His life would become an endless journey of love with Leila, travel to different lands, motorcycle rides, and a secluded home somewhere on the ocean shore of British Columbia.

A sudden thought tossed him from his dreamland: What if she didn't wait for him? What if she found another love?

Leila was the only human in his life who had ever cared about him. She was not only his lover but also his friend. His parents were dead, and he had no relatives or genuine friends. Without her, loneliness would be his destiny to the grave. This thought terrified him more than death. He jumped up from the bed and pounded the door.

"I wanna talk to Serge. Now. It's important," he said, when a policeman came to the door.

When such a witness says that he has something important to say, guards don't wait long. Serge came at once, this time without a smile. With the instincts of a wild animal, Claude sensed that something serious had happened. But there had been thousands of serious things happening since he'd gotten involved with the Devil's Knights. He couldn't care less for anyone else's trouble in his current situation.

"I wanna meet Leila," he said.

"We can't do that anymore," was the response. Serge stared at him with a blank face.

"Listen. This is very important. I'll help you a lot. I know that it's against the rules to let her in, but let me have just one last exception."

"It's not my decision. I never minded . . ." Serge cleared his throat.

"Leila is dead."

"What?" Claude stood still. "You said 'dead'?" he screamed. "Is that what you said? What are you talking about?"

Serge bent his head, as if studying the cracks in the wooden table. Claude stood, dumbfounded. A professional killer, who had seen many deaths from his own hands, he was unable to comprehend that Leila could be dead.

"Sit down." Serge cleared his throat, again. His invitation was timely because Claude's legs could not have supported him much longer. He collapsed on a stool and placed his elbows on the table, grasping his face with his large hands.

"When did it happen?" he croaked, coming to grips with reality.

"Two days ago. Three men were there, allegedly from the Iron Ghosts. They spent a few hours with her."

A minute of thoughtful silence made Claude look twenty years older. His face grew pale, almost green.

"How could you let that happen?" Claude asked. Serge said nothing. A trace of compassion, unusual for a crime crusader, flickered in his eyes.

"Take me back to my cell," Claude said, hardly moving his lips. "I need to rest." He was afraid of asking more questions. He didn't have to have much imagination to guess what had happened during Leila's final hours. He walked, blind, to his cell, and threw himself on the bed. In a fit of depression, Claude pulled the blanket over his head, covering himself from head to toe, seeking refuge from the terrible reality, and then lay motionless, as if in a coma.

He longed to be magically taken to a desolate, distant land where no human existed to watch his misery, where he could die hopeless and defeated. Instead, memories took him back to his childhood, which was devoid of anything even remotely resembling love. His mother, an alcoholic prostitute, performed her sex trade in broad daylight, just across from his bed. Everyone abused, kicked, and humiliated him, including his mother. She'd died when he was ten. By that time, he had already reached the point of no return. As far back as he could remember, there had only been one source of light, warmth, and tenderness: Leila. Now, that light had been put out. Disoriented, he could see neither present nor future. A message from heaven had been brought to him, to the Messenger of Death: "You have nothing to do on Earth anymore. You have no place among normal people, no place even among outcasts."

Epilogue

This meeting of the Ministry of Justice was to be devoted to summing up the government's efforts to curb the activities of organized crime. All members of the task force who had worked on the anti-gang legislation had been invited. As had become her habit, Monica arrived fifteen minutes early to have a cup of coffee and chat with colleagues and acquaintances. The first person she saw was Bertrand, who was consuming a Danish with the determination of a hungry soldier.

"Nice to see you, Monica," he said while she settled in across the table.

"We're having dinner after the session," she reminded him.

"True. That's why I'm eating a Danish. It whets my appetite."

"I've heard that you locked Marcel in jail for life," she said. "Congratulations on the huge success in fighting organized crime, Bertrand. I hope that the anti-gang law that was adopted by the government helped to achieve this goal."

"It sure did," Bertrand nodded. A mocking smile appeared on his face.

"You're one of the speakers tonight," Monica said. "Your speeches are always interesting and informative."

Bertrand gave her an appreciative nod.

"Thanks."

"As I understand, the judge did accept the testimony of the informer, Claude Pichette," Monica said. "Otherwise, it would not have been possible to convict him, I guess?"

"It's not quite that simple. There was another witness against Marcel by the name of Norman Vincent. You must have read about him in the newspapers."

"Yes, I did," Monica confirmed.

"The informer admitted to killing Norman's wife. After Norman's testimony corroborated that part of the informer's story, all allegations from the informer were accepted at face value. But there were numerous pieces of other evidence, of course, that also supported the fact that he was telling the truth. Many crimes and many mysteries have been solved with his help, and each of those resolutions gave even more credibility to his testimony against Marcel."

"Very interesting. Who's the leader of this gang now?"

"A very remarkable personality, I'll admit. Techie is his nickname. He's—" Bertrand didn't get to finish his sentence because an announcement was being made directing them to enter the hall. They moved inside, and Monica took a seat at one of the tables in front of the podium.

The first speaker was a representative of the Ministry of Justice. In a monotonous, dull speech, he drowned the audience in countless facts and statistics, supporting the view that the government had achieved great success in fighting organized crime. "Gangs are not fighting on our streets anymore," he concluded. "We broke their spines. Seeing as life in our city has returned to normal, we're reducing police funding to the level that existed before the war between the two gangs erupted. I believe that we taught a good lesson to the whole underworld. It won't be very soon, if ever, that they return to their former capacity."

The next speaker was Bertrand. As usual, he had no notes with him and did not resort to a computer that showed exhibits and charts, but his speech impressed everyone in the audience. He told them that more than ten high-ranking Devil's Knights had been arrested and were being kept in prison until their trial dates. And a much, much greater number of their associates were in jail with an abundance of proven evidence against them. Almost half of the top echelon of the Iron Ghosts was in prison, too, he announced. There had been massive arrests of bikers and their cronies all over Quebec, and beyond. He agreed that the campaign had been a smashing success.

"To say that we achieved our goals is understatement at its best," he concluded. "We closely monitor organized crime. Our staff is well versed in coping with different aspects of the biker problem. Our ongoing alliance with RCMP has proven very effective. However, with the police budget going into a shallow dive, we might be tempted to forget about the biker's threat. It may not be long before we discover, to our great surprise, how serious the problem has grown again. Still, I'd like to take the time to thank each and every one of you for your contributions over the past few years."

After Bertrand finished his speech, questions followed.

"How soon should you be able to eliminate the remnants of the biker's gangs?" someone in the audience asked.

"Instead of giving you a direct answer, I'd rather mention some statistics, which may help you understand better the new reality that I mentioned.

"In the past few months, the number of Devil's Knights has doubled. The number of their sympathizers and associates has grown proportionally. Their rival gang, the Iron Ghosts, has grown even more.

"They have opened additional chapters in Ontario, Manitoba, and Nova Scotia. Both gangs have more money than ever. In addition, law enforcement agencies have come across some very puzzling information: Many new members of these gangs have no criminal record, have never been in jail. Some of them have a formal education, and even respectable professions. We know for sure that no one could become a member of an outlaw biker gang if he had not committed numerous crimes.

"That's something to think about."

Bertrand looked around for more questions. Silence in the auditorium was the only response.

"Thank you for your attention, ladies and gentlemen," he bowed, and left the stage.

The End

Also by Alex Markman:

Payback for Revenge

The Dark Days of Love

Alex Markman

An excerpt from Alex Markman novel

PAYBACK FOR REVENGE

Hatred, densely blended with blood, was spreading through the Balkans like a poisonous pool. In anticipation of inevitable death, men took to arms and indulged in a rampage of atrocities. As they saw it, the only way out of this mess was the complete extermination of their neighbors— now their enemies. At such turning points in a nation's survival, great diplomats and politicians with vision are needed. Instead, primeval instincts easily subdue intellect and common sense. That's what I saw in the first day of my journalistic venture in Yugoslavia.

The reality of war is a shock and a burden to anyone unaccustomed to it. I wouldn't have believed it if I hadn't seen it with my own eyes. I almost cracked under its weight in the first encounter.

The driver of our battered military Jeep did not slow down on a jolting narrow road. The fresh craters dug by exploded bombs made his sharp maneuvering very risky. According to Jovan's account, the driver was a colonel, the commander of the regiment in which Kosta was in charge of an infantry unit. To convince us of his driving skills, the colonel steered the Jeep to jump over one of the shell holes, almost throwing Jovan and me out of the rear seat. The colonel looked back with a careless smile, as if expecting our approval.

"I greased his palms with one thousand dollars for arranging this interview," Jovan said, gasping from the continuous shaking. "He said that today is a particularly good day for it. Kosta's unit just drove the enemy from this village. It would be natural that an American journalist would want to get information first hand."

The deafening sound of an artillery shot tore the air, pushing my heart into my throat. I had never been so frightened before in my life. The colonel turned around and, observing my face with a fleeting glance, said something with a grin. I looked to Jovan for an explanation.

"He said," Jovan translated, "that there is nothing to worry about. The fighting is now far away. We are out of the reach of the guns."

"I don't care," I said, recovering from the shock. Jovan translated my words to the colonel. The colonel turned around again, said something very fast, and laughed.

"What did he say?" I demanded.

"He said …," Jovan took some time answering. "M … mm… He said that there is a much better place for a beautiful woman to be brave, other than the battlefield."

"Thanks for the elegant translation," I snapped, boiling with anger. Jovan chuckled.

"Slavic men, you know. Besides, it's a time of war."

We were approaching the village where ruined houses were still smoking. The colonel pulled up close to one of the armored vehicles, stepped down, and gestured for us to get out. At the same time he spoke to one of the soldiers who stood nearby. The soldier nodded, and walked briskly toward a house where people were milling around. The howling of women mingled with the rough, abrupt shouting of military men.

I jumped down onto firm ground and, while stretching my legs from hours of sitting in the shaking car, I suddenly noticed a man lying on his back about a hundred feet away. He looked as if he were taking a rest, endlessly tired and deep in his own thoughts. His right leg was twisted in an unnatural manner, as if someone had tried to twist it out of its socket. His eyes were open, as well as his mouth. A pool of blood under him told me all. This was the first dead person laying outside a funeral home I had ever seen in my life. I had always had an instinctive fear of death in any form. But now the time had come to show my strength. And I did. With firm steps I walked up to the corpse, pointed my camera at it, and took a shot. Next I took pictures of the ruined, smoking houses. With the same deliberate calmness, I returned to Jovan and the colonel, who were now looking at me with some respect. The colonel pulled out a pack of cigarettes and held it out to me. Although I had stopped smoking many years before, I took one.

"Thanks," I said casually, moving the tip of the cigarette to the flame of his lighter. "Why doesn't anyone attend to this body?"

Jovan translated. The colonel shrugged his shoulders.

"He does not need any attention," Jovan came back with the answer. "We'll soon take all the dead out of here."

The soldier, who had gone off to fulfill the colonel's order, came back with a tall, dark-haired man, about 40 years old, with a commanding posture and steely gray eyes. The colonel said something to him, pointed at me and Jovan, and left. The man nodded and stretched out his hand toward me for a handshake.

"This is Kosta," Jovan introduced the newcomer. "He is surprised that the commander chose him for the interview. But he kindly agrees to give one."

Kosta gestured for me to sit down on a fallen trunk, and settled on a rock opposite me.

"What brought you here?" he asked. Jovan began translating back and forth, fairly fast for a non-professional interpreter.

"I'm an American journalist from *Around the Globe* magazine. May I ask you what is going on here? What provoked the fighting for this village?"

"It's a long story," Kosta said, looking bored. "The two villages there, one Muslim and one Orthodox, attacked the Catholic village on that side. Then the Catholics combined forces with some Muslims and attacked this Orthodox village. And then…."

"Wait. Wait a moment," I interrupted. "I don't get it. How could these arch-enemies, Muslims and Catholics, combine forces?"

"Not all that simple, Madam. It is a stupid war—the most stupid one ever on earth. People who need each other try to kill each other. It's a long story and I don't have time to tell it."

"Okay. Perhaps you can explain this to me later. How many civilian casualties are there?"

"Not many. Most people ran away, but one family had the bad luck to miss the moment. Croatians captured the house where two young parents with their two small kids were about to have dinner. The soldiers cut the children to pieces in front of their parents and put them into the oven. They promised the parents a nice dinner. When our soldiers came, the bastards were gone. The husband was dead, his wife mortally wounded. She died a few minutes ago. She told the story." Kosta was watching my reaction with keen interest, as if evaluating whether I was fit to be a war journalist. Gathering all my strength, I suppressed the urge to vomit.

"Do you wish to see the house?" he continued. "It's over here. The parents' corpses are still on the lawn. The smell of cooking is still there; the whole house reeks of it. Want to go?"

I gave him and Jovan a scornful look. If I had heard of this sort of atrocity back in the States, I would probably have been impressed enough to mutter "Oh, terrible," only to forget about it in an hour. After all, this would have been only one of many frightening stories printed in publications I had worked for, and there were more that were never published. We journalists couldn't eat our hearts out over them. Cruelty happens in other places where the minds and deeds of the inhabitants are different from those of normal human beings like us. But now I was about to see the real thing. Should I say, "Yes?" The very thought of smelling burned human flesh and seeing children who had been roasted in front of their parents for dinner made me sick. I know I went pale, and the soldier turned a superior smile on me, the smile of a stronger male to an understandably weaker and emotional female. I felt an urge to spit in his insolent face.

"No, not necessary," I muttered.

Kosta began talking about the battle, but I didn't listen, trying to cope with nausea, for I had now caught a whiff of burned flesh. When Jovan finished his translation, I simply nodded in acknowledgment.

"Now I want to ask you something else," I said, regaining control of myself. "You witnessed the abduction of a young Serbian girl a few months ago." I unfolded a newspaper with an article on Lilia. "Remember it?"

Kosta frowned.

"Yes, I do. Why you are interested in it?"

"I believe that it would be of great interest to the American public. American people are very sensitive about cruelties against civilians, against helpless and innocent people."

"How do you know about me?" he asked rather sharply, with a note of menace.

"I've talked to the detective," I lied. "He told me that you'd been the only witness who stepped forward. That's odd."

"Why?"

"According to the newspaper article, the girl was murdered by Croatians for revenge, supposedly in response to the rape and murder of their girl. How come nobody else wants to be a witness against a mortal enemy? Could you tell me what you saw?"

"What else did the detective tell you?" he insisted.

"Not much. He told me that you were not cooperative. That's odd too."

"Bloody jerk. I can tell you what I said to him. On the way home I noticed a very pretty blond girl, about 14 or 15 years old. She had a very short skirt, nice legs, a mane of blond hair—not a mature woman yet, but almost ripe, you know . . . .Not that I'm that type of a man, you know . . .. I have a daughter too . . . but this one did attract attention. All of a sudden a car stopped. Two guys jumped out of it, grabbed the girl, and threw her into the car. Next moment they were gone. The whole thing took a few seconds."

"Thank you. Have you identified them as Croatian men?"

He shrugged his shoulders. "Who can tell that for sure? There were so many mixed marriages for centuries. After all, we are all the same people, just different religions." He turned his attention to the group of soldiers, who were busy removing something heavy from the house. A light wind brought a murmur of their conversation and an already familiar, revolting odor.

"Would you be able to recognize any of them, if they happen to cross your path?"

"Perhaps." He turned to me again. "Take my advice, Madam. Drop it."

Now I sensed something that made my heart pound. He was quite sincere in giving his advice. Why? My journalistic instincts screamed inside me: 'Push him! He knows something." I took a one-hundred-dollar bill from my purse and held it out toward him.

"If you give me meaningful information, this is yours."

The sight of hard currency did marvels. He became softer, if not friendly.

"I don't know if what I am about to say is of any use to you. I don't think so."

"Doesn't matter. Take it."

I darted a covert glance at Jovan. His face was rigid and impassive, as if carved in stone. I continued to hold out the money, and finally Kosta took it.

"Make it confidential, though," he said, hiding the bribe in his inside pocket. "I haven't told you anything. Okay?"

"Okay. I'm all ears."

"The guys are local pimps." Jovan's voice was smooth in the translation, as if the conversation was about cooking.

"Pimps?" I cried. "Are you sure?"

"Quite sure. I have seen one of them once before."

"Where?"

"In one of the bars. I'd call it a brothel. I was there with a friend of mine for a couple of beers."

"In what brothel? Where is it located?" I asked impatiently.

"Hey, hey, lady," he protested. "I thought that you were interested in political matters. What could be of interest for you in this case? It has nothing to do with the war or politics."

"Prostitution is of great interest to me. It's an international problem, as far as I know."

"I can't help you with that," he said, rising. "I haven't told you anything. Okay?"

I stood up as well, looking him up and down contemptuously.

"Are you afraid of pimps?" I asked. "A Slavic soldier is afraid of petty criminals?"

This ostensibly macho man fixed me with an angry stare.

"Do you know how much per day a pimp makes?" he asked.

"I have no idea. How much?"

"From five hundred to a thousand dollars per girl per night. If he controls 10 or more girls, how much money would he make per day?"

"It's an impressive statistic," I said.

"Smuggling girls to other countries is no less profitable," he continued, ignoring my remark. "Hordes of them from Russia and Ukraine pass through our country now. Because there is no law and order here. No control over people."

"Why do you tell me this?"

He stepped back and crossed his arms on his chest, slowly lifting his eyes from my legs to my hips, then to my bosom and my lips. He gave me an ugly smile.

"In our troubled times, money and insanity rule the world. These people have enough money to buy everyone's silence. Good luck, Madam."

Choked with indignation, I turned my back on him, ready to leave.

"Oh, by the way," he said in a merry, mocking way. "Take my advice, Madam. Stay away from this business. Another death won't change the world."

This made me turn back.

"Whose death?" I asked, looking into his sharp, narrowed eyes.

"Your death."

Waves of horror ran up and down my spine.

"W..w..what?"

"For your own good, Madam. There are thousands of criminals in this international syndicate. You will be like a small insect standing in their way. Our police work together with them. One wrong step and you are dead. Stay away. Thank you for your donation to our army."

Jovan and I walked in silence toward the road. The colonel was already waiting for us. Back in the Jeep, I looked at Jovan's face; it was pale and grim.

"What's your take on it?" I asked.

"Something's fishy in what he said. The autopsy concluded that she was a virgin. Pimps wouldn't have killed her; they would have raped her and sold her to another country. They wouldn't have dared to force a local girl into prostitution here. Locals would have killed them and burned their brothels."

"True," I agreed. "And yet, my gut feeling is that he's told the truth. Something is seriously amiss."